Chapter 1: The Balloon

Soundtrack: Fat Les – Vindaloo

We've all seen a balloon taking flight. It's an awe inspiring sight. Unfortunately this book has fuck all to do with hot air and wicker baskets. The balloon in question is me. Ballooning is a very British type of behaviour which has undoubtedly become part of our mad dogs and English men culture.

My balloon isn't set up to fly but once upon a time I threatened to see if it was. I performed a mock leap from of a second floor pub window in a way that scared and entertained my friends drinking in the square below in equal measure. It wasn't a premeditated act. The thought just came into my head and the entertainer took the stage. My creative, in some part rational, but mainly destructive mind subconsciously calculated a complex mathematical estimation; if I propel my twelve stones of man-fat out of that window - which has approximately a twelve inch gap - at roughly 10mph then raise my calves and heels before the lower half of my body exits the building, this should in theory stop me completely flying out of the window and falling to my death. Then I had to count on my friends in the pub to spot and retrieve me. Thankfully I managed to execute that ridiculous stunt without inflicting death or serious injury upon myself. I even managed to drink most of the pint I had in my hand even though I was hanging upside down pulling funny faces at the crowd below. In my head at that time I thought that was great. The lad who saw the stunt from a few feet away inside the bar still reminisces about that afternoon over twenty years later. Now I'm approaching forty and my son isn't too far away from getting his adult wings. The thought of him taking such risks really gives me the shits.

Blackpool is the land of balloons and it's quite fitting that I was inspired to write this book on a visit to chav-dom. In 2011 I took part in the Blackpool marathon. I was very surprised by the lacklustre support around the course. Nobody cheered, nobody clapped. That's a lie, about twenty people around the course did, twenty good people. The rest ignored you or stared blankly at you. Hens heckled, Stags leered, 'Run Forest, run!' Beer cans were launched, all in jest, you know the crack.

It was as if the people of Blackpool had, had all the goodness and life sucked out of them. My overwhelming feeling is that a large number of English folk are that uneducated and naive about what's right and proper, it's become normal to be un-normal.

This book is actually about my life and how me, a 'normal lad' got lost like so many other people do. Millions of kids like me have no idea about what the fuck they are doing. Responsible living is now a minority sport.

I think adolescents and potential balloons will appreciate my honesty and relate to some of my crazy stories. Hopefully they will then grasp why they and their mates are on missions of self-destruction and hurt. Pretending to be people they are not and doing crazy things they don't really want to do. As I will go on to explain in this book up until my 30th birthday I, like so many people in our great country had no idea how to live.

I was a lost but good soul and I mention the word good because at core I am nice. Even kids that are out of control are in the main nice. Just because someone is living a selfish, piggish existence doesn't necessarily make them a bad person. Everyone is fixable. Such a person just needs to realise they're doing it all wrong. Unfortunately if you don't get the education I believe each parent and school has a duty to deliver, then normal kids are gonna be broken and they just don't deserve it.

I'm sure there are a thousand journey books out there explaining how people have done the do. Everybody's story is worth telling. Each and every human has to take that learning journey through life. Some are born into a loving wholesome environment, many are not. I'm a fairly normal fella who when I look back, has experienced what is now considered a fairly standard upbringing. So I'd like to share my experience and the details of how I became a balloon. What the consequences are of such a lifestyle and the battle to reclaim the real me.

As you read on through this documentation you'll realise I'm quite spiritual and I feel fairly connected. I've deffo felt a calling to share this book with the world. Don't get me wrong I'm not the thirteenth disciple and I'm not attempting to add another chapter to the bible. I've never even read one. However this shit comes from my heart and I hope you can feel that.

Chapter2: The Hindsight Manoeuvre

Soundtrack: Travis - Driftwood

People always say hindsight is a wonderful thing. Wouldn't we all like
to turn the clocks back so we could study harder at school and
waste less time on beer, drugs and manipulating girls that you would
never ever want to show to your mum? Some would say no actually,
that was the best time ever and I wished I'd donated a few more brain
cells to partying.

I find perception a very interesting subject matter. I'm not the first
hippy to realise that we are all on a journey of constant
change. You're not going to be the same person at forty that you are at
sixteen. Your views are going to change. That's a given. Even so it
amazes me how horrified I am when I recall some of my antics down
the years. It's almost as if it wasn't me.

Every time you make a decision, you make what you think is the best
decision for you. This is based on your perception at that time. Your
perception, the way you compute the thoughts that come into your
mind is influenced by so many things. Young kids that miss out on a
proper family upbringing don't get a pre-loaded responsible and
positive decision making computer. They have to learn from their right
moves and their wrong moves, their mistakes.

Unfortunately you can only do that if you know what's right
and what's wrong and parts of our society are sadly lacking here and
it's not just the chav class either. There is a whole generation of kids
that never get told off by their parents. At each level of society in this
country there are spoilt brats absolutely ruined by their parents. In my
opinion there's nothing to be gained from this approach. Most kids will
resent their parents because like it or not humans do have a killer
instinct. Just like the lion in the jungle we can sense the weak and the
feeble and where the opportunity arises we have to strike, to take the
piss. Parents become injured wildebeests bullied then devoured by
their own kids..!

It's not just at home that kids are left to drift. Across society there is a distinct lack of discipline and guidance. Bible boundaries have gone. Even the police and the schools have been stripped of their powers of intervention. This creates kids without conscience. Once a human being takes no responsibility for the consequences of their actions anything can happen. Drifting with no moral code a lost soul can do untold damage to themselves, those around them and the community at large. I've been a drifter. I once crapped on some poor unfortunate's doorstep on my way home from a night out in town. I did it for no other reason than it was convenient and the plants in the garden had sphincter friendly looking leaves. I had no shame or guilt. I chose not to care. I can remember retelling that story with
pride. Now I'm ashamed and it's rather cringey that my mother in law might read this. How does that complete shift in perception come about?

So in writing this honest account of my life experiences and my decision making I've tried not to serve every antidote with a side salad of then and now perception thoughts. I've tried to leave the old hindsight manoeuvre until later in the book. Even so I'd like to share some of my shameless stories in the hope that reading this can help young people along. Give them a start with the old decision computer.

Chapter 3: Milkspermboobstitswank

Soundtrack: Black Lace - Gangbang

The human brain is a complex and wondrous machine. I love my brain but the way it operates can be quite infuriating at times. I have an awful short term memory you see. I'm one of them that puts the coffee in the fridge and the milk in the cupboard.

I decided to go back to college and have another go at GCSE English as I only achieved a D grade at school. I had to go for an assessment at my local college to find out if I was suitable for the course. I had to write a letter and admittedly my command of the English language ain't the best. I couldn't really spell or punctuate very well. On completion of the test the teacher looked at my masterpiece and said "Sorry you're on course for a D grade so we won't be able to accept you into the class".

I said "I'm on course for a D without any schooling so by the end of the year I'll be greatly improved and on for a better mark". "Sorry you haven't met the criteria I'm afraid that's it". I knew right there I would get into the class and show the old reptile.

I tried to sign up at the pay desk without the assessment form. No chance. So I sussed out the times of the classes and just turned up. Funnily enough I wasn't on the register. The lovely Northern Irish teacher said "They must still be processing your payment". After three weeks I left her in no doubt I was her most keen and committed student. I came clean and she got me registered.

Soon enough my teacher Mavis said "Your spelling is awful. You obviously have a spelling memory dysfunction. Let me teach you a method of remembering words and combating memory loss." She explained that the mind retains naughty or filthy information. Basically you just need to tag something rude onto what you're trying to remember. What kind of information you're trying to recall really doesn't matter. It could be a spelling, where you last left your keys or even the name of a person. Just by adding something a little porno to that information seems to trigger the brain into memory action. For example if I was introduced to a lady and I wanted to remember that she was called Karen, I would silently name her 'Cum face Karen'. The little devil in me will remember that every time.

The only reason I played out the little ditty above is because my only memories of nursery school are all filth. I remember orgies in the wendy house. I remember full on showing and touching of willies and being shown girls bits too. There was also a sandpit. Now that was a real fondling hotspot. For the dare devils there was a large plastic barrel thing which could hold three to four kids at a squeeze and when I say squeeze I mean it. You got felt up rolling down the hill. Surely my life as a four year old couldn't have been so sexually charged? Maybe not but that's what my dark side remembering function recalls! Oh yeah before I forget I do remember the cute milk bottles with straws they served at play time but I'm starting to worry I only remember that because milk comes from TITS!

As for the cold blooded college entry assessor I fluffed a GCSE A* in her honour and I still can't spell or punctuate!

I think it's important to realise the dark force, the negative, your demon, the grim fuckin reaper. It's strong in us all. That's why gossip is remembered, it's why mud sticks and it why life is not always fair. It's not all bad though. It's great news for bad spellers, dyslectic's and people with dementia.

Chapter 4: Glee Club

Soundtrack: Fame – Irene Cara

At primary school I was what the yanks would call a jock. I was good at sport and from an early age this filled me with a lot of confidence. From day one I felt blessed and I mean I felt absolutely magnificent. Home life was alright but school was a holiday camp; football, girls, singing, stories, shows and fights. Everything a young scamp desires and I took each and every opportunity to go for gold. I was in a state of complete fearless innocence. People search their whole lives for happiness and at seven years old I was fully conscious that I'd found it. It was like being on tour with 'The Stones' and being on 'It's A Knockout' and 'Superstars' all at the same time.

The school was a 50/50 split of council and not council estate kids. It wasn't Beirut but I was aware that not every family had money. Clothing was expensive in the eighties. A jumper could cost thirty quid at a time when beer was around 50p a pint in the local. For financially unblessed parents it was a straight choice between sixty pints in a row or stay in and save for a sweater. No contest really and therefore skegs as they were known had nowhere to hide.

I felt particularly sorry for one young lad and his sister. At a time when skin tight jeans were the law he was sent into school in half mast mega-flares. Not only that he wore moulded football boots instead of shoes or trainers. Whatever his family circumstances they'd sent him out as a sacrificial lamb and as soon as he and his little sister arrived in the playground the wolves tore the lambs to shreds. I still get upset thinking of him being surrounded and taunted as his undersized little sister cowered under his armpit. 'Flarey Mary' was the chant and it went on and on and on.

Throughout my life I've always been a defender of the Vulnerable. I tried to talk to them two but they were too scared to notice I was genuine. If they weren't barking when they arrived then they must have had serious mental health issues by the time they were hounded out of school at the age of eight and six respectively.

They weren't the only stand out characters. Bobby and Tommy were two brothers who were proper scrappers. Bobby was my age and he was an absolutely lovely lad to talk to. He looked a bit like Rowan Atkinson, his eyebrows were epic. He was funny and naughty and he hated teachers. Whatever he and his brother faced at home meant they could not handle authority and at a time when teachers chucked chalk, spanked you with metre sticks and banged desk lids on your fingertips these two met fire with fire. Male or female teachers, they didn't discriminate. If they were physically touched in any way then they attempted to beat the living shit out of their assailant. Bobby had a playground ruck with a middle aged first year junior teacher known as Mrs. Polski. She made the mistake of trying to take him on. He gave her a right going over and ripped off her blouse. I'll never forget my first glance at a pair of tits. He was restrained then dragged down to the headmaster's office for caning. Fuck knows how that situation panned out.

In our last year at primary school he took it to another level. In music class he hid in a large cardboard box and half way through class he sprang out of the box and started beating the elderly female piano playing teacher before running out of the fire exit.

His younger brother was less selective when it came to picking winnable scraps. He attacked the six foot four deputy head who pinned him to the wall in a Darth Vader style death grip. He kicked him repeatedly until he went limp after being almost strangled. It was absolutely fantastic viewing. I didn't understand their pain I just thought they were fearless and crackers.

The school bully was hilarious. He looked quite intimidating and regularly bullied and robbed kids. In my self-righteous mind I was a force of goodness. So I took it upon myself to Police him and anyone who was terrorised by him knew to come to me. He was game but so piss weak I gave him a controlled hiding on a daily basis often taking back stolen goods and attempting to teach him moral lessons he was clearly never gonna learn.

Looking back there was a selection of bullies in each year group, always penniless, every one of them trying to divert their pain onto others and doing what they had to do to get by.

As I became an older junior and the landscape started to change, the bullies got a bit scarier. Glue bags and porn were found in the sandpit and the news on tele was all Tory doom. My innocent youth was finally coming to an end.

Chapter 5: Garden Party

Soundtrack: Pointer Sisters - Automatic

We had eighties normality in our house, a very hetro football dad,
Home brew and Findus crispy pancakes.

Yeah dad was cricket, footy and all that. Mum was also a buzz. She
was a grammar school girl. You could tell because she liked
crosswords. She'd also used to play fight with us and she gave as good
as she got. She liked to fight on the inside rolling around, getting us in
death grips and making us submit. She had good core strength. She
once taught me the art of how to take the pain of a Chinese burn. You
silently repeat the mantra: doesn't hurt, doesn't hurt, doesn't hurt and
for some reason that makes you hard and it doesn't hurt, much.

Years later I tested this theory on a boring visit to a French Industrial
History Museum. As the guide was telling us about the French farming
techniques of the last hundred years I took the opportunity to insert my
penis in a workshop vice. As he wittered on about the effects of the
industrial revolution I started tightening the vice around my cock.
Once I had the full attention of the group my knob was as flat as a
pancake and about to explode. It wasn't the first or last time I'd use
mums pain resistance technique. My pals were falling about laughing
and the French bloke didn't make a fuss. He must be that boring that
this sort of defiant display happened regularly or maybe he thought all
English people are on the sex register and he was cool with that.

So back to family bliss. We had a big Ford Granada with an electric
ariel, a Yorkshire Terrier, a Grifter and a Tomahawk bicycle. All was
well until they called our kid and me into the front garden of our two
up two down semi. At the time we were aged ten and seven
respectively. "We are splitting up. Who do you want to go with?" Just
like that, the cheeky Bastards! Not wanting to make a boo boo and
being a self-righteous, judgemental little tinker I asked the question:
"So why are you splitting up?"

"Because I've met someone else!" was my mother's reply. So that was it, I took the moral high ground and Findus pancakes became badly done boiled ribs and cabbage, just like that.

There was a brief reconciliation the day after. Mum woke us up in the middle of the night, said she'd never leave us again. She hugged me and sobbed for what seemed like hours but by morning she was gone.

I've never found the truth out on that one. Mum says Dad forced her to say that so she would have to stay with us. Dad says that's shite. That passage of savage game play turned our lives upside down.

Not only was I a self-righteous and judgemental little chap but I also bore grudges and on the basis that my mum had just broken my heart twice I was having fuck all to do with her again.

My old man did nothing to dissuade me and at the time I thought that was right. Now I'm a parent I struggle to see how a dad could let a ten year old make a decision like that, let alone stick to it for six years. My dad was angry. We realised that when he told us to wait in the car while he beat up Mum's new fella outside of his workplace. To my knowledge Mum made no real effort to bridge the gap with me. She saw my brother. He needed her. The poor little bastard needed his mum. He still does.

From that point we were left to our own devices. Dad worked hard. He was a working class fella with what I would describe as a privileged job. He worked in a grimy factory fitting out tractors. That may seem like a contradiction but I have friends who worked with my old man at Massey Ferguson holiday camp for grumpy blokes. You know the crack as it was the kinda place where the union was king. They took the piss to a fine tune: Brew time, lunch time, washy hands time, shower time then maybe a spot of graft here and there.

To be fair it was a world class product and in a capitalist society at worker level it's best to keep output and market expectations low. Because next year you're spanked into beating the previous year, every year! They were geniuses in that respect the lazy fuckers!

Dad was famous in the factory for being able to locate the trouble spot on any machine that was losing fluid. Hence his nickname, Leaky! He had good knowledge and the respect of his peers. He even grew his nails long to use for twisting screws. I would say he'd found his vocation and he literally grew into the job. He was attempting to grow Swiss Army hands.

Hangover, illness, earthquake (1984). Nothing stopped him going to work. 7am he was up and out of the door and I love him for that. He was a grafter, he kept the house going.

Chapter 6: Boys Will Be Boys

Soundtrack: Sabrina - Boys boys boys

There was definitely an element of shame attached to being part of a one parent family. I really felt that at junior school. Gossiping two faced back stabbing bitches and bastards aren't just exclusively part of the adult world or maybe it's a case of the paranoia I felt wasn't. Either way it took the shine off my last year in juniors and I was glad to comfortably fail the 11+ exam for grammar school entrance and safely slot into a school where most kids had an average of four dads.

The divorce affected us all in different ways. We were all heartbroken in our house. Not least with Dads cooking; it was shite. We were used to no fuss ham and chips off Mum. Dad went all five-a-day overkill and tried to make us eat proper stuff. Things like meatloaf served with vegetables like beans and spaghetti hoops.

We won out quickly. First our non-gourmet dog put on two stone from eating our under-the-table backhanders before we got sussed out when poor old Scoob choked on a chicken bone. From then on he spent torture/meal times locked outside.

Being forward thinkers we started squeezing all the food the dog usually took off us straight down the back of the radiator. Dad was very unimpressed firstly with the mystery smell then the mystery flies.

Suddenly he changed tactics. He went all Kramer vs Kramer. He introduced stand off situations where first up he'd threaten us into eating and when that failed he would try and silently stare us into eating. You chewed and chewed but his food didn't disintegrate. It was absolutely minging, pointless and painful. We gagged, we cried, we rolled around on the carpet like we'd been poisoned and fairly quickly we drove the poor guy nuts. He was done in. He must have thought, why did I give them ungrateful little fuckers an option to stay here? He had tried, he did his best but he wasn't trained for this. He soon gave up and threw himself in to work and the pub. I was suddenly deemed old enough to baby sit and I became a self-sufficient housewife at the tender age of eleven.

My poor little brother just didn't get it. He just needed his mum. Dad
grafted, home for tea then off to the pub. That was how it was in those
days. We often got scared as there were a lot more burglaries back
then. Dad once caught one of our bin men who must have spotted
something worth a bob or two trying to climb through our downstairs
back window. He was promptly punched back through the window and
didn't come back. We kept thinking he would though. Every night we
were waiting for somebody to break in. It was fuckin' harrowing
really. We patrolled the house tooled up until we heard a noise then we
hid in Dad's bed under the heavy protection of a duvet. When
Crimewatch hit the screens we stopped watching the T.V.

Spending all that time together in the house might make you think two
brothers would have come together to comfort each other. The trouble
was our kid was in that much emotional pain that he just kept lashing
out. I was three years older and bored, so most of the time I was happy
to scrap with him. Boys will be boys and there is a sick sort of
gratifying pleasure you get from overpowering someone who's just that
little bit weaker than you even if it is your very own tormented little
brother.

One day I came home and my little brother was unconscious in the
shed with a half empty gas canister and a towel beside him. I was
naive. I just didn't know what that meant. Dad slapped him round the
house when he came round. Dads answer was often violence and more
disturbingly ridicule. Here was a little fella still at junior school and
way out of control. Dad just said he was nuts and I had started to
believe him.

Just like the teachers at school the only adult in our house didn't shy
away from confrontation. My dad would occasionally lose his rag. He
wasn't a puncher or a belt whipper but when his head went he was a
power restrainer. Bruv got dragged by his hair and pinned in an
attempt to subdue his own very violent outbursts. I didn't like it as Dad
seemed to tease him once he had him locked down. I honestly think
my dad had no idea he may be partly responsible for this gorgeous
little fella being so messed up. He seemed to view his temperament as
a genetic pass down and not a problem really. He just thought he had a

natural bad temper.

Our kid would sometimes want to move out and that's when Dad went really crackers. I remember two occasions when he transferred all Trev's belongings to his desired new addresses. The first one was the park and the second was my mum's new front garden. It was all very messy, extreme and unnecessary.

My relationship with my brother was also deteriorating. One night when Dad was in the pub we got into a fight and he ended up purposely throwing something through the kitchen door, smashing the big double glazed pane in the process. Next door rang my uncle and he brought Dad home from the pub. I hid upstairs fearing the worst whilst our kid concocted a crime scene and alibi that led to Dad whacking me without asking for an explanation. I did bear grudges and I'm ashamed to say I was starting to write my brother off as a nutter. He moved out of the bedroom we shared and into the front room of the house which contained his beloved terrapins and a large keg of home brew bitter.

One and one equals two and pretty soon he smelt of fish shit and was often quite pissed. We were at breaking point. One day I held him down on the stairs and pissed on him. I knew it was very wrong but I was at a point of wanting to hurt him in a way that had some effect as he seemed to be unfazed by normal violence.

Trevor's outbursts, rants and rages were all a cry for help, his inner defense mechanism. All he needed was love but in eighties Manchester men didn't know about that shit and both Dad and I ended up meeting force with more force. Although he was unable to express it Dad loved him more than anything really. He just didn't understand him. He spoke of him as a mental case and as if it was his own fault that he was like that. Eventually he moved to Mum's. Then he'd fritter between the two because the poor little fucker didn't know what the fuck he was doing. He was lost.

He and his mates started doing acid to escape from the shit world they found themselves in. I had no idea what acid was or that he was doing it. We had drifted apart.

Chapter 7: We Fuckin Hate City

Soundtrack: Eric Conner - Manchester United Calypso

In the previous chapter I hope I didn't make my dad sound like he was ever a bad 'un because that simply was never the case. He just didn't know what to do with feelings and kids in the same sentence.

He was a top dad in many ways. We knew that he loved us. He would never say it but actions speak louder than words and he'd do stuff like sneak out of work on a wet Tuesday afternoon to be the only dad on the touchline at a school team footy match. I'd score, he'd nod, Say no fuckin' more.

He did that for both brothers and he treated us both the same on all levels. He was generous. He never spent money on the house but when he was off work it was all about leisure. For him life was football, concerts, pubs, curries, kebabs, friends and birds. That's how he operated. The house was shabby but he was always cash rich. He did live music concerts with our Trev and with me it was the footy.

Going to Old Trafford as a kid was a real experience. Before a match we always visited a smoky club complete with swearing, cards and shagging talk. It was a different world. One which made my hair stand on end. Not all the adults treated me as one of the lads; they just acted as if I wasn't there. This suited me fine as my vocabulary was expanding rapidly and I was learning so much more by staying quiet than you could ever hope to by asking questions.

Walking to the ground with thousands of pissed sheep you felt like part of an army on the verge of something big. You could hear the different battalions firing off war songs in the distance. The closer you got the louder the call. A male mass of red cladded testosterone marched down the Warwick Road.

Once you got inside the Stretford End it was at first a wall of smelly arses. About ten thousand stood between me and my space on the railings at the front. Northern blokes drank bitter and mild and their arses all seemed to smell the same. That was it then until Dad would find me at half time with a sloppy meat and potato pie and possibly a life threateningly hot Bovril.

Some of the new words I learnt in the club were sung at fever pitch. Fuckin' this, blue cunts that, it all took some getting used to but it didn't take long to tribalise me. I was in my dad's gang and it felt so good. "We fuckin hate City..!"

At the end the pissed sheep squeezed out of the ground en masse and I really felt like my dad's son as he ushered me over the Stretford End Bridge like a joey in his kangaroo pouch using his sizeable gangly frame to fob off overly exuberant piss heads. It was a long three to four mile walk from there but I didn't care I was with my dad.

Soon enough Dad got a bird and she had a young son. Dad treated him exactly the same as he did us. He was good like that.

Chapter 8: Arise Sir Derek Trotter

Soundtrack: Chaka Khan - Ain't Nobody

Not unlike my initial primary school experience, secondary school fitted me like a fanny. I love people and there were loads of them there. My initial assessment of my new school chums was that they were full of life. Footy at break time was intense. Some lessons had lively debate. There were alpha males around every corner. Violence was much less common place at this school though. People would challenge you at sport or just take the piss because if you had a scrap the headmaster simply kicked you out. How very civilized, I loved it.

Fashion was more of an issue here. The girls wore their socks in a certain way; long and perfectly ruffled. There was a lot of talent and I liked their socks.

By Year Two strong friendship bonds were formed and about half of the year travelled to France en masse for a school holiday. For many this was their first trip abroad. Men's fashion was all over the place at the time. My boys went for chinos, paisley ties, waistcoats and acid house smiley face badges. Some of us took it up a notch donning tweed jackets, navy blazers and black and white tap shoes. We were throwbacks to some bygone era. Which one? I really don't know.

I must have looked a right plonker as I volunteered to go to the bar on the ferry and order the drinks. "Twenty eight pints of Woodpecker please!" She didn't crack a smile. She must have been on commission. She just typed it in the till and took about forty quid off me. I couldn't fuckin' believe it Derek Trotter the second had arrived!

Everyone was waiting outside on the open deck to see if I'd been arrested. As I walked out into a stiff sea breeze I toked on a fat cigar and held on tight to the first Holy Grail tray of about eight ciders. After a group hug I told the youngest looking one of us to go back in and get the rest of the apple juice. The commission pig must have thought what the fuck have I done? Apollo 14 had just been launched in my stomach. You couldn't beat this.

By the time we got back on the coach some kids were spewing. Others were getting all romantic with each other. All this from twelve year olds only half way through the first day of their first school trip. This was team bonding of the highest order.

Sharing that experience had to be replicated and sure enough the best dressed under thirteen drinking collective you ever saw started meeting regularly at Gorse Hill Park.

My old man would finish work at 1pm on a Friday and go for a pint in the cricket club house onsite at his workplace. I would join him and they were happy for me to have a shandy or a cider with him. Dad always gave me a fiver as we went our separate ways after the club. That fiver, my friends, was equivalent to four bottles of Peach Concorde and a lung-busting Hamlet Classic cigar. Amen!

On the park the basic rules of conduct were simple. Most importantly secure booze. Some resorted to robbing it. We were lucky as my mate had facial hair and he'd usually get served at one particular Offie (Off Licence). Then it was all about the birds. The beauty of the set up was that The Gorse Hill Park Posse was a collection of smaller groups of friends all looking to get pissed and cop off.

Closer to my home you had The Chippy Wall Gang and the V.P, The Vicky Park Gang. Both of these firms were different. They were all boys and I'm sure they had a lot of fun along the way but their path to fundom included intimidation, robbing, fighting and drugs. They would certainly never wear tweed. I used to have nightmares about them. I think a lot of kids did.

Our group was much more peace loving. Every group entered the park already steaming so there was no messing about with nerves or anything. You would walk straight on and ask a girl to go with you and either start necking with her in front of the group or take her off somewhere more private for closer inspection. When you came back you could ask another one. There were no limits to how many you could cop for really, we were free to go with as many as we liked and then your mate would go with them too and no-one bore a grudge in the main.

I had a bird right the way through school who I'll talk about later. She and her pals were connected to the V.P which probably explains my nightmares. She will have been playing the same game in a different bush I'm sure. I was happy she didn't come on our park I didn't want to upset her but this was an education opportunity that may never come around again. I wasn't gonna miss out. No fuckin' way!

This spit on your fingers, straight in type of human transaction suited me down to the ground. I didn't have the social skills to talk to my own bird, never mind chat up another thirty or so. In this cave man, free love set up, you didn't have to worry about all that.

I was happy with a snog and a titty grope. That was my level. Plenty went home with grassy knee's though. Whatever you wanted you could get and of course if you didn't want or get it, you could always pretend. That's where I was at. Of course I shagged them all!

One girl heard I'd shagged her and she also heard she had a fishy fanny. They were older than us and I bumped into her and her four mates on Greatstone School. They beat the fuck out of me and stripped the clothes off my back. I was three miles from home. That was a lesson learned. I ran home crying with a trainer over my little bald cock.

Chapter 9: Wildlife, On One

Soundtrack: Tight Fit - The Lion Sleeps Tonight

Zammo and the Grange Hill smack-head storyline of about 1985 hit me hard. I didn't like needles and that's what I thought drugs were. So I didn't like drugs. In my Hurcule Poirot persona I liked to have a cigar. I liked the sweet taste of a Hamlet Classic but I didn't like the idea of smoke going inside my body. So I wasn't really interested in smoking or smoking weed. Therefore I was late into trying drugs, almost middle aged at fourteen.

Mad stories were going around school about trips (L.S.D) little bits of paper that made you get chased down the road by Mars Bars. The lad that told me about that experience wasn't a bull-shitter. He was usually a level headed dude so I had a feeling there was something to it. A close friend of mine became a regular trip head and he confirmed lamp posts did bend in half and Mr Soft off the soft mints advert was a real dude.

Kids on the park started taking them and they just seemed to laugh for hours. It seemed fuck all like the Zammo adverts so in the end out of curiosity I decided to give it a whirl. We scored some Purple Om's for 50p a trip and had half each. We decided to placebo the guy that sorted it out. Just to see what he did. He was fed a piece of cigar box.

We were fourteen and boozing in the company of a load of middle aged benefit swindlers in the nearest boozer to our end of the park. We gobbled our trips whilst quaffing Woodpecker. I was nervous but not overly. I didn't expect it to be too different from the cider buzz.

Sure enough half an hour later all of a sudden we were crying with laughter. This fella came over and started saying in a very Cornish tongue." Ave you got a light boy? Av u got a light?" It was the song of the time off the Ovaltine advert and he just kept doing it. Not one of us could strike a match between us as we were just rolling with laughter, Placebo man included, it was like doing ten thousand sit ups in a row. Our stomachs were laughter strained to fuck.

There was an arty member in the group. He kept rambling on about being an animal man and about the amazing powers he had in terms of controlling animals. Whatever fella!

After dark we left the boozer and walked down by the gas works in the general direction of my home. The spotlights dissected the railings in the most amazing way. We were all mesmerised apart from gibbering animal boy. He shot off down an alley, probably to befriend some cats or rats.

We slumped on a wall and started to dissect the evenings goings on. Without warning Terry Nutkins shot out of the alley. He had a fox just behind him and a number of low flying birds flying at running speed just around his barnet. About twenty feet behind him a bald and very angry dude carrying a four be two inch piece of wood with nails in it. He was locked onto Noah until he spotted us. The wildlife documentary went one way and we went the other. He chased us over the canal and through the Moss Road estate which was a bit rough. As we gave legs all the car lights started to look at us. By the time Hulk Hogan gave up all the cars were looking very mean and angry.

The council houses that were half rendered looked like they were held together with zips. The four of us didn't talk; we just walked quickly for another half a mile to my house.

Dad was up. He was never up. After beer he always went to bed. But he was up. He said " What the fucks up with you lot?" We sat down and said "fuck all." Next thing the Channel four sign was spinning around and reforming in the middle of the room. We cowered then said "See you later Dad we're off to bed."

The dungeon master style computer game posters in my room haunted us for the next five sleepless hours or so. Placebo case still doesn't believe me to this day because he saw the same shit we did. LSD was on another level it was definitely not for me.

While we are in the Gorse Hill area of Manchester I can't move on without mentioning a special guy and very interesting puzzle.

His Mum and Dad went out on the piss every weekend and he let pretty much everyone who went on the park come back to his house. It got absolutely mullered and annihilated every single week. The fridge got emptied and weed bomb burns tormented the couch. A normal night went something like puke, fires, broken beds and soiled sheets.

Once the mob split into two on the landing and staged a tug-o-war battle with a rolled up carpet which eventually got yanked in half. The fuelled up domino's inevitably tumbled down the stairs and ripped the banister clean off the wall.

Our host didn't flinch. A can of Special Brew and a spliff and he were happy. Even if someone was busy up stairs borrowing his mums sex toys and negligee it wasn't a problem. He was never bullied into it. He just got pissed and seemed to forget last week. Everyone worried about him a bit but it was like a car crash, you couldn't help looking!

It was one of life's great mysteries how he squared it with his folks and then repeated the crime scene on a weekly basis. I saw him recently, thirty years on, in real life. He's a nice and normal bloke. When I asked him how he used to work it. He just giggled.

Explanation 1

His parents were getting that smashed that they thought they had caused the damage when they came round in the morning.

Explanation 2

Maybe they were the most submissive people in the world but you can't imagine parents like that would go out. Surely they'd stay home and guard the house.

Explanation 3

Was he feeding them Purple Om's and convincing them they lived in the Mississippi Delta? Did they think that Nansen Close was Tornado Alley?

Chapter 10: Outdoor Expeditions and Back-door Adventures

Soundtrack: Gary Jules - Mad World

From then on I stayed away from acid, most of us did. I smoked a bit of weed. Less than the national average though. All that didn't really appeal to me. The appeal of Life on the park was dissipating too. The Quady lads and other unrulies had hustled in and there were more and more scraps kicking off. They were the type of scraps you had no chance of winning either so we simply jibbed it.

We started going into town, firstly to traditional middle aged holes like The Ritz. We wore our dads suits and 'Past it mingers' from exotic sounding towns like Beswick and Ordsall were happy to pretend that we were our dads. It was a happy time.

Dad spent more and more time with his new family round the corner. I approved as they were nice. Our kid didn't so he stayed away. My mate's families became my family. Two mobs in particular made my life special and I'll always be grateful that they let me share the warmth of their families. I often didn't want to go home and sometimes I didn't. One school night my pals parents were less than impressed when at 2 a.m. they spotted my leg hanging out of their boy's wardrobe door.

I was in more than one social circle and one other pal I knocked about with was more arty and interesting. He smoked spliffs and listened to The Doors and he also drew amazing pictures. He was different to other lads. He played basketball not footy. He secretly liked City not United and what I liked best about him was his spirit of adventure.

We slept on active railway bridges, in cricket scoring sheds and often in our garage. There was a pirate radio station called WBLS with DJ Drac. That was our bag and they played soul2soul going into early dance music. Between this and my dad's pretty robust record collection we were developing a pretty eclectic taste. Before school other pals picked out Motown and The Beatles records. I like the theatre of putting a record on. I dug all things cultural.

My outdoor squatting partner was in with 'The Quady' the tastier firm from Old Trafford. He started bringing bags of whizz with him to Madchester venues like Isadoras and Devilles. Both places had a room full of indie/classic rock heads and the other room was full of the seedling ecstasy generation. We were firmly in the Talking heads/Madchester retro camp because the fitter looking birds were still in our room. Not that it made much difference to me. Whizz made your cock retract into a little rubber stump. It made for very chatty bus rides home though. I mainly spoke to lads.

At home things were cool my dad never told me off. The boundaries between dad, son, housewife and friend were blurred. He got it all very wrong one night though. Me and my pals had decided to stay in and have a gentleman's evening at my house. We challenged each other to get some porn. The best we could muster was a carry on style American seventies soft porno called 'Truck Stop' that one of the lads managed to acquire from the top shelf of a Gorse Hill video rental shop. We were happy with that and stashed it midweek under the sofa.

Dad lingered like a bad smell on the night of the 'Manfest' before he said "I've only been hanging around to make you sweat, you bunch of sex pests! If you want to watch a real porno there's one under the chair."

He was buzzing off us the cheeky twat. Anyway, best not to look a gift horse in the mouth and as soon as the door banged to, we were all on the floor feeling for porn. We found it and settled down for a trip to Flange-land.

The video crackled at first, we were mesmerised. Then all of a sudden this pretty hot slightly cross eyed nun came on screen. She held her cross with one hand and this hairy dudes cock with the other. We all looked at each other. Fuckin' hell! Yes. She sucked him off before he pulled up her nun's Habit skirt thing to reveal a shrivelled little cock and balls. The next thing we were looking at a dry bum fuck. The guy then proceeded to punch him, it, her unconscious and then started shitting all over what was starting to look like a corpse.

Either my dad had not watched this film before or he was a very sick individual indeed. We stuck 'Truckstop' on for a bit but our minds were elsewhere. Is that what goes on in the real world? I didn't even know nuns had tits and dicks.

This wasn't an isolated incident either. Thankfully my old man wasn't the only wrong 'un. There was another time when we sat down with my mate's sister in their family home. We held cushions on our laps as a mark of respect for her. Then we watched in amazement as West Country Dairy farmers went about the business of milking their animals in various different ways. This was my first screening of Animal Farm and it was disturbingly wrong. The cushions certainly did not bulge.

We learned to find humour in all things. Even knowing your parents were if not into, then at least tolerant of bestiality, buggery and what looked like attempted murder. It was a funny old learning curve. I believe a child's innocence should be preserved. Even in dysfunctional households like mine. That is not cool. I knew that then and I haven't changed my mind.

As for school in every subject which had an interesting teacher I managed a GCSE B.In any with a teacher that didn't care I got a GCSE D. I got three of each: Average! The last day of school we got steaming at ours before we went in.
By 8 am we were right on it: As a fitting tribute we burnt our school uniforms in the garden. I loved a lot of people at that school. It was the end of a golden era. One I'll always cherish.

Chapter 11: Double Bluffed

Soundtrack: New Order - World In Motion

My dad was a wind up. He liked to tease and well, wind you up. He repeatedly said to me in jest "Sixteen and you're out son." He didn't mean it. He just had a rather twisted sense of humour. Anyway I double bluffed him. I signed up for the Royal Navy at fifteen years old and half way through the 1990 World Cup I was off. Dad waved me off at Piccadilly station, his little chin was going bless him. He was gutted but no doubt proud. I loved the old boy. He'd always looked after me.

The day I joined the Royal Navy I'd convinced myself and all my friends I was a stud. The truth was I'd tried long and hard to penetrate my long suffering high school sweetheart. She was fit. She had gorgeous auburn red hair. She also had great boobs, pubes and everything!

We didn't have much of a relationship. We sent each other letters but we never talked because both break and lunch times at school were for footy. About once a week I went to her house and we snogged. We kissed for hours until our lips were crusty. Her parents never talked to me either. They just opened the front door and let me go straight up to her room and get stuck in.

Each time I tried to impale her with my monstrous bone Mr Floppy came out to play. We never discussed it and we tried quite a few times but it was always a case of now he's hard, now he's not!

Looking back at that droopy situation with my hippy spectacles on, I feel that a greater force was controlling my todger density because the scary truth is that one shot of the good stuff and we would have made a real mess of some poor kids life. I suppose there's a minute chance we could have learnt life's lessons together and have grown up into great and responsible parents but the reality was that I would have messed up hers, mine and the kiddy's lives and spent my later years hating myself for being such a misguided selfish tosser.

Two of my best pals shared their goo at sixteen. Twenty years later they both love their kids and their kids are cool. Both lads do carry some baggage regarding the way they didn't really engage with their kids early doors. They simply existed beside them. They both struggle to connect with their offspring to this day.

For the record I loved my bird and her mate and about five others. I was always a little obsessive in the emotional department but unfortunately if you don't love yourself then you can't love anyone else. Mr Floppy was living proof of that.

My long term nearly lover was always an on and off sort of set up. We ditched each other at least once a fortnight and the bad news usually came in A4 hand-written letter form. We were never too devastated as we both knew that it was very likely that a hand-written A4 sheet of good news was always around the corner.
Snogathon respite periods were very convenient for exploring other opportunities and going with other birds. That was the way of the plastic gigolo.

My only other close call regarding popping the old cherry was with a bird in my class. She came to our school as a mum, a really young mum. She was blonde, bonnie and a lot more experienced than moi.
I took her to see the soul singer Alyson Williams who was big at the time in more ways than one. We went to the Manchester Apollo. I thought I looked the part in the usual chino pants, shirt and paisley tie until we walked into the concert hall and everyone else in the building was black, stoned and wearing sports gear. I wasn't too bothered we stood out because whilst Alyson belted out her quality signature tune 'I Need Your Loving'. I was prodding my new friends bum with a right old stonker. We quaffed a few halves of Woodpecker and black before a triumphant touchy feely black cab ride back to hers.

A great night got greater as we got straight down to business on the rug in front of the fire. She was much more experienced than my real love and I could feel myself amongst her hot wet underbelly. Up until

this point I hadn't had an orgasm and I didn't really know
what one was but I was sure something was happening.

I was quite pissed and pleased with myself, a few beads of sweat
appeared on my forehead before she announced "I'm going to take my
tights off now." I was devastated. I rolled off, pulled up my kecks and
did one! A few weeks later I sat in the cinema wanting to puke as my
pals and I watched the same thing happen to a young soldier in the film
'Biloxi Blues.' When quizzed about my date at the Apollo I told my
best pal she was mad for it and he popped round the very next day and
gave her a proper seeing to or maybe he was full of shit too.

So although I'd been naked with a couple of chicks I essentially joined
the Royal Navy a virgin, a virgin with no pubes! This isn't a great
starting point in the macho world of single sex Navy Basic Training
School.

As ever I blagged it. I showered at 3a.m before the rest of the
Silverbacks arose and luckily enough I started sprouting the
odd spider's leg from there on in. It was rumoured the naval hierarchy
put bromide in our tea to suppress us and make us less horny. That
simply can't have been the case because each morning the whole mess
(dorm) rose en masse, willies pointing northward!

Pretty soon I, like the rest of the hair-bears learnt the art of
masturbating in silence. Picture the scene. You're in a mess with thirty
five other blokes all lying there in their rickety steel framed single
beds. Any sudden move produces a noise.

So here's the technique. First you convince yourself everyone else in
the room is asleep. Then you picture in no particular order every
woman you've ever come across, putting your knob in her mouth. I
often liked the thought of my English teacher doing the detention
thing. Then very slowly and gently you would have the most
tender wank imaginable. It would take quite along time to get there
and it was almost impossible not to celebrate on completion. I was
quite good at passing it off as a yawn. Some weren't so polite.

The fact that wanking in a room full of men is wrong made it
so much more intense. That seems to be the way this life is set up. The
naughtier the deed, the bigger the hit, then you pass out and wake up to
bad Karma. Yes you're stuck to the sheets or even worse later that day
you come back from the parade ground and somebody has exchanged
your sticky sheets for sticky and pissy sheets.

You can find the same story at the start of the bible; Adam's apple and
the tree of temptation or in the film Trainspotting regarding heroin
abuse. The fact is every single action you take has a consequence and
the more you wank, pinch forbidden fruit or shoot up, the stickier your
life will become.

Life in H.M.S Raleigh wasn't all about spanking the monkey. Overall I
breezed through the Navy Training School. At sixteen I was physically
and mentally stronger than most. I was a fuckwit when it came to tying
knots and operating weapons. My mind isn't set up for that sort of shit.
I wasn't too worried that I shouldn't be trusted with a gun or a rope.
My inner force guided me through the tests and I knew they weren't
skills I'd need anytime soon. After all I was going to be trained as a
chef.

We also had to learn to march because at the end of the training
program there was to be a passing out parade. The parade ground held
no fear for me. We weren't marines but we were one of the last all
male classes to come through the place so the instructors had their last
real chance to bully an intake because pretty soon girls or split arses as
they were known would be in the mix. Political correctness was just
around the corner, but not for us. We were still fair game and lots of
young kids just crumbled. One Scottish lad who had somehow crapped
his pants in the night was made to stand at the front of the whole intake
with his shitty knickers on his head. He was about six foot three and
the poor fucker cried like a baby for what seemed like hours whilst we
all looked on.

I found it quite easy to keep my head down. Being a housewife from
the age of ten set me up for military life. I was self-sufficient. I could
wash and iron my kit no problem. When it came to marching I was
pretty bad. We all were. There is nothing funnier than bad marching or
tick-tocking as it's called. The most fun came when the instructor

would give a command to turn right or left and the poor duty muppet would turn the wrong way. A bit like one man and his dog when a sheep gets disconnected from the group. The farmer whistles and the dog chases and barks the lost sheep back into line. I struggled to take it all seriously. The louder someone screamed in my face the less real it seemed to me. My strategy to avoid intimidation was fairly simple. As I'm being screamed at I'd send my assailant a telepathic message right back. Usually something like " I bet your wearing suspenders under that uniform?"

My class was clearly the worst marching collective. We were ritually chastised and belittled before the other classes. We seemed to be a collection of lost sheep. Each Friday we were on parade and each week we got slightly better. The week before the pass out we fluked a near perfect march around and from nowhere we were chosen to be the Guard of Honour for our passing out parade. Manufactured or not it was Billy Elliot stuff and we were transformed overnight into a very proud bunch of crap marchers.

On passing out they sent a big cheese admiral to inspect us. I telepathically told him he had bad breathe. It was all going so well until one of our lads collapsed. He narrowly missed the upright bayonet of the sailor in front of him. He was spark out and bloodied. The silly sausage never bothered with breakfast and unfortunately if you pass out holding a gun only the cement will break your fall. We'd failed and botched the whole event. It seemed rather fitting really.

Later that evening it was all rather surreal as our proud families celebrated our success inside the pub they used for the passing out party venue. The injured sailor and I were present in a line of five young matelots that were being wanked or sucked off by a number of Wrens (split arses) who were very easily led after their first beer in six weeks.

My mum attended the parade. It was the first time I'd really seen her since the split. I sent her a letter inviting her. I decided this was a new start for me and we could start again.

Chapter 12: Cold Fish and Warm Oats

Soundtrack: Shades of Rhythm - Sounds of Eden (Every time I see the girl)

Naval chef training was stellar. We probably had the same experience every small class of eight chefs that ever came through the place did. I would call it the Auf Wiedersehen Pet experience. Young fella's, daft accents, big fun. One Scottish lad was a shit hot cook, the rest of us burnt things and cut ourselves.

I can't move on without mentioning a tragedy that highlights the damage evil bullies can inflict on vulnerable people. There was a lad in our dorm who was an ex sea cadet. He'd obviously been tying knots throughout his adolescence. He was a bit of a know-it-all and somewhere along the line he must have rubbed up the duty fat, ugly Glaswegian bully the wrong way.

Each night a number of alarm clocks would go off around the sea cadet's bed. I used to register it subconsciously but by morning it was always forgotten. Nobody knew or cared who was planting the clocks until one afternoon the Glaswegian fiend was caught red handed planting a sleep disturbing device behind the nearest radiator to the victims bed. I honestly don't know if it was his first offence but the finger of mean shame pointed towards the highlander.

I remember coming back from leave to hear the clock prank victim had jumped off Blackpool pier and drowned. I have no idea what was going on in that lad's private life but Shrek must of felt partly responsible even if he was only a bit part bully. His poor mum and dad! He was living out his dream and evil got in the way. It's hard to justify that sort of tragedy. Once you get suicidal. little problems become life threatening and the devil got into that poor lad. We never got asked a single question and to be honest we did what lads do. We made a joke of it: nothing like throwing yourself into a weekend off! That sort of shit.

We were taught from day one that looking after number one was how to survive in the services, that humour was part of the process. As I've matured I've come to hate that sort of joke or text message. It takes away our humanity and symbolises all that's wrong with society. Self, self, self gratification. It normalises horror and wrong doing. They are usually sent by people who have little going in there dull and dreary lives.

My first Naval draft was to deepest darkest Cornwall. I arrived in January and they did not roll out the red carpet. In the early nineties Navy kitchens were run by grumpy and often alcoholic chief cooks. They had little responsibility and would fritter between drinking in their living quarters to wandering into the kitchen and dishing out indiscriminate bollockings.

The chief cooks henchmen were heavily tattooed bullies called leading chefs. In the main they misled teams of baby chefs on their daily duties. Most of these fella's weren't out to help and educate you, they'd rather belittle and embarrass you. There was one particular prick that would heat a ladle in a deep fat fryer. When you were digging out in service he'd sneak up behind you and burn the back of your arm. I used my mum's 'doesn't hurt' trick. He wouldn't get a reaction from me. There was one nice fella. He seemed almost embarrassed to be normal though.

They would try and send you to stores for tartan breadcrumbs for the scotch eggs, all that bollocks. I got the humour and I knew there was a pecking order. I was just a bit disappointed nobody showed a personal interest in you. They were cold fish.

Three months later I'd made my mark on the football pitch. Mr Hot Ladle got snapped in half leaving him in no doubt I was a physical match for him. It seemed to matter little in the kitchen as I still felt like a bit of a spare part but everything changed when I laid eyes on a slight framed stewardess polishing the silver. Fuck me I don't know what it was about her but I needed to ask her out. She looked confident but vulnerable at the same time and I think it was that vulnerability that that gave me the confidence to approach her.

"Hiya, can I take you out? " She looked up. "What?" Somehow I got her to meet me that night. We met at the main gates. I was on my

Vespa scooter. She was so fit I thought I was gonna puke. I pointed for her to walk out of the camp and round the corner. I gave her my helmet and I wore none. She smiled and I was putty. I felt like Jimmy in Quadrophenia tearing down to the beach. What I would have done for a Leslie Ash knee trembler.

A week later my knee trembler came. I'd waited over seventeen years for it, and to say she knew her way around the bedroom would be doing her a great disservice. She Kamasutra'd me left right and Chelsea Not only that, she was vocal, she swore. I was gob smacked. I lay in bed watching her do her hair and make-up in the morning. She was perfect. I had always been susceptible to a love job. This was it. I knew I was fucked.

After an encouraging start to my fledgling sex career I couldn't stop ejaculating and I don't mean inside her. I just had to hold her hand. It was all too much for me. She thought it was cute. I liked that point of view, she said it was a challenge. We moved into a cottage by our beach. I challenged her further. She trained me up. I was grateful. I was more fucked.

One Saturday morning I awoke with a pleasing stiffness and made an approach. She freaked out, a panic attack. She broke down and told me her step dad had been abusing her since childhood and for a second she thought I was him. I told her I'd look after her. I meant it.

Later that day I went for a crap. When I was done I rolled some extra bog roll down and wrote will you marry me on the paper and rolled it back up. It just came to me. When she went in for business I heard a scream. We were young, daft and in love.

Elizabeth Duke came up trumps at about £150. Her mum came down. She knew, I knew she'd always let the abuse happen. I wanted to murder her. Her attitude was repulsive. She said it was unavoidable. She was still fuckin' with him. I was freaked out.

Chapter 13: Piggin' Blew it

Soundtrack: Billy Ray Cyrus - Achy Breaky Heart

Life was stale in the kitchen but things were taking off at home and on
the football pitch. My adventures in football are another book but I'll
give you a brief synopsis: I wasn't a fast sprinter but when I was on
one I had the determination and unstoppability of a runaway train.
Being in love seemed to strap rockets to the back of that train. I was
grateful too for my natural talent. I could see a pass and I loved the
game.

To cut a long story short I got selected to go and play for the Navy
youth. My job was not suited to this. Chefs are one of the few branches
of the Royal Navy that do hard physical graft. At weekends people still
needed feeding. That meant one in three weeks I had to work a long
day Saturday and Sunday. Now in my new life the Navy Youth played
in the Southwest Combination League. They had to release me to play
footy. The bitter chief cook tried to stop me but the club-swinger (On
Base Sports dude) made sure I went every time. I was grateful as he
helped me out a lot. The younger chefs warmed to me. They liked my
spirit. The old guard detested my special status.

I came into the team half way through the season. They got battered in
this league. It was boys against men but it was insignificant. Your
focus was staying in the team all year to make the annual trip to play in
the Dallas cup.

At home my sex training was gaining momentum. She was
unquenchable. I'd run the three miles home in the dark with a boner on.
Forest Gump on naturally produced Viagra. Testosterone was
pulsating around my being, I liked it.

The Missus was okay about me going away at weekends, she said she
was proud. One Friday I ran home after breakfast service to get my
gear prior to going for the train to Portsmouth. There was a flash car
outside the house. This dude got out of the car and I instantly

recognised him as a pilot off the base. I made this twat's breakfast and she served it to him. He said he needed to speak to her, he was holding a letter. He started to get emotional. I chose not to hear the details. I punched him all the way back to the Jag then I started to dismantle the vehicle. He was upset but also in defence mode. He dove off fast in a much devalued automobile.

I knew everything deep inside. I chose not to know. She thanked me. She said the freak wouldn't leave her alone. If he'd reported me, then assaulting an officer is worth about six months in nick. Screwing a junior rate was a discharge. He stopped coming in for breakfast.

I arrived in Pompey around 10pm. My team mates were in the Mucky Duck pub. From there it was off to the famous nightclub Joanna's a real Naval School of Dancing. However much I got caned, the next morn I prayed thanks for my new love. Kissed the badge of my new blazer and went into battle. Amazingly my granddad played for the same team during the war. I took great pride in this and I made the Dallas flight no probs.

So two months before my wedding I flew off to Dallas. One of the chefs from basic training was the keeper. We set the tone on the flight. We decided to disregard the brief about listening to your body in terms of no beer and lots of water. We took on the points about representing your country though. Chef produced a bottle of Jack Daniels and challenged me to a wanking competition. The British Airways club class packs contained socks that we put on our ears and grey blankets for over our laps. I had recent good form behind me in this discipline and fired one off in no time.

Scouse was a key member of the team and a cracking player too. Showed exactly what a player he was as he took what looked like a fourteen year old into the toilet. Her dad seemed to be sat opposite and seemed not at all interested. Turbulence seemed to be occurring just inside the toilet cabin and then she came out all of a Bambi. The tour was off to a rather disturbing flying start.

On arrival in Dallas we were greeted by some very enthusiastic families who were very excited to share their homes with real English sailors for the whole length of our stay. My host was far less jovial.

Rosanne Barr seemed to be wearing at least one glass eye. No hugs for me she grunted out a "Hi." It looked like I'd bagged another cold fish. The only cold fish.

Somewhat deflated the quiet bloke they'd paired me off with loaded our bags into a clapped out Toyota. We watched aghast as the other lads boarded luxury air conned MPV's, sports cars and monster trucks.

On arrival in the hood Rosanne's husband grunted in our general direction. Their daughter greeted us very enthusiastically, big hugs. She was sort of attractive. Long hair, cap, skinny jeans, flip flops. She was all American.

She addressed us both and said "Do you Boys wanna come and see my pig?" We both said yes. She said to me "I'll show you first, you watch T.V until we get back, then I'll show you me darlin."

Apparently each pupil at school gets a pig to feed up until you graduate. Then you get judged on your pig pedigree. Hers was prize. On the way to the farm she told me about her violent boyfriend, her drug habit and how she and her dad were at war.

We walked round to the pig pen. The skinny jeans came down and she bent over the middle bar of the fence and showed me her pig. It looked nice. "Mrs, I'm getting married". "So what? I won't tell". I declined. I'd just seen her pig now she saw her arse. We drove back mainly in silence but she did mutter intermittent expletives.

I walked in and my team mate associate walked out. I was pleased for him. We spoke later and he was very pleased for himself. He was no longer the quiet man of the team. From then on we called him Porky.

The young livestock handler spent the next two weeks devouring the majority of the squad. This suited me as she drove us around all the luxury residence's the other lads were staying at. She introduced herself to almost everyone. Apparently she'd been at it for the last three tours.

The opening ceremony of the footy was like the Olympics. When they announced the Royal Navy the place erupted. It was too much for the balloon. Suited and booted I broke rank grabbed a union jack and started running past the packed stand whipping them up into a frenzy. This went down like a lead balloon with the management team.

We partied hard and played shit. There was a party held at the house of the toilet nookie young looking one off the plane. Thankfully she was of age but she had no shame. Scouse did her in the Jacuzzi then in front of everyone on the pool table. She loved it. Our big and daft chef/keeper jumped in a pool he wasn't supposed to then nearly drowned in the pool cleaning chemical stuff. The police were called.

The next day management played a video of his fully clothed pool bomb back to the group. Keeps and I were made the scapegoats and our punishment was? No more footy!

We celebrated not training in style. Keeps had copped off with the millionaire's daughter he was staying with. They were grateful as she was ugly. They let us have the run of the place.

Flying back to Blighty I felt a huge pang of guilt. I could have played footy all over the world for the Navy for the next twenty years. I'd sacrificed it all by letting my selfish little inner beast control my thoughts and my actions. I couldn't see past the party on each given day. This is a pattern of behaviour that I and a lot of the misguided youth of England just fail to see past.

Through the guilt I always saw a positive. At least I could spend more time with my wife to be.

Chapter 14: The Big Bang

Soundtrack: Talking Heads - Once in a Lifetime

Before the wedding we had three epic visits. The first was from a
Geordie I met in basic training. His family was amazing. They were so
wrong and so right at the same time. I went up there for part of my first
summer leave after basic training. You walked in the door and you
were family.

His dad's appearance was somewhere in the middle of Terry
McDermott and a chuckle brother. He seemed to be an alcoholic but a
nice one. He didn't seem to get angry and bitter like most piss cans do.
He was warm, generous and fuckin' funny. He was well sauced from
breakfast onwards. He'd position himself next to a stash of Ace
branded lager and seemed to be on the periphery not really paying
attention to the high brow 'change the world' weed head waffle that
was being branded around the room. Then about once an hour he'd
deliver an 'on the money' one liner. For whatever reason he'd got his
life wrong but he clearly loved his family and I loved him.

Mum also had a Terry McDermott mullet. She was a gorgeous person.
Her softly spoken Geordie was so soothing. She was in a wheel chair
because she broke her back after falling down some stairs in a shop.

The two of them met when she was a stripper in Amsterdam. My pal
seemed to hold that against his mum. I got the feeling I hadn't heard
the whole story.

If I thought my old man was chilled. Sunday dinner in Pendower was a
whole street affair and they all brought drugs with them. They loved
the Happy Monday's and Wrote For Luck was the soundtrack for
copious weed intake.

They were doing hot knives, buckets & bongs, the whole shebang. It
was like a mad science demonstration. Then we all took turns gulping
big clouds of harsh, bitter, acrid smoke. I wasn't a smoker but there
was a camaraderie here that I couldn't resist. I got as stoned as a crow.
I couldn't knock back hospitality like that. The atmosphere rivaled the

Rio Carnival.

Geordie turned up at our little cottage with a lump of weed and some Ecstasy pills. I had no interest in mixing Navy time and narcotics normally and was surprised to hear Plymouth was now hosting its own version of the Rio Carnival.

Even so my beloved was delighted to receive such lavish gifts and to my surprise she rolled the biggest spliff I'd ever seen. We'd never got smashed together before. We all popped a pill & thirty minutes later we were in a three man rave rubbing each other and expressing the true love we were feeling. I felt like a walking orgasm. My chin went west. My wife in the making had the filthiest looking 'shag me face' I'd ever seen.

What followed was not of this world. Upstairs at least 35,000 vaults shot through my penis then reverberated around my body. Feedback from the lady confirmed this. We had just experienced an explosion that in our minds at that time ranked alongside the original big bang at the start of time.

We couldn't leave Geordie out. I would never be the sort of guy to wife share but those pills let you feel love on a different level and it was a level that also included friendship: man love! That doesn't mean I wanted to touch him. It meant without even discussing it we had agreed as human beings we couldn't let a fellow human miss out on that. We came down and explained the situation. No strings. My friend from up north was welcome to go and engage my fiancée. If he didn't then as a human he'd missed his gift from whichever side of the other side it had come.

He was such a geezer that even with the purest MDMA love medicine ever sampled manipulating his being, he managed to knock us back straight away. His head popped.

We went back up for more far reaching experiments in his name. When we all came back down to earth a couple of hours later he was obviously promoted to world class friend. Again I chose not to question her suitability for wife duties. This was it for me.

A few weeks later our next visitor was my old railway sleeper pal. He endured thirteen hours of National Express torture to visit us. His gifts were of a similar persuasion: weed and whizz. He still had great music taste and we got talking and dancing to Talking Heads and other non-rave material. He and the missus started having mega-spliff roll up comps. They hit it off as friends. They had something in common: they were that proud that they took photos of their artwork. I couldn't keep still. I enjoyed the extra energy of the amphetamines and danced my cock off in front of them all night. You talk a lot on that gear and by breakfast we thought we all knew each other inside out.

Two weeks later the Naval Police came and removed me from the kitchen. They took me home and like the Gestapo they turned the house right over. Straight away I focused on the photo of the 'Spliff-Comp.' In a frame over the fireplace was a picture of my fiancée and our guest arm in arm sucking on their mega-spliff creations. For half an hour they emptied every drawer, nook and cranny. They never clocked the photo.

When they had finished trashing the gaff I was taken to the base in a van in which I prayed. It paid instant dividends as I came up negative on the urine test. For hours I was interrogated over drug use. They told me one of the chefs claimed I was a user. I told them that just because I'm from Manchester doesn't mean I'm a druggy. I explained I'm a footballer and certain fat bitter chefs were jealous. They couldn't break me I was at my peak.

Chapter 15: Reality Check

Soundtrack: Leslie Garrett - Dome Epais Duet

I'm writing this book as a guide to right living and not as an advert for hedonism. So I feel it's important at this point to make it clear how very dangerous having a mind blowing drugs experience is. As explained earlier in Milkspermboobswank your brain holds on to the filth and the naughty bits of life so much more than it does the right and the proper.

Once you bring a mind blowing high into the mix on top of filth and naughtiness or even on top of pure love and naughtiness. It's a fuckin strong force. One that can lead ultimately to your death. It takes a super human to put an experience like that in a box and be able to cherish and celebrate it but to leave it in the box and never try and replicate it. For settled souls, never mind kids that don't love themselves and struggle to do emotions and or life that sort of experience is gonna resonate in your head and soul for a long time. Untold damage gets done chasing that sort of buzz. When normal life becomes shit you're in trouble. When you enter a world where offering the services of the spouse that you love to a friend is normal. Wise up, it's not normal. You're damaging your brain and your soul.

IT'S VERY FUCKIN 'DANGEROUS!

Chapter 16: The Start of Hate

Soundtrack: Nomad - Devotion

I've never told anyone what I'm about to write such was and is my shame. I have a feeling lots of people have similarly never made confessions. Back to the Bible, the apple and the tree of temptation. I can't quite explain how it works but the forces in charge of this world throw up tests at big moments throughout a man's life. I failed my first such test dramatically and it's such a good example of why making the wrong decisions in life in return for short term gratification will always be the wrong option.

The Thursday before the wedding I hit the town with some of the chefs and stewards from work. A helicopter dude I'd rattled at footy bumped into me in the Lady Street nightclub, I looked up and he said "You want some?" I was about five beers into the evening, of course I wanted some. Outside I hit him with an unanswered flurry of about ten digs. He crumbled and I felt an adrenaline rush on par with the drug induced ones of recent times. I wasn't a nasty man I never kicked a man when he was down. In my mind I'd just won a duel like a gentleman back in Shakespearean times. I went back into celebrate and the bouncer shook my hand on the way in. My ego was getting out of hand.

Back at one of the chef's houses I got my head down. The chef had a bird and his bird had a friend and at roughly 9 am she walked into the room where I was lying on a mattress on the floor. She was about 17 and bare arsed naked. She was dark haired, pretty, skinny and white. She pulled back the sheet and helped herself to breakfast. I could have stopped her, I could have banged her. Sadly I chose option two.

As soon as I came I felt sick. She knew it and I never saw her skinny white arse again. Self-destruction had struck again. The test was offered and I chose to fail. This was typical of me. I'd passed all the minor tests along the way but when whoever sent that girl, sent her to make me hate myself and it worked.

I lay there for a while and started the process of punishment until I heard the screech of a hand break turn. Horns a blaring half of Manchester's raving fraternity had just turned up for my stag do. Look out!

Chapter 17: A Big Fat Cornish Stag Do

Soundtrack: Terry Wogan - The Floral Dance

Fuck me! All my pals turned up in a mixture of boy racer mobiles and dad's pride and joy. For most it was their first holiday drive and they were full of spunk. It looked like the Dukes of Hazzard as I looked at them all skidding into the chef's cul de sac abode.

We hit the town early afternoon and Mungo from school decided my Scouse chef pal wasn't to his taste. He hit him with a haymaker on the way to the second pub. He crashed against a shop front and slid down the window. I reprimanded Mungo and he duly picked him up and said sorry. The poor chap had gained a black eye already. He shrugged it off like only a lad could and we went down to sample the world famous Spingo Special real ale. It was about 8% proof and flat minging. Mungo and friends got started opening up their gullets. It looked like a very dangerous game. I just had one.

Over the road in the next boozer there was talk about a stabbing in the town the previous week. The locals were blaming the Navy and they wanted revenge. Next minute a local clipped my pal and a small melee ensued. Ten minutes later we were in the main road facing an angry mob of about forty tooled up farmers and fishermen. They had spades, shovels, iron bars and God knows what. It was totally unjustified. I gave the command to retreat: "Fuckin leg it!"

Leg it we did but we met a bit of resistance going up the hill. Scouse with the black eye got a spade across his face. He was definitely having a bad day. My auntie spotted me and ran out into the action totally oblivious to the carnage she'd just stepped into. "Can't talk right now auntie, see ya tmoz!"

It was like a scene from Zulu without the black people. Fighting our way out of town we started to splinter. My group made it up by the church, the scene for the following days wedding. It was dusk and a group of hippies complete with fiddles and medieval style dress played and danced in front of us just across the church yard. We hid in the long grass as the angry mob raced passed. We pissed ourselves laughing. Scouse did too. It must have hurt his spade flat face. We stayed there for quite a while until it was deemed safe. Then we started climbing the hill up to the chefs house where we would all crash. On the cusp of the hill we were faced with two lads, one holding an estate agents' sign.

Suddenly they identified us as enemy and raced down the hill. The young fellow aimed the stake for my face. I stepped to the side and smashed him in the grid. He collapsed in a heap. His pal said "What did you do that for?" I said "He tried to kill me." He wasn't happy and kept gobbing off until one of the other lads had no option but to chin him.

We pegged it back to ours where most minor injuries were being repaired. Everyone had a story to tell. I was proud that the lads had travelled the length of the country for me. I was glad they were buzzing they'd had an epic day. I lay down and reminded myself what a pig I was then I passed out.

Chapter 18: In The Family

Soundtrack: Terry Dactyl and the Dinosaurs - On a Saturday Night

Morning broke on a gorgeous English summer's day. My mind was messy with guilt but I told myself to get a grip. At least I wouldn't live my life wondering if I'd missed out by being a one woman man. It was a quality control test which confirmed my product choice was far superior. I awarded my fiancée the British Kite Mark for excellence.

The economics of the day were quite extraordinary I earned only £600 a month at the time. Our cottage wasn't cheap but somehow I scraped together £900. Everyone helped us. The baby chefs kindly stole a buffet. The only nice leading chef on the base made us a cake and doubled up as the D.J. I really couldn't thank him enough.

On Sundays I played for Goonilly F.C. I was proud to kiss their badge and their manager who was a smashing Cornish old boy loved the passion I displayed when I played for his team. He arranged for Goonilly's arch rivals Helston FC to donate their club house to us for the day in return. No charge. I was humbled.

That left me to pay for the dress, suits for me and my two best men, the vintage car, the church, the honeymoon and an overnight B&B stay after the wedding. We just about scraped it. Both sides of my family attended. It was the first time they had all gathered together since I was ten. It was all too much for me.

Wife looked stunning. She was beautiful. She had a tear in her eye I hoped she felt safer. I was so disappointed with myself having to take the vows full of guilt. It was so unnecessary and it ruined my focus. I held it together in the church but two pints into the reception my little brother was crying. He was so proud of me. It did me in. I cried for the next two hours. My family formed a queue to console and congratulate me.

My old man produced a telegram from Alex Ferguson wishing us all the best along with his and hers United tops with our new matching names on the back. He'd thought about that. It was his blessing, bless him.

The alleged sex pest was in attendance. I told him my thoughts. He said if I did anything to him then bad things would happen to the younger sisters. They were young innocent, blond and beautiful, I wanted to puke. He was working for the devil and his wife could burst into flames at any minute. I wanted them in prison: adopt the kids. Wife wasn't in that mind-set. I just didn't get it. They went and sat in the other room I prayed the little ones didn't know why.

Wife stayed with me and we got beered up. All the speeches were brief, we were only kids, we had no words of wisdom. There were very few wise people in the room. I stood up anyway and through the tears promised to look after her.

That sparked wild applause and the start of a relatively drug free rave. The lads had brought all the current rave tunage. Mungo was on the mic shouting out stuff like 'Man-chest-or you know the score!', "In the family!" and "We fuckin hate City!" We all lapped it up.

The normal sections of my family all enjoy a good party and we had it large. There was a circus pitched on the football ground at the club. Just as we were reaching fever pitch a gaggle of clowns, jugglers and blokes on stilts came in. I don't know who sorted that out but it certainly cranked it up a level.

As the atmosphere got more frenzied a good friend of mine got carried away with it all. His missus searched the whole club-house for him before flying into the little boys room where Kernow Kate had found a big boy and was sucking the end off it. I can still see his face, his natural reaction was to laugh and that was the last reaction his missus was expecting as she took in the scene. You wanker! To be fair she didn't kick off but it must have been a long drive home for those two.

We stayed out by the Gweek Otter Sanctuary. They let us have BLT and chips at 1am. I sat on the bed with my new official missus. She looked proud and ready for business. I thought to myself "I bet otters don't have it this good."

Chapter 19: Where's the wife gone?

Soundtrack: Gotye - Somebody That I used to know

Next day we travelled north by rail for our honeymoon in Stretford. It was a rather memorable trip for more than one reason. Firstly we joined the 125mph club. When the train guard finally removed us from the toilet we looked like a pair of greasy otters from Gweek. We felt no shame.

For some reason that shag triggered the confession. ”I've got something to tell you.” “Me too I thought, ”ladies first” “I used to be on the game to feed my drug habit and my pimp still controls me when I go home at weekends.” We were travelling at speed but everything stopped bang bang still. “What are you saying that for?” I replied. She wasn't on the verge of tears, if anything she looked sort of pleased with herself. I decided to keep my pathetic confession to myself as I'd just been well and truly super-trumped.

On arrival in Manchester we both kept our confessions to ourselves and I invited everyone to the pub. I needed a large one. Dad agreed but wife suggested to my soon to become wicked stepmother that they stop home and give her a haircut. That seemed pretty reasonable as she was a hairdresser and they could do girly stuff.

Two hours later, meat and potato pie chippy dinners in hand, Dad and I made our merry way home. I walked through the door to be greeted by Sinead fuckin' O'Connor. Lucky me I'd married a bald, junkie prostitute!

“Why have you shaved my wife's fuckin' head?” “She asked me to do it, said she needed a new start.” I looked at Mrs Edward Scissor Hands and asked the question; “Are you for fuckin' real?” Dad looked at his feet.

Never before had pie and chips looked so unimportant. I scranned them anyway then lay in bed holding hands with a complete stranger.

Chapter 20: Our Time

Soundtrack: Liquid - Sweet Harmony

Life on honeymoon all felt a bit hollow. It was hard to look the Barber of Seville in the eye. I sort of got used to looking at her victim. We had come north to meet my Nan. Nan didn't come to the wedding. She'd witnessed all that sort of teenage love nonsense before. Meeting Sinead wasn't gonna change her point of view, but meet her she did and what it was I don't know but they seemed have something in common. Nan was cool, always! She still gave me a pound coin every time I saw her. This time she gave us two.

The pre-planned highlight of the week was a trip to Shelly's Lazerdome in Stoke-on-Trent. At the time it was one of the top nightclubs in the world.

Some of my school pal circle lived for this experience. Sunday through to Saturday the transition from recovery to excitement then onto euphoria was planned out pretty meticulously.

We were part time ravers in need of some respite from the dullness that had come out of the bombs that she'd just dropped. That lethargy was soon replaced with the butterflies of anticipation as we met up with around twenty five other cars worth of giddy youth ready to drive convoy style to Stoke.

Ecstasy was not cheap at the time of its rise to prominence. Up to £15 a pop and there must have been a few bobs' worth commuting down the M6 that evening. We travelled in a gold mark 2 Ford Escort which hovered down the motorway on pre-drug taking nervous energy.

Sinead had her hot pants on. Her pimp was onto a very good thing. I chose to smile not sulk. I'd decided tonight was gonna be a celebration of life. I had a feeling we may never do this again.

Stoke was and is a shithole. We piled into a tiny boozer and got on the beer. It was a pub straight out of the seventies: flock wall paper and brass tat everywhere. Even so it had a blinding juke box and the joy of youth was all around the building. Everyone had made it through college, work and love trauma to be here and together we all started to climb the sensory buzz ladder.

In the big and fervent queue people were on tiptoes like meerkats trying to see what's for dinner. You could hear the boom of the base. The front walls of the club quivered. We popped our pills to avoid having them taken off us at the door where you got well and truly frisked. Half an hour worth of fidgety nonsense talk and we were in.

We timed it perfectly. Just as we were greeted by a wall of sound, blinding lights and a mass of mad for it man love the pills kicked in. She dragged me off for a snog and it was a desperate and dirty kiss. My cock was rock solid and adrenalin was shooting not just through my manhood but through every cell of my disco bits. I had no bad feeling in me I loved her and every fucker else in the room. These were nice pills. They were a pure buzz. You didn't feel heavy or restricted just loved up and ready to rock.

The music was so perfectly balanced it see-sawed between filthy, nasty hardcore sounds which plug into your dark side and have you growling and stomping and pulling all sorts of crazy faces as you struggle to burn off the excess energy blasting through ya. This contrasted with the love generating beautiful, clear and true piano tunes with soulful diva sounds thrown on top that sent rushes of joy and adrenalin up your back and out through your smile and limbs. The M.C professionally and passionately guided us rebel forces up and up and up like Jedi conductors of a supreme orchestra.

As the night went on the extremes in the music would intensify. D.J Daz Willot was the champion of the time. Each generation has their thing and this was ours.

The joy of it all was endless. Everyone was full of love. That meant no fighting. People would talk to everyone then hug them and rub their spines to give them a buzz before moving onto the next. "What's your name, where you from, what you on?" That was the standing joke but you could not help but say it.

Everyone had their own thing they liked to do. Some liked to puke as you get a massive rush straight after. This led to people subconsciously becoming toilet monitors. Because everyone was so helpful and loving you'd have people hanging round the toilets helping pukers recover and get them on a good one. Toilets were also great for chatting shit and a necessity for people that had to screw. They sold ice pops and space crackle candy and water out of the hatch by the bog. These all helped keep you alive and stimulate your senses to the max. I liked to put Vickes Vapour rub on my chest for clear clean as a whistle breathing and on my nuts for a burning buzz which helped me to enjoy the stomp.

In the car ride home we got in sleeping bags and smelt like bacon frazzles from the chemical laden dried sweat. A brew from a flask and a spliff to come down. These kids were organised pleasure seekers. Everyone told there story of the night. "Did you puke, kop off, see someone jump off a speaker? How many pills, trips, whizz did you have?" There was a slight ringing in your ears but in the main a great calmness settled over us all as we finished the night at an after party at Rivington Services on the motorway.

What an experience. This suited wife, she was right at home. We got home and tackled a chicken and mushroom pot noodle. That balanced our chemical P.H. perfectly. Nighty fuckin' night.

Next day we travelled back to Cornwall. We had a good booze on the train. You need it after a rave. Back in Cornwall life was all over the place. We had three days to collect our stuff and move to Plymouth. I was joining my first ship and my temporary life partner was to join a nearby shore base.

Chapter 21: Sea Dogs

Soundtrack: Cornershop - Brimful of Asha

We moved into Naval housing in Torpoint. It was basic but if she wanted to she could start a new life here. Her strings could be cut if she wanted them to be. We didn't really discuss a game plan. We both new I was going away to the Med in a week's time and I just hoped I'd come back in a couple of months to someone that had missed me and had chosen a new way of life.

My first day onboard was in a leave period so there was only a skeleton crew onboard. As I walked up the gangway and onto the quarterdeck of this creaky old grey warrior of death I realised this thing was my new home and would be until they decommissioned the poor old bugger the following year. I did wonder what the fuck I was doing there. I felt rather fraudulent and not at all like Popeye. Maybe that would come later. I hoped I wasn't a land lover. I'd always wanted to travel.

The ship was deserted. I was shown down to the mess (living quarters). It was in total darkness with just four lads in naval attire watching the opening credits of the Silence of the Lambs. "Hiya I'm new, where can I pu..", "sit down and watch the fuckin' film." So I did just to avoid the possibility of one of them eating me. After the film it was clear that there were more cold fish aboard this vessel. The warmest of whom showed me my pit and locker. When I re-entered the T.V area they were watching a film where a woman was sucking and fucking an Irish wolfhound. I said "what the fuck is this?" I was passed a video box and on the front it said 'Linda Lovelace fucking an Irish wolfhound'. No shit. What I really meant was why are you freaks watching sex between humans and animals? It was violent, the dog started to rip her back off. I snuck off to bed, my animal farm insecurities about a big sick world confirmed. I went to sleep without having a wank.

A couple of days later we set sail for the Med. I was soon impressing nobody in the kitchen as my chef skills weren't the best but I was a grafter so I held my head high. The older chefs had decent knowledge. I could learn from them.

In the mess there were a few interesting characters. There was one lad who was about twenty five, we secretly called him Psycho. He was intense, he demanded total submission. He liked to beat on us young ones. He would order you to go weight training or boxing sparring or even defence technique training. Whatever 'Sensei' showed you it always ended in pain for his subject. He'd usually batter you then make you thank him. He seemed relatively friendless apart from a mild mannered young Brummie who would secretly call him by his full name: Mr Psycho.

There was also a time served (approaching 22 years service) Cornish boy. He was a family man who never left the ship. Home or abroad he never spend a penny. It was his dog video and he was a gossiper. He was a mean and creepy fucker. Creepy fuck was a total contrast to 'Burnley' a slightly overweight dreamer from Burnley. He over-spent and over-ate. Best of all he liked traditional human porn. I bonded with a Cumbrian Liverpool fan: Nobby. We had a lot in common. Our bunks were side by side up in the rafters amongst the pipework. We were baby cooks, football players and masturbators alike. If we were off watch (day off together) we would have all day wank offs. That doesn't mean that we wanked each other off all day. We competitively and repeatedly wanked ourselves to see who could come first. We could whack off up to seven climaxes each in a day. Whoever came second had to get the other one refreshments and tissues. Our favourite was tea and toast with lime marmalade & salted butter. We needed to replace the salt.

There was also a Jabba the Hut type sloth. He was constantly releasing gases into the mess atmosphere. His head was lurgy scabbed and he constantly wore the same overalls with no kit underneath. In the Royal Navy such ratings are known as Crabby Fuckers. Beneath him slept the unfortunate Janner a nice lad from Plymouth.

Opposite my bunk slept another beast, Dawlish slept naked and his bed sheet was always pulled back exposing possibly the hairiest arse in the universe. I tried yodeling into Wookey hole a few times but the forest seemed to spoil the acoustics. He was a very intense, sincere and likeable sort of a chap. Each morning the sight of his gaping orifice made me feel very thankful that I wasn't a girl, a gay or a toilet roll.

The old boy of the mess was known as 'The Bastard'. He got his nickname from playing rugby. He loved to sneaky punch people in the rugby scrum. He was a hooker and he also loved hookers. It was all he ever talked about. Every time we approached a new port he'd tell us about his last visit there. He loved places where the staff would wash your cock before and after the business transaction. If you washed this mans penis he was happy. We all got that point.

We sailed Monday morning and in terms of sea legs I did okay. I felt a bit squeamish but managed not to hurl. Lisbon was my first foreign run ashore. We hit Estoril and Cascais which were cool beach resorts but the highlight of the visit was a visit to the famous Texas Bar in the old part of town. It was a well-known Naval haunt full of pig ugly hookers. A belly full of Superbock beer and Scouse and I had a ball dancing and taking the piss out of them. We both agreed there must be worse jobs than this.

Next to France for a few vin rouges en Toulon. All the chefs walked into a bar where the whole of the stokers (engineers) mess were doing there party piece 'singing in the rain' ala Bollocky Buff (naked). Thirty bearded smelly beasts singing their hearts out Tommy Steel style. It was a crazy type of tribal camaraderie. It was daft and seemed fairly harmless. Pyscho And Brum got stimulated by the cabaret and started french kissing before spitting beer at each other and play fighting to make light of their YMCA moment. From that point we just them saw as a construction worker and an Indian.

Istanbul was a bizarre experience 'The Bastard' had organised a coach trip to 'The Cages'. This was a government run brothel in a prison. Like in Amsterdam all the tourists walk around looking at the ladies. Difference is these ladies are incarcerated and if you want to screw them a guard stands there watching you. I bet 'The Bastard' didn't ask the guard to wash his todger for him on this occasion. With my wife being in the same trade union as the inmates I felt sorry for the poor fuckers. Apparently most of them were just regenerating the taxes their husbands had failed to pay. Rumours circulated that Crabby had enjoyed some prison hospitality but surely nobody had a tax bill that big.

Onto North Africa where folk weren't too friendly. It made little difference to the ship bound 'Creepy Fucker' but it did to us as our leisure time options became go ashore and risk a beating or stay onboard and endure dog porn. Nobby helped me up after a local down the town elbowed me in the face without warning. I ran after him for an explanation. He just gave me the universal sign to fuck off! We discussed whether to drop him or not but in the end we decided to fuck off and go for a kebab as we both agreed they were looking for any excuse to bum us in prison.

Last stop was Gibraltar and our last chance to pick up mail. I got nothing from the wife. I'd written quite a bit to her but I didn't hear a sausage. Lying in bed each night I feared for her life and I wondered what would become of mine. I prayed for both causes and listened to a lot of Kool And The Gang.

The mail I did receive was most unexpected. It was from Rio, a medium sized brown enveloped stuffed with around 70 photo's of a certain Geordie boy. He was bollocky buff and beside him were two world class light brown Brazilians also in the buff. They all had 'reefers' on the go. I knew he liked a spliff but I wasn't aware that sex and smoking at the same time was ever an option. I felt a bit health and safety over that.

These photo's were undoubtedly hilarious but I feared for my pals career. I had a cheeky wank over the birds and reluctantly chucked the pictures overboard. The crazy little fucker. He'd taken the carnival full circle from Newcastle all the way back to the Copafuckincabana! His days In the Royal Navy had to be numbered. Surely such open drug taking would be his downfall. You had to tip your hat to his birds though. Whoever they were, they were shit hot.

The highlight of Gibraltar was the tale of 'Burnley'. He had been harping on about his Asian bird the whole trip. What a top curry she made and how her fanny hair had a different coarseness to it, all that. They were engaged to be married on his return. He liked his food and the whole trip he was also banging on about trying to lose weight for slimmer wedding pictures. He'd starve himself all day then go training. Then have a beer in the mess before sneaking back upto the kitchen for midnight scoff. He was never gonna shift a kilo. You couldn't not like him though; he was a trier.

When a ship arrives in Gib the deployment is almost over. It's only three days off Blighty. 'Burnley' had managed to stay in all trip to save his wedding pennies. For some reason he decided to venture out for a few scoops on the last night ashore of the whole trip.

The morning after the night before he strolled into the kitchen at 5.30a.m where I was the duty breakfast bitch. He looked hung-over and flustered. "Morning Burnley, do you want a butty?" "Bacon, egg & sausage mate please." (Fat bastard) Then I spotted that the whole of one side of his neck was covered in love bites. You had to laugh. This was fuckin' blatant, the daft twat! "I want you to burn me!" His plan was for me to burn his neck with the Grill tray I was cooking the bacon with. Turning a bite into a burn which he could explain away. I was reluctant at first but he was upset and before you could say Burnley cross faith marriage I was branding the fuck out of him. The blisters didn't take long to come up. He looked like a mutant cauliflower. A week later he was back early from leave. Asian Annie had binned him about a month ago. The poor sod.

My prospects weren't looking much better. As we came alongside and docked in Plymouth I was shitting myself. I had to work that evening. The following morning it was time to face the music.

Chapter 22: Lamped

Soundtrack: Samuel Barber-Adagio for Strings

I was on duty the first night alongside in Plymouth. Geordie rang the ship, bless him as he'd received my reply to his brown envelope. We talked and I explained my lack of contact with her indoors. He suggested I meet him the following lunchtime for a couple of scoops of Dutch courage before I went for the ferry home. I agreed.

We met in the Frog and Frigate up on Plymouth Hoe. It was a sun trap and instantly I could feel the vitamin D rays on my face. Geordie was full of tales of the Rio experience but since he got back he'd fallen for a pot headed civvy. He said that each one of her tits was bigger than his head. They'd moved in together. It sounded dangerous to me. He was only little, he might suffocate. His company was easy and I was getting comfortable. As the sun started to frazzle my face he kept the lager coming. Four hours later I gave him a hug. The time had come and instantly I felt alone.

Only people that have used a cable crossing will understand the groan of the Torpoint ferry. My insides were in perfect harmony with the chains as they ripped through its underbelly and dragged me closer to all that I feared. It was surreal walking up through the town wondering if I would be welcome in my own home. At least I had a tan. My face was stinging like fuck. I had no real agenda I just wanted to know what she was doing. At core I'm a lover not a fighter and I approached the door in a submissive frame of mind.

My key no longer fitted in the lock. I spied through the glass part of the door and couldn't believe my eyes. A man that wasn't me was wearing my dressing gown. It looked like he was talking to her in the kitchen, my kitchen. I started kicking the bottom panel of the UPVC door in. It was solid but I'd chosen my point of entry. Next thing he was at the door saying fuck off or he would kill me. I registered the voice; he was an ex-street robber from London. I remember her saying they had a lot in common with their upbringing. They worked together cleaning spoons. He was some sort of kickboxing champ. All of those things flashed through my mind and if I wasn't in kill mode already he then announced through the letterbox that I should fuck off because she was having his baby.

The panel soon buckled and I ploughed in head first. He was repeatedly booting me. I never felt a thing. Before he knew it I was up and at him continuously raining blows until he upended and we both fell to the floor. He seemed dazzled I pinned him and I started beating him. She was screaming like a Banshee then she started trying to pull me off. I went in for the kill I grabbed the lamp and ripped it out of the wall then set about strangling him. She stood behind me and dug her long nails into my face I could feel blood start to trickle down my sun stained face. Next thing I felt huge hands on my arms and seconds later I began fighting with Naval policemen. I threw numerous potshots at two officers before one rugby tackled me and the other one got the cuffs on. Just like in a crap soap opera I looked up exactly at the moment I was about to be thrown in the van. She was holding her small bump belly at the door. I got my wish I knew exactly what she'd been doing.

Back at the ranch I was still crying. I'd cried through the whole battle scene. It wasn't a cry of sadness. It was pain, raw and uncontrollable. The coppers weren't happy I'd decided to fight them but they could tell from my condition that it wasn't personal. I would have battered my granny. My face was a mess, she'd scraped tiger markings into it and what was underneath was silly sunburnt. For the next day or so they left me alone. I carried on crying.

They interviewed me then spoke about charging me with attempted murder. I hadn't even considered that. I suppose that's the way it was going though. They said "Don't worry too much. We are aware of the mitigating circumstances here and there is a lot of sympathy for your situation. It has all been documented and you'll be able to represent your point of view before your commanding officer. You'll notice you've not been charged with assaulting my staff. They have chosen not to acknowledge your behaviour towards them. We are holding you for another week while you cool off. Then you'll return to your ship. Do not come back on this side of the water or my staff will not be so accommodating. Your father has been informed and he is visiting you tomorrow."

Dad came and laughed but in a way which made me know he felt for me. Back onboard the hearing was a farce thankfully They did what sailors do best and made a huge joke of it. The only serious bit was the skipper who said "If you get in trouble for fighting again you will be dismissed." I was glad it was over and as much as it hurt I gave up on the pregnant one. My first big love job was over.

Chapter 23: Handshakes and Fisticuffs

Soundtrack: The Rolling Stones - Street fighting Man

A week is a long time to think. I was sad. I don't think I was ever mature enough to actually save her from all the shit she faced and the cycle of hurt she was addicted to. I desperately wanted that though. It seems she gave a lot of pleasure to a lot of people but it was such a waste of a special person. Even so, she was beyond help. I had to accept that.

On release, exactly how much I'd been pissing in the wind with her started to become clear almost immediately. The first confession came from the club swinger from my old base in Cornwall. I bumped into him in Gus (Plymouth). The same kind man that secured my release to go and play football in Portsmouth each weekend told me that while I was lacing my boots he was filling his: in my bed! He, like all the ones behind him told me with a smile and a handshake. She was good for my football career, he said. That got fucked too unfortunately.

I'd been so naive. She was a fuckin' nymphomaniac. Quickly I developed a humour coping mechanism. I didn't want to as I cared more than that, but it was the only way. From then on if anyone asked about it or confessed to having naughty times with her was told the same thing. "What can I say I married a nymph. It was good while it lasted: Two weeks!"

Days later like a gypsy of the sea I was able to sail away from all the turmoil in the South West. The lads took the piss. 'Burnley' was overjoyed that I was in his club. There were lots of rumours about what she'd been up to. Creepy Fucker was like a dog with a bone. The sad bastard!

It was the lads from the other messes that I felt staring at me. I felt that they thought I was a mad man. It was a funny feeling. Subconsciously I stopped looking people in the eye. I think around that time I stopped loving myself.

It seemed crazy in light of all the misdemeanours of the ex but more than anything I was struggling to come to terms with my betrayal the day before my wedding. I could have walked away from this experience just feeling silly and sorry for my ex. Instead I hated myself. I hoped that would go away.

I was a good man that had started doing bad things. My inner balance was out of synch. All the guilt that came from that should have shown me the way to right living: It's that simple!

I, like millions of young kids in this country failed to grasp that concept. I thought escapism through partying was my path to peace. How wrong could I be? The problem is when your soul isn't settled you have little control over some of the crazy decisions you make when you drink alcohol. An inner beast takes over. So while I was able to sail up to Sunderland and feel liberated and funky free in Annabel's nightclub on a Wednesday night, the escapism was always accompanied by the threat of violence. Testosterone, alcohol and an unsettled soul do not mix.

Back to sea, we went into defence watches which are continuous spells of eight hours on shift, eight hours off shift. So you could end up going to work twice in a day. The good thing was on the night shift we made the ships bread. This was the first time I'd been impressed by a Naval foodstuff. It was fresh, crusty, even artisan. The smell drifted through the ship and attracted all types of sailors on the scav.

The chef in charge of the kitchen was a cockney geezer who had limited knowledge in the kitchen but liked the cleaning side of things. He was a bit of a space cadet like myself and what went on outside the kitchen around the ship didn't really concern him. In his eyes we were a self contained unit of special forces cooks. We were the engine of the ship.

I became fully aware of P.O cockney's disinterest in 'out of kitchen' ship activities when I turned to (clocked on) for a night shift. No more than ten minutes after I got out of bed he ordered me up to the boat deck to drag eight bags of potatoes down to the kitchen from the spud locker for peeling. I unbattoned the door clips and forced it open into a stiff breeze. I stepped out into the darkness and started to feel my way towards the locker. Then I got the shock of my life. A SeaCat missile was launched only metres away from my position. Not only that, it seemed to stop and look around for a target before it decided which way to go. I lay still and lifeless praying while it made it's choice. Then with a crack of thunder it lit up and fucked off. Scared shitless and spud less I was back down to the kitchen in seconds. I was sworn to secrecy over a cup of tea and some warm crusty bread and butter. The ship was at action stations during a firing exercise, the dozy twat nearly killed one of his stealth caterers.

The ship headed north. We hugged the east coast which was absolutely stunning. I'd often hide by the warm fans on the boat deck and take it all in. Wildlife and oil rigs were added visual treats but just the sea was enough. I found sitting there both exhilarating and melancholic depending on my mood.

This trip threw up one of the opportunities I loved the Navy for. The notice board always had weird and wonderful trips and challenges to put yourself forward for. Aalborg offered a cross country challenge against the Danish army followed by an initiation into the Aalborg Freemason Society.

Nobody else volunteered to represent the ship but Nobby and I. We were decent runners so the pride of our great nation was in good hands. Two hours later we realised we were shite runners. These Danish fella's were machines. I came last and Nobby second last. Not to worry, it was great to tear through the Dastrup Forest and burn up testosterone in a civilised manner.

We lost the race but won the reception. The machines weren't allowed to drink alcohol. They had to watch us demolish a crate of Carlsberg Special. We only semi-disgraced ourselves with a few glass breakages. It was weird getting drunk in front of people that wanted to participate but couldn't. We were conscious of our clumsiness but we couldn't help it. A few beer puddles later we began over-thanking our hosts who were probably very pleased to see the back of such a pair of out-of-shape drinking lightweights.

They laid on a giant bus into Aalborg just for the two of us which made us think the whole crate of beer wasn't really meant to be consumed by only two people. The Freemasons were already in good spirits when we arrived almost as if they had been drinking someone else's beer too. They taught us their funny handshake and presented us with keys that gained us access to their drinking den twenty four hours a day!

Why? I have no idea. There was a large picture on the wall of Ronnie Reagan the U.S President accepting the same key. I looked forward to sharing a pint and packet of pork scratchings with him at some point in the near future.

From there we made the effort to go clubbing. It was like they had a local Whigfield/Abba cloning factory. Very pretty blonde girls were all around us. Both of us could hardly string a sentence together although we did understand it was about £8 a pint. Back at ship there were stories of very liberal Danish husbands asking our lads if they minded screwing their wives while they watched. We couldn't remember seeing any blokes such was the talent on display. This had been a trip to remember and I was grateful for the experience.

Two weeks later back in Plymouth. Geordie called me round to his ship. His shipmates insisted guests drink a pyramid's worth of beer cans. I didn't want to offend anyone. One Jockenese alpha male amongst them was pushing my buttons and testing me out. I didn't rise to it but I wanted to bump into him on a football pitch soon. After Captains rounds at seven o'clock we hit Union Street which is the Las Vegas Strip of Devon. We span some Sea Dits (stories) and drank up to silly level. Pretty soon we were all gooey and talking broken biscuits.

At midnight we gained access to Blondz nightclub. This was Plymouth's premier rave cave for non-ravers (drug free). Even before I'd got the first round of drinks in, Geordie had stumbled into confrontation. Somehow he'd upset two Americans. He walks over to me with his two new friends and says "These two Yankee Lifeguards want to fight us. Are you up for it?" Without a thought for the skippers warning, my career, my health or my family I agreed to this very unusual type of pre-agreed tear up. Yank and lifeguard were too much of a challenge to refuse after fifteen pints. The fact they were gobbing off in typical over the top Yank style just got me even more excited. As this complete stranger threatened to fuck me up, inside my demons were already dancing. Beer + Testosterone = Devilbeast and mine was never gonna pass up an adrenaline feast like this.

We didn't sneak off to an underground car park for fight club. No, as soon as we got down the stairs and out onto the busy main road we went at it. They were genuine lads. They weren't gonna stab us. It was proper fisticuffs. By rights the Naval police should have picked us up in a few minutes as they patrol the strip all the time but somehow our scrap just went on and on. Not much came back from my guy but he was game and reluctant to go down or run off. Geordie was faring a little worse. So I ran over and we swapped opponents. We scrapped past all the food outlets up to the next roundabout. This guy was tougher and we traded blows. I felt my knuckle explode as I caught him with a haymaker and he fell down into a railing and smashed his head. His mate ran over to tend to him and we celebrated like we'd just scored a goal to win a legitimate sporting match. The buzz was ridiculous. We must have looked frightening with our shirts ripped and bloodstained. Geordie's eye was gashed and my hand was smashed. We walked arm in arm triumphantly up to Stonehouse Hospital. Our perception of life at that time was very wrong. We thought we were the dog's bollocks. In the morning a chef would need his hands and I wouldn't feel so clever then.

Chapter 24: Snags

Soundtrack: The Police-So Lonely

Unfortunately a good man had become stuck in a cycle of destructive behavior. I was still kind, helpful, hardworking and considerate on the 9 till 5 but when the bell for playtime rang I didn't know I had any other options. I didn't think my behaviour was anything other than normal. My family didn't advise me to take stock. If anything my parents seemed proud of my crazy tales. Most dangerously my ego was out of control. I couldn't not listen to the thoughts that were encouraging me to crack every other like-minded idiot in town. Letting off steam fighting was becoming the norm. It didn't take long for me to feel the clasps of steel around my wrists again.

The Scottish alpha male from Geordie's ship was my next opponent when I got nicked. This type of thing happened all the time. We just disliked each other from the start. Whether we were too much alike, jealous or maybe our inner demons just needed to have a piece of each other, I don't know but unsurprisingly we got it on the very next time we met. We were only thirty seconds into our fracas when the blue light brigade came and had their fun. They gave us both a good kicking before a cold night in a cell and another visit to the captains table. The Jock admitted he attacked me but only because he'd seen me first. I was all too willing. The skipper again showed mercy to me, fourteen days extra duties. I kept my career for now.

This is how life progressed. Even worse I developed a subconscious strategy for not getting locked up. I'd only ever fought with people who wanted to get it on and I'd always fought by the Queensbury rules. My inner pig moved this strategy forward to a new more cowardly level. I still only identified willing victims but my new innovation was to crack them and leg it. It was ridiculous. Friends would come out with me for the evening and bang I was gone leaving them stranded. The initial bang and dash gave me the fix that my beast needed without any risk of police intervention. It also gave me an awful sense of guilt. The more I did it the less I liked myself. On special occasions I'd not run but I was becoming a cold and calculated individual. The common phrase for such a person in Naval terms is a snags rating. If you had snags you had mental hang ups and weird behavioural patterns. That was me. I didn't see that though. My ego told me I was cool and when I was out playing Mr Mad Fuck I believed it. Unfortunately that ego was overpowering my right side which was starting to turn guilty sour. That's how it works I think, the dark side feeds you the highs you crave as a trade off for taking a good piece of your soul away.

Fortunately there is good news for mankind. Every time you reject a destructive thought your good side reclaims part of your soul. So it's never too late for anyone. Whatever type of shitty mess you might be making of your life, stop, act right and fix yourself. It's there for everyone unfortunately at nineteen years old I was a world away from that sort of knowledge.

Chapter 25: Kavos Spar

Soundtrack: Bill Conti -The Theme from Rocky

Even though my ex had already given birth to someone else's child. I received my divorce papers through stating the obvious: Unreasonable behaviour on my behalf. I agreed. No point dragging it out.

Well I'd been on bread and water in relation to the ladies for some time. A holiday in Greece might give me a sniff of romance but I doubted it really as my travelling companions were twenty eight Mancunian wrong 'uns. Navy snags? In Manc company I just had a bit of an edge like the rest of them.

We were taking no chances on the pharmaceuticals. Most of our drugs cache travelled in our pots of Brylcreem. Clingfilmed white pills are virtually invisible. My dad dropped us at the airport. I travelled in the company of my brother and school chum Easy.

Before the plane took off, we took off! We were off our tits on pills. So the moment the plane actually left the runway was like a well delivered knee trembler. I was loving it. Immediately I repositioned myself next to two darlings and all my insecurities of the past year and half were gone. I was on form and I'd managed to half talk the green eyed stunner I was stalking on the flight out of her imminent wedding.

I talk a lot about demons in this book. This particular dark force symptom is different though. When I got good quality Ecstasy in me and I wasn't dancing or shagging, I had a funny demon. I know that drugs can make you think you're funny when you are actually a ball bag and maybe I was a veiny testicle carrier but these were magical comedy pills. They used a part of your brain that remembered every intricate part of a conversation then sometime later skillfully regurgitated the relevant minor comedic point that the person had forgotten at exactly the right time. When I talked to someone like that they usually laughed hard until they got freaked out by the memory trick.

Green eyes and her pals were stunners. We had made our mark. Bruv and Easy were a pair of gigglers. All our jaws were aching by the time we hit the hotel at 5am. We knocked up the birds next door and started chatting shit to them. Ecstasy was such a sociable tool. I was glad we'd brought a suitcase full.

Being with so many lads was a real spectacle. We were all outdoing each other in terms of silliness. One lad got off the plane and stayed out on the piss/pills for five days from landing without going to bed. For days he'd just had a stinky beer towel on his head and some skimpy shorts which were only half in tact after someone set him on fire. Finally on night five he passed out with his head against a monster speaker and we stretchered him out on a sun lounger back to his gaff with his unopened suitcase placed on his lap.

That very same night I pulled a size 6-8 sexy little blond Cockney. After an uncomfortable clumsy effort at a shag on top of a pile of sun loungers on the beach we went back to hers. She was really nice in character and in the nude. She really impressed me when on climax she said let's get a kebab and a beer.

It really was cool nookie and I fancied her. The next day when she came over something in me decided to fob her off. I decided I wasn't there for a love job. She protested that we could have something special. "Sorry love." The boys were impressed. When you get on a flow like that women can smell it. The same way they can smell desperation when you couldn't trap your cock in a vice.

The very next night and full of funny pills I set my sights on a dark haired posh bird. She was very confident and initially she thought the funny demon was dull. I returned to the scene of the line three or four times before she cracked. Suddenly she went all Sigourney Weaver (On Ghostbusters when she needs the devil dog thing inside her really badly). So, taxi back to mine. It was relatively early so we wouldn't be disturbed.

In the taxi she started lightly slapping me and asking me if I was going to hurt her. "Oh aye, no danger love!" My confidence was high and I was quite liking her approach. I disembarked the taxi with a boner with bad intentions.

A few minutes later a pair of duffle coat hanger style nipples were on display. I got straight on the job and fairly soon the cheeky cow said "I thought you were going to hurt me?" "Is this no good for you love?" "No hit me!" I just giggled and carried on gyrating. Then she started slapping and punching me in the face. I panicked, put the brakes on and started to think about my defence plea. She said "don't you stop. Hit me!"

Bells were ringing here. I'd just left the company of a nympho sex abuse victim. I explained my position and she said "look I've never been abused, I love it hard and when I say hit me, fuckin' hit me!" I butted her, not full on but semi hard. It was a tester. She came back with a filthy smile: test passed, ding, ding round one!

We went to town on each other. She got off a few decent shots on me and also nearly chewed my nipple off. Her favourite punishment seemed to be a rear entry with a serving of hard hair pulling and kidney punches. After a high cardiovascular boxer-sexercise we touched gloves in the shower.

As I fell asleep I could feel my eye swelling up. I wasn't expecting that. About an hour later our kid came in and crashed fully clothed on the bed next to us. He was only seventeen. As he came around he nearly broke his neck. I've never seen him move so quick. I began to do her whilst sort of strangling her at the same time. It was just for effect really. She loved it, he didn't! He dived over and rolled me off. She was laughing her tits off as I introduced him to my new sparring partner. She explained she liked all that and for just a second I thought he was considering laying a headbutt or karate chop on her himself. My brothers mis-education had gone up to the next level.

Hours later she limped up the beach to where all us Mancs had gathered. The Rocky chants echoed around. She took it all in good spirits. I had two days more in the ring. You couldn't spend your whole life with this bedroom grappling champ but it was certainly a three day education I'd never forget.

On the last night I knocked back Twiggy again. It would have been wrong to have gone back with her after that. But like I say when women smell that smell they are as naughty as us and sure enough Green eyes from the plane turned up and temporarily called off her engagement while she blew me up on the beach.

HEALTH WARNING

When you take drugs that make you much funnier than you usually are and give you untold willy strength, reverting back to your normal self can be a real disappointment.

Chapter 26: Top one, nice one Mum

Soundtrack: Queen - Tie Your Mother Down

Yes everyone has their poison whether it be Coca Cola, cigarettes, White Lightning cider or crack. For me it was e's. In normal life I didn't love myself or anyone else, I didn't have the tools. On this gear I was tuned into peace and love and pure escapism and that's quite a contrast to the pent up aggression and sporadic violence alcohol could evoke.

I craved the 'E' buzz, it was medicine for me. On a weekend home I met my mum in the pub and explained the whole thing as I really couldn't see a downside. She said you need to take me out so I can understand. The next weekend I took her up on that offer.

In her local I issued her with all the essentials. Chewing gum of course. Once you come up you really need to focus your jaw movement otherwise you could easily grind your teeth down and risk chewing your tongue off. A no gum policy could also lead to some pretty disturbing temporary slow- mo 'E' gurn facial disfigurement. I also explained that I had some menthol cigs for a mountain spring clear breathing sensation. It was a bit surreal explaining the do's and don'ts of Rave-land to your mum. Her new fella looked deeply troubled by the prospect of our educational field trip. He gave her a 'I might never see you again hug and we jumped a cab.'

My plan was to go to grab a granny night in the 'Ritz'. Me ma liked Motown so I thought it would be like a Wigan casino style northern soul experience.

In the small queue I popped two pills and gave mum a half before we had a beer at the bar. Mum always got a bit complex just on beer. So it was no surprise she didn't display the typical rave behavioural pattern. She came up heavy and clumsy. This place was a bad choice on my behalf as there was no baseline to focus on and the dance floor was sprung, so you felt like you were on a cruise liner. She was barging into people and acting like a bum. I'd seen this type of thing before.

You can't help it when you come up like that. She was a little surprised when I got her coat and ushered her out into another taxi to the 'Boardwalk'. Bless her she looked a bit twatted. I gave her a hug and she seemed to like it.

It was a smart move shifting venues as in no time she started chewing her gum in a beneficial manner. She was responding to the sounds and doing what can only be described as a frog challenge dance. She still had a bit of an edge and was going up to the girls in the room and twisting down 'let's twist again' style into a crouching frog position. She looked very pleased with that. I couldn't decide if she was trying to have a crap with her clothes on or mop the floor with her fanny, either way she was having a buzz now and I started to relax a bit. These pills weren't doing it for me so I gobbled two more. When I got a bit of a strut on I dragged her off to another club called 'Home' where the music went up a notch again. She was less clumsy now and we had a good old dance together. I didn't smoke in normal life so again it was surreal to share the buzz of water and menthol cigs with my mum. She got it and we shared some nice hugs. She loved me. I didn't feel like a bum and it didn't feel a great mind blowing coming together with the woman that brought me into the world, I just felt like a parent taking their kid for their first messy beer.

She did it her way which looked like the beer way because as soon as we came out of 'Home' she asked for a kebab. I was horrified. Fair play though she mullered it and seemed to be not at risk in terms of a taxi reflux disaster. I dropped her off with a big hug. She'd enjoyed it. This was confirmed when she rang me from the supermarket it the morning to say she was buzzing her tit's off in the frozen meat section.

Mums intentions were good. They always were.

Chapter 27: Under Attack

Soundtrack: Edwin Starr - War

Back to sea. New ship, new start. It was quite a young sporty mess so I slotted in without too much fuss. In the kitchen my skill set was steadily improving. Ecstasy taking had had a definite impact on my demeanour. I was a bit more confident. This was possibly down to the holiday shagging. I felt a bit more at home with the Naval mentality. I was starting to get the banter. It was all about doing outrageous minging things to outdo the previous minger. It wasn't real behaviour, just a game. That wasn't really the way I needed to go but I needed to fit in and it all came very naturally.

I say naturally because I'd always been an entertainer. I have a funny trait that sums it up really. I loved to jump over things. Static objects that is. I had a good spring and sometimes I'd get the urge to jump things in my own company but I usually didn't bother. At school and later on in life on the piss, give me a crowd and I had to jump things. Crash barriers were the norm. Stuff like cars and people came later, very rarely did I come a cropper, though I must admit I once grazed many a pointy railing. My sphincter led a very charmed life.

My new mess had a gronk board on the bulkhead (wall) which contained photographs of the least pretty women that the lads in the mess had pulled over the course of the previous trip away or time alongside if the ship was in dry dock. It was all part of the game.

Yes the sailor who had trapped the worst gronk of the trip won a case of ale. It was more about the prestige though. Each night when the duty officer conducted their rounds they would always enquire who was top of the gronk league or ask for a tour of the board.

So it was a back to front mentality in terms of trawling nightclubs for hot women. Quite often the big girls were the ones copping all the free drinks and the propositions. Once you start getting into playing those sort of games with people. It's obviously wrong but there is a strange 'Team Pig' bonding sensation that comes with it.

I liked big girls and big personalities, I was often drawn to them but I saw a couple naked and it just wasn't for me. The only time I ever pinned a picture on a gronk board was a shocker. I had a few beers in the mess and entered a nightclub very early on at about 10pm. This bird comes over and said "do you want to come home with me? I'm going now." There was no reason for me to go but I just did. I fell asleep in her car and when I came round it was straight in for the cocoa. I set an alarm for seven to start work at eight. After a forgetful exchange of bodily fluid I came down stairs bang on seven to ring a cab. There was no dial tone. I went back up to ask her for another number and she said "You're in Southampton my darling." Holy shit she lived twenty miles from Pompey that was me in the shit again. I came downstairs and the family portrait over the mantel piece winked at me. A black dad and two cross eyed kids. That was a big gronk score.

This is an honestish sort of make believe book and that was the reality of the humour. The few black lads in the Navy at that time understood the crack. They were heroes because they were different. Everyone respected how they put up and often seemed to thrive on the Ron Atkinson type language. It was a sick culture, one that's thankfully long gone. Inside I'm sure they were as screwed up as me and the next guy because when you compromise your ethics, morals and what you stand for to conform I think you suffer in the soul. They just wanted to survive like the rest of us. They suffered at the hands of sick Alf Garnet style jibes but it was also their defence strategy. Everyone has their own shit going on.

After reporting in late I placed the portrait over the whole of the gronk board. I'd only been on-board a short while and the Dry Dock Re-Fit Gronk Championship was secured. I did feel awful on the bird though afterwards. She said she was divorced. If she was lying she would have a job explaining that one away. Bad karma!

I too suffered bad karma when it came to this kind of caper. Stealing was now added to my list of things to feel bad about. I missed having a wife or at least a bird. Point scoring gronking: I had a dabble. It wasn't great. You felt like shit.

When it came to scoring sicko extra points some lads claimed to have shit in their victim's drawers. So instead of robbing the family portrait as their parting gift they claimed to have crapped in their hosts knicker draws. I didn't believe them at the time. What you would get out of that I don't know, points I suppose. A couple of years later in Weymouth I did see a leading steward turd in a pint pot and put the steaming log on a busy bar. So maybe they did. Logging wasn't my thing.

Round about the same time the Bosnia conflict had kicked off and we were deployed to support the United Nations in the Adriatic. About a month into the trip the ship received a request from the Army. Some of their chefs were cracking under the strain of working continuous eighteen hour days so would any of our chefs consider swapping roles and letting them come on-board for a little rest and recuperation. That ticked every box for me I was the first to put my hand up.

One other chef volunteered. We had a 30 minute refresher on the SA80 rifle and the next day we were sat in the back of the ships helicopter trying to take off in a rough swell and dense fog. Not your ideal flying conditions. I'd never really thought about the risks the ships pilot and his number two took. The pilot and the vicar are always the top shaggers onboard out of the officers. Women at cocktail parties are susceptible to funny vicars and cocksure Biggles types. Sat in the back of the ship's budgie listening to them crackling over the radio's waiting for an opportunity to lift off safely I had a new found respect for these fellas. It was pretty hairy stuff. Soon enough we made the noisy flutter to Split in the Croatian region of Yugoslavia.

I was greeted by a red haired Geordie called Ginge. He had a bullet proof vest, a helmet and a gun for me. The other chef went his own way with his own chaperone. As we made the long drive to wherever the fuck we were going he explained we were sitting ducks. Snipers and road mines were hazards but the worst threat came from ambush from kids. They would pelt the wagon with stones to make you stop then loot the wagon.

Sure enough about an hour into the drive Ginge said "Here we go!" The local lynch mob had built a temporary wall across the road forcing us to stop. For a second I thought I was gonna have to try and use a fuckin gun. Fortunately Ginge ordered me to get a cool box out of the back. Already the little Ewoks were helping themselves to complementary supplies. Ginge cracked the first of two cool boxes which seemed to contain a load of oranges. "Watch and learn!" he started launching them at the kids who totally ignored him. They were fully focused on the looting. It was only when one connected with a young lads skull I realised the oranges were frozen. He was spark out. The rest just carried on. Ginge had a big grin on and started to explain that lone convoys rarely got their stores through in tact. He couldn't shoot them so this was the sport they had developed. I never threw any oranges. I could see these people were desperate. Ginge was obviously hardened to it all. He was just scoring his points and playing the game.

On arrival at the school that was doubling up as a military base and U.N convoy feeding centre, I was escorted to the kitchen. Instead of the chap in charge saying "young man, thanks for coming over we appreciate it", he started screaming in my face parade ground style. "When you are in my kitchen you will do this, you will do that and I won't accept this." All that bollocks.

I wasn't wise enough to think this is how this mob work. He's just doing what they do. I reverted to my basic training telepathy. I posted him "Are you taking the piss? you fuckin limp dicked pongo!" On the way over I had every intention of happily pulling my ring out in the kitchen for Queen and country. Eighteen hours a day. No probs.

This fucker had just sapped all my team spirit. I came over to help but I was now here for myself. Kissing his arse in the kitchen wasn't my focus. I didn't have to work until the next morning so I went to find Ginge. He showed me to the bar which was a classroom with a fridge and a lot of people smoking.

Within minutes I had locked onto a guy who was working as a translator basically in the interests of the opposite side to his own people. He said he was being paid a fuckin' fortune and it beat working in a munitions factory. You could see he wasn't really cool with it. He was feeling guilty as fuck. I helped him forget about it and we got absolutely mullered. We spent the late evening in the yard. We could hear shelling and see traces in the sky. This is what living near war felt like. No wonder this guy was troubled. It was disturbing enough for a temporary tourist chef. God knows how the local kids felt.

The next thing I knew I was being screamed at to go for physical training. It must have been 4am. I'd been in bed for about two hours. Usually I like PT and I would have loved to run about with these lads but I'd been tasting the local firewater with the traitor bloke. I was minging so I declined the offer. I was informed I'd have to face the sergeant from the kitchen if I didn't turn out. Sorry lads I'll face that knob, cheers.

I turned up on time for all day kitchen duty. He gave me a mega-bollocking over my running no show. I said "I've come here to give you a lift in the kitchen not to do a bleep test at 4am" "You are a wanker" etc, etc. As he insulted me he was turning blue.

When he'd finished I got on in the kitchen. This place was busy. They did a lot of meals four times a day for hundreds of people. I felt for the chefs. They never got a day off. I did my graft and got chatting to the pot washers and cleaners who were locals. They were surprisingly friendly and good humoured. I hit it off with a bird called Suzie and we had a giggle ball room style dancing with mops. Sergeant Gruffalo gave me a stop enjoying yourself stare, so I went and looked serious whilst chopping onions.

At 11pm I left the kitchen. When I got over to the dorm Ginge and a few other Pongo's were having a little party. Within an hour I had us all doing crazy underpant photograph poses with all the military hardware and cleaning equipment. Guns and feather dusters, it was a joyous evening and I even got to jump an ironing board. There were some really nice fellas in the room. One guy was a career private. He was a bit dim but with a heart of gold. He was getting sponsorship to shave his head for charity the next day. I gave him a few shekels and wished him all the best. These guys had a tough life. They earned every fuckin penny they got. I was proud to be in their company.

Next morning I was a bit pie eyed in the kitchen. Gruffalo gave me about five jobs to crack on with at once. Chop veg for this, that and the other. Make a spog bol and a veg curry and turn on the deep fat fryer as the veg for lunch is already in there. They had no steamers so they used the elements in the fryer to boil up water around large tins of veg. I followed his instructions and went a chop, chop, chop. Two hours later I was feeling quite pleased with myself as I cleaned down my bench, all tasks done.

Without warning we came under attack. Everyone hit the deck and an air raid siren started blaring. An explosion ripped through the kitchen. Some of the equipment blew up and food and shrapnel splattered over the five chefs on duty. I felt a hand grip my T-shirt neck from the back yanking me up and causing me to choke. I was covered in mushy pea spray. "Did you put any water in the fuckin fryer?" "Oh shit!" As he dragged me through the kitchen by the scruff of my neck I took in the scene. There were at least two holes in the roof, some of the veg had shot up into space. The rest was splattered all around. I felt sick. I'd dropped a major bollock here. The base thought they were under attack and some sort of response force was now running around looking for infiltrators. Sarge simply said "fuck off and don't come back!"

I slouched over to the dorm feeling bad. I should have checked but the tosser should have explained it better as well. I got cleaned up and changed clothes. One of the other chefs came over and said that it was the funniest thing he'd ever been involved in. I was just glad nobody got hurt I had a few scratches and a slight pea burn on my neck. Nobody was close to the explosion thank God. The chef said with a big smile on his face, "Don't come near the kitchen, he'll kill you!"

Not long after, private Dim from the night before came in. He looked a bit freaky as he'd had his head shaved with a Bic razor. He was wittering on that the bastards had charged him with something along the lines of having an unsuitable haircut. This summed up the arseness of the army for me. Here was a guy who had got sponsorship off his pals including high ranking officers to raise money for Christmas pressies for local orphaned kids, but because he didn't ask permission from his officer he was looking at a fine and a beasting. Just so everyone was reminded of the pecking order. You're not allowed to think for yourself. I told him my story and he instantly felt better. I gave him a hug and had a feel of his head. I obviously couldn't go in for dinner so I went back to the beer room and filled my boots.

I reported back to the kitchen in the morning. Sarge said "fuck off, come back tomorrow in your combat gear, you're going map reading." I asked for food and he told me to fuck off. The lads shared their personal nutty stash (chocolates & crisps). We all celebrated the kitchen explosion with a few tins and I got my first decent kip in.

The closest thing to combats I had was my number eight uniform which was basically shirt, pants and a beret. As I walked over to the kitchen I could here the grumble of engines. Waiting for me in the square outside the kitchen were 'Kelly's fuckin Heroes!' There was a troop of about eight tanks ticking their engines over. A very posh officer called me over gave me a map and told the chaps I was a thick as fuck navy piece of shit. Fair one!

I got my own body armour and a hat with a radio in it with a Madonna MIC bit too. He pointed to my armoured vehicle taxi and we started to roll out. I was grinning like a Cheshire cat. I let out a celebratory woohoo! About twelve "shut the fuck up's" came through my helmet speaker. We were all linked up. Oops!

I was to hang out the back and read the map. I was clueless but I tried to look interested in the map. It was easy really, just follow the tank in front. We seemed to be on a steady ascent and it was getting colder the higher we went. The two other guys in the tank were cool. Geordies always seem to be fun. I asked where we were off. They just said "To see some communists."

Up and up we went until there was snow on the hills. There were a lot of burnt out vehicles around. Quite often we would stop to clear mines. They were big old things in the middle of the road. The guys just got out and kicked them out of the way. I wondered why they weren't slightly buried. I thought they must be for blowing stuff up in the dark.

We stopped on the cusp of a hill and the lads said we were there. As we rolled down the hill I could see some of leaky's handi work.

Outside the log cabin style house was a Massey Ferguson tractor connected to a trailer which contained some sort of rocket launcher.

As we stopped outside the hut pointing our turrets threateningly their way the door swung open and two burly dudes with yes, you've guessed it communist red starred hats on appeared.

The posh bloke went up for a gabble with them. Then waved me over. Fuck me I'm being sold as a wartime rent boy. I inwardly told myself "This is the British army. People don't disappear, surely not!"

Sure enough Tim nice but dim officer bloke explained I was to stay with these chaps while they went off on classified business. He shook my hand and said "Good luck!" Just to pickle my head. I stood on the porch with hairy and hairier and watched the troops roll out waiving to me as they went. I waved back, I didn't get the feeling this was my Stephen King 'Misery' time but I was shitting myself all the same.

The two warthogs beckoned me inside. It looked like an eighties working men's club on pay day. It was smoky, very smoky. There were cards and dominoes on the go. I was introduced to all the lads. None of them spoke English. I used my international communication skills and smiled a lot and tried to appear grateful. They poured me a clear white spirit drink. I smiled and pointed at the beers a couple of them were drinking. They all beamed and made it clear I had to drink the firewater. I tried it but it was a red hot burner. I couldn't drink it. They kept pointing to it for me to drink. Eventually the nice guy at the table got up and fetched me some Fanta. Game on!

I tried asking if this was my permanent new home. They had smarmy looking faces. This indicated I wasn't gonna get killed or bummed. The army had planned something and they wanted me pissed.

I wasn't hot on cards or dom's but fifteen minutes later I was steaming and putting on a show. I did animal impressions, TV show theme tunes and football chants. They were a good audience and we had a lovely jolly boys' time. The funny Fanta kept coming and I had almost forgotten about England when I heard the hum of the tanks coming back over the hill. The Commie's gave me a good send off. We'd had fun. I briefly wondered who the fuck they were.

Timothy thanked them. I waved at the Army, they made wanker signs at me. It was fuckin' freezing. Timbo locked me in the back of a warrior and I thought "Nice one I'll get my head down." On the way I don't think we topped 15mph. We took off at about treble that. Within five minutes I'd sussed my fate, we seemed to be off road and they were ragging the arse off the machine. I had a strong constitution and decent sea legs but pretty soon the room was spinning and within fifteen minutes I started puking. It was relentless. Sick was dropping down off the low ceiling back onto me. After what seemed like years I passed out and I remember people's fingers in my mouth. I was ill. I had to tip my hat to the twisted fucker who came up with this. Sergeant chef had his revenge. Good one.

They let me lie in bed for a day to recover. The day after that I was allowed back in the kitchen. I saw Suzie and she was grumpy. When I asked her friends why they said she'd been raped and the men in her family had been taken away. I couldn't believe she'd come into work to mop the floors.

Sergeant Gruffalo finally shook my hand and we smiled at each other. He warmly called me a wanker. In a way I was pleased he'd forced me into blowing his kitchen up. It was brilliant really! At Split airport the other chef asked if I had enjoyed it. I said "Mate you'd never believe me if I told you."

Chapter 28: Ear Ear

Soundtrack: The Cranberries - Zombie

I am a great believer in fate. You experience the stuff of your life for a reason. It's up to you to suss it out. I also think if you pick the wrong road you'll be given an opportunity to take a better one soon enough. You just have to learn the lessons of going down cul de sacs and the one way streets the wrong way.

I'm gonna flip back to 1982 to start this story. In junior school I had a fairly camp pal. He was very similar in manner and humour to David Walliams. I loved this fella and his family that had been very good to me. It was our first ever trip on a bus. His mum gave us the fare and £1 spends each for a chip barm. We were going to Stretford Arndale which was less than a mile down the road.

We got on the little single decker bus called a buzzy bee. The only space was on the back row. We were dead giddy and sat ourselves down. The bus stopped and two lads got on that were maybe a year older than us, one big, one small. The small one did the talking. "Where are you going?" Young Dave Walliams answered: "To the Arndale." "What for?", "Chippy." He punched my pal in the face. "Give me your chippy money you fuckin' queer." He started crying and handed the cash over. I just froze. They shouted obscenities at us as we got off. I looked at that cruel bastard celebrating through the window. "One day I'll have you." I knew I would. We both got a bit flustered. My mate cried most of the way home. His mum was heartbroken too.

Through my teenage years my pal drifted away into different company. The little fella on the bus got more and more notorious. He didn't go to my school but he would turn up to sporadically 'tax' people. I'd see him but I wasn't ready to challenge him. He had around ten older brothers and it was a proper hard family. They annoyed me further when one of the brothers started bullying my uncle when they moved in the flat below.

Six years after leaving school I was home for a weekend. I met up with some ex school chums at the local celebrity drug dealers flat. He was only tiny but he was a big United hooligan and dished out harsh punishment in fights. He would two finger poke big 'uns in the eyes and smash what ever was handy over them before they regained their sight. He had a nice way of speaking, almost a whisper. He was a fuckin' drug dealer at the end of the day but everybody liked him including our parents' generation. The police once raided the local pub. He slipped my dad a 9 bar big lump of weed under the table. Dad coolly nodded at the old bill and walked out with it in his suit pocket. They were mates then and he got a few free spliffs every time they bumped into each other. Dad thought that was funny. Why my old man risked prison for him I don't know. He was just that sort of fella, people warmed to him.

Friday afternoons at his flat were messy. Some good lads from school had lost their way a bit and made this their lives. They were there five days a week. He had whatever narcotics you wanted. His thing was amphetamines and he liked you to sample his very cheap phet paste as that was his poison. The guy never went to sleep, he talked and talked. Every one there talked, you couldn't help it on that gear. One lad who was known for bullshitting was the easy target. He got dogs' abuse and the drug Tsar led the way on that. The golden rule of the flat was don't fall asleep. If you did you'd lose your eyebrows, that was the law. Bullshit Billy still looked a bit freaky as he must have lost his over the past couple of weeks.

Drinking on drugs is different to just drinking. You don't really get pissed. You can drink all sorts and just enjoy it really. You don't really get a hangover either. Recovery from drug taking is more in the mind. Moods swings and insecurities that sort of thing.

So we hit the Offie and got a load of boozage: rum, alcopops, white lightening, Stella, everyone had their own jungle juice. Skins and poppers too. This was a sinful shopping facility.

Up in the flat the Tsar held court. There were white lines being tapped out all over the place. Soon everyone was whizzing their tits off. Tunes on, jibber, jabber, talk, talk. Billy couldn't help talking shit on whizz. He was a really nice fella but he kept contradicting himself and always ended up looking foolish. He spoke in a really loving way about his dad. I thought "Your dad wouldn't want this for you." We smoked spliffs and sniffed poppers which made everything go dizzy slow. It was a sensory play centre. Each lad that was there was a nice person but I could see they were on a rocky road. I never considered I was too. This life wasn't me, I was a narcotic tourist, I dipped in and I dipped out.

About five of us went over to the local and carried on the session there. The pub had bouncers at weekends. One of them used to work with my dad and they didn't get on. We were pretty wired. I was waffling all sorts of shit. I'd found two lovely girls from school and was giving them medium strength Jedi mind trick waffle. Not to entrap them, just for fun. I asked them what they were drinking and approached the bar. I ordered the drinks and had a good look around to select my next group of listeners. I couldn't believe it when I spotted the chip barm thief. The time had come.

"Two quid dick head hand it over! You taxed me and my pal when I was ten and I want it fuckin' back." "Fuck off weirdo" was his reply. I let a big right hand go, he had his back half turned so it was a cheapish shot that caught him on the side of the barnet. Fuck me, within half a second my dad's enemy cleared me out with a flying head butt stroke rugby tackle. He was a fat bastard and he'd damaged my shoulder. It moved backwards in its socket. There was lots of heckling as we were escorted to the car park. This plan was going tits up. A school ground scrap crowd had gathered and was intrigued to see a local bad boy get challenged by a no gang individual. I couldn't back down now.

I laid into him like Sugar Ray until he went down. Now even though I wanted to make a point with this fucker, I still didn't have it in me to finish him off when he hit the deck. I couldn't stick the boot in. It wasn't me.

I suppose I just wanted to either knock him out with a punch or for him to give up. Bad decision! I put him down three more times. Each time he got up he seemed happier. The fucker was smiling now. The snap had gone out of my punches as my shoulder was fucked. We got into a grapple and started rolling round the floor. I felt him bite into my ear, the scruffy twat was a fuckin' zombie. He seemed to be locked on for minutes. Although it was probably only about thirty seconds I knew I was at risk of losing my ear. I heard a thud and the teeth released. Billy Bullshit stuck two more boots into the human kebab eater. "Come on let's fuck off!" said my saviour. We sprinted back to the Tsars gaff. On the way I told Billy I owed him a big favour. One day I would help him. The Tsar loved the story but was disappointed I never reclaimed the two quid. He issued complimentary drugs, gave my ripped ear a salt wash and then a Savlon rub. I put a plastic clothes peg on it to stop the bleeding. The drugs kicked in and the shoulder felt a bit better. At the time I thought I'd done what I had to and I didn't feel sorry for him. I genuinely thanked Billy for saving me again. You could see he instantly felt more credible and worthy in the room. He was a caring lad, I was thankful for that. We both agreed the chip barm thief was a tough little fucker. About six hours later I got a taxi to hospital. There was no way I was gonna risk losing my eye-brows.

This do-gooder type of vigilante violence wasn't an isolated incident. The tallest lad in school was being bullied by a gangster type on the bus. The bully went on to be a big player in the criminal fraternity. The big guy was upset at registration one morning after another tormented bus ride. He explained and I agreed to meet the bus in the day after. "Just point him out." I hit him right on the chin and he flew back onto the bus, crumbled. I legged it. Two days later his boys came to school with bats. I saw them but luckily they didn't recognise me.

I did it again in my early twenties. My pal was checking himself out in the mirror in the pub/club toilets. The local head started having a go, "Who do you think you are?" He'd done nowt wrong. As he approached my pal on the dance floor. I dropped him. He got up and came over and groggily said "Outside!" Luckily for me I dislocated my shoulder and immediately he filled me in. If he didn't win he would have eventually. People in those circles have to save face. Luckily for me this gangster shook my hand as I lay on the deck with my arm out of place, "I like your spirit lad" he said.

So how does this all fit into the big lesson life plan? Well even now I wasn't ready to learn any real lessons. I believed my ego demon. I had my self down as 'freedom fighter'. Even so, looking back I only took whizz about five times in my life and for the school bully to turn up just as I was getting all invincible growly and likely to take such a crazy decision, well for me it's too much of a coincidence. Was that situation cooked up by a good or dark force? I can't decide. I think the drugs dimension is the realm of the dark side. LSD users will tell you the coincidences on that gear are unexplainable. I know lads that went to The Woodford Air show tripping. One lad said "Wouldn't it be mad if that plane crashed?" Seconds later it ditched into the crowd. Weird devil shit is that.

This fight may have been the work of the good side. Putting all these coincidences together to damage my shoulder and slow me down. Stop me fighting, to help me. The bouncer had his own revenge agenda but what force put the thought in his head to attack. Was he just doing his job? I don't think so. Later on in life I'd start to recognise the coincidences and tap into the lessons.

At this point of the story though I still had a lot more destructing to do. Such events and tales made me popular amongst the single lads in my Manchester circle of friends. I wasn't the only fruit loop, there were a few. The couples were starting to get a bit wary though. I didn't get too many dinner invitations!

Chapter 29: Wrong Bird, Right Good Time!

Soundtrack: Atlantic Ocean - Waterfall

The next summer I was still womanless and like the previous summer I was hoping for a bit of romance on holiday. This year in Ibiza I made the trip with a different Geordie pal of mine. It was a twenties holiday which was something like an 18-30. It wasn't really for us. We didn't want to pay money to go on a pub crawl and watch the crusty cocked Reps cop for all the birds. "No offence, we'll be doing our own thing thanks."

On arrival we went straight down to the San Antonio strip and sank a few cocktails. It was like fishing for mackerel as soon as we walked in the first bar. We cast the line and in seconds we were fighting at least six hungry fish. The mackerel that caught my eye was making some favourable shapes in a catsuit dancing up on a podium. We didn't really speak we just got off with each other. George copped for her mate who explained we were in the same hotel. She came to our room. I went to theirs. I was glad English girls went on holiday because they were at least ten times easier to pull on holiday than they were at home. I was on a holiday streak and not just with plain women. I kept pulling novelty birds with weird and wondrous bedroom tricks. This year I'd latched onto a human garden sprinkler. She was a walking orgasm. As soon as you touched her she started spraying her juices all over the shop. It inspired me. Her room looked and smelt like a tsunami had swept through it by the time we'd finished. I'll not elaborate on this story but she was proud of her skills and she took great pleasure demonstrating her talent. About 6am I walked up the corridor to our room. As I entered George was strangling his victim with the hotel telephone phone cord. I sat on the other bed and watched him do his comedy strangle sex thing. It was funny. She bent over and winked at me as she gave him a kiss and said see you later. "What was her pal like mate?" "Brother she was like the Trevi fuckin' fountain!"

I had a feeling these chicks were serial shaggers. They had brought £50 between them for a week away. I hoped I didn't have a dose. You could have worn as many jonnies as you liked with this one. A space suit and fishing waders would have possibly saved you from her upshots. As tremendous as the experience was I decided to let the next best man ride the wave for the rest of the week. I saw her around the pool. She was cool. She wouldn't go without.

We stayed round the beer side of the bay for the next two nights and had a good beer buzz. We watched a few brawls kick off but we had no wish to fight. We were here on a love buzz and the next day we went for haircuts as we were going proper raving in the evening and we wanted to look the part. I asked the barber where we could get some pills and he went in the back and came out with a voluptuous bag of pick and mix E's. "Wow which ones are best?" "The pink ones" he said with the face of a seasoned pill muncher. So we blew our budget and bought all his pinkies. About ten in all. It wasn't a bad haircut either. The Balearic Gents grooming experience was far superior to the British one. That's for sure.

So we were fully prepared for a big night out. We had sun tans, white jeans, Es Paradis T shirts which was a club over the bay. My Manc boys had been over earlier in the season and they recommended the Star Club and Space so we plumbed for the Star Club.

By now I was an experienced pill head and my 'E' tolerance was a bit higher for this reason I took three pills before we went in and kept two for later. George made do with one as he wasn't a regular. We looked at each other, we were in our prime, we felt that without speaking. We soon came up and spent the next twenty minutes man hugging. These pills were crystal clear buzz top. We got some water to drink that was absolute nectar. Then without warning water and foam start shooting out of the walls. Fuckin' hell my brain struggled to contain the excitement. We weren't expecting this. Fuckin mad one. The rushes were intense. I fuckin' loved that feeling. The force and whiteness of the water blew our minds it was like hedonistic heaven. It was like sitting on a cloud having a long and wondrous all over orgasm. There were people belly down, legs against the wall shooting themselves across the dance floor. There must have been a lot of pink pills in circulation as everyone was loved up. John and I were still in a loving embrace when a Welsh bird came over asking for pills. She asked if we were gay and we explained "Nar but we do love each other. We are crusted." She legged it and came back with two mates. One was shit hot, gorgeous smile, curly hair and the most amazing tit's you've ever seen. Her pal was porno. A red head. She wore big, big boots, hot pants and she looked rude. We gave them a pill each and fifteen minutes later we reaped the rewards. We were all rolling around in the foam having a grope. Porno was locked onto me. Arrrrgh. No! I was mad for the other one. It's near enough impossible to knock an advancing horny bird on pure ecstasy and I failed. We only had a snog but she'd put her marker on me and I felt that. This place was mad there were people shagging on the floor, there were people sliding down the bar. The music was very euphoric and there weren't many stomp off beats to bring you down a peg. The buzz just went on and on. Without warning the music died and the lights came on. The white jeans were now black. All our hands were bath crinkled. All three girls looked horny sexy. The five of us walked along the harbour holding hands and watched the sun come up. It was the best of Ibiza.

We spent a brilliant next few days in the company of the girls. They were staying at plush apartments so we chilled round their pool. I avoided shagging porno as I really fancied her mate. I should have just said "Hey you with the big boobs, I like you best." Unfortunately I didn't and the red head started talking like we were already married. I just let it drift I liked the boots but already I knew I'd dropped a large bollock. George didn't manage to cop any of them and the next day they were gone. Such a fun trip was once again soured by poor decision making. It wasn't just the fit bird's breasts I wanted, she was great company and the sort of person I'd been longing for. If I was ready to calm it and settle down I'd never know as I'd managed to create another crappy guilt heavy situation.

George and I finished the week in a twenty four hour rave in 'Space' which was exhausting and a bridge too far. The pinkies had raised the buzz bar. Alternative pills weren't the same. We were knackered!

Chapter 30: Nessum Dorma

Soundtrack: Pavorotti - Nessun Dorma

For some reason I kept in touch with the Welsh Porno. If I'm honest there were two reasons and they were both on her best friend's chest. I was also fuckin lonely.

I invited her to meet me in Manchester. North Wales wasn't too far away. She turned up with her pal with the norks. I thought this isn't normal. I can't be imagining her pal wants me. She just would not have come otherwise. I found it bizarre that she didn't read that herself.

Sure enough the first night we went raving in Manchester. We were all suitably pilled up and busy having a good stomp off when Miss Boobs told Miss Boots she was gonna puke. Everyone was twatted. Boobs spoke to Boots then said to me "She wants to keep dancing so can you look after me?" I took her to the toilets and thought she was genuinely going to puke. She took my hand and guided me into a loo. Puking wasn't on her mind. She told me that she loved me and she'd been waiting for a man like me. She couldn't believe I was seeing her best mate. "Surely you should have seen I was the one to go for in Ibiza." "Of course I saw it but she just sort of jumped on me first." We had a loved up kiss. I was impressed she didn't want screwing in the loo because she obviously did. She either cared about the lack of respect that that sort of initial liaison can generate or she felt some sort of guilt for her pal. I was throbbing. My inner love demon was dancing.

Back at my family gaff I shared the bed with both girls. When Boots went to the loo Boobs gave me a quick squeeze. It was a mad old situation. My ego was throbbing.

We met in secret about three times and had fantastic dates. She ticked all the boxes for me but she did come out with some weird shit. She told me that she fancied her own dad! She said "I know it's weird but he's gorgeous!" Snags yes, but as usual I chose to overlook those.

I should have just finished with Boots but we agreed she would be less suspicious if I stayed with her. So I got the green light to see them both. Boobs arranged to come and go raving on the following Saturday.

By this time the price of E's had dropped to about £8 each. I started to buy up to thirty for a weekend. This incurred a further discount down to 30 for £180. By now I was gobbling big multiples to guarantee the buzz. I thought little about the risks.

As we queued to get in the vicious security blokes found drugs on a guy ahead of us in the queue. They abused the poor twat. The unofficial drugs policy was if they copped you with gear your options were to eat all your drugs yourself or eat all the money you had on you. This sicko policy led to numerous harsh confrontations and some near death if not death experiences.

The incident in the queue encouraged me to eat all my ten pills at once and for my new mistress to gobble her three. I went blind within about ten minutes. I managed to get inside and lie down. I'd experienced this before and liked it. I was buzzing my cock off even if I looked dead.

My new fit bird was holding my hand protecting me as she got her own buzz on. "Oh shit!" she said as her best mate and my newish bird entered the fray. "If she sees me here I'm dead." I didn't need too much convincing to be led out blind through the fire exit to my motor.

Boobs had lost it. She wanted me to drive blind with her giving rally driver type instructions. I said "No, just chill." She wasn't having it. As soon as I could see we hit the road. It was suicide I was out of my mind. She started stroking my knob as a thank you for driving. That didn't help my concentration but it did feel nice.

Quickly we formulated a plan. Drive down the motorway and straight into the airport and mooch around the terminal till morning when we'd come down.

It was a shit plan. My chin was all over the place I was shivering with a pure Ecstasy rush. I was trying to be a window licking sensible driver but it just wasn't happening. I kept missing the exit for the airport. I did this at least five times.

On the fifth pass a storm broke and the rain started to bounce. On E's like this as explained earlier you were just full of love. So when we spotted a guy broken down and in trouble, we just had to share the love and stop and offer our help.

As the guy looked through the window he may have been slightly concerned to see a naked driver humming along ecstatically with Pavarotti 's Nessun Dorma as it blared out of the radio. The slip road wasn't too far away. "Just drop us at that phone box. I'll ring the AA." "No fucking problem mate." A minute or so up the road the AA arrived in police cars.

We were taken to the local station. She was briefly questioned and was free to go. She didn't. I could hear her gabbling on trying to secure my release for a good few hours.

I was crusted and just wanted to hug all the dibble. They did a great job. I loved good people. That was my in station mantra. I just had undies on now. One officer let me hug him and had a buzz. The doctor was less impressed. I wouldn't give a sample until he gave me a cuddle. After an hour he crumbled and reluctantly felt the love. The custody Sergeant said "I've never seen anyone be as happy as you to get nicked." "Come here!" I said. I gave him another hug and he giggled to himself.

Two hours later I was still very fuckin' happy. I pretended not to be and they charged and released me on the condition that we fucked off home in a taxi ASAP. The only reason they let me out was because she had talked and talked for four hours on reception, completely doing their heads in.

We held hands tightly on the way home. It was a very short love affair. I'd never see her again.

I have to look at this with my fate glasses on again. So many coincidences triggered this grotesque life threatening behaviour. A small bad decision in Ibiza led to many worse ones at home. Was that guy's engine failure God saving me? Looking back I'd have to say so. We had no right to get off the motorway alive. I could have killed innocent children that night. At the time it was a funny story, one that could admittedly lead me to prison for manslaughter. I was such a lost sheep I was just drifting from one mess to another.

Chapter 31: Mini Penis

Soundtrack: Barry White - Can't get enough of your love, babe

Sub consciously I think I felt I'd been saved because I started praying. It was a totally selfish prayer. It was a prayer for help. I was staring down the barrel at the end of my career at sea and possibly two jail terms. One civilian and one military.

The case ran and ran and in the military world I was innocent till proven guilty. I'd been tested for drug driving no more than that. I didn't really know what to do. So I just kept drifting.

I still travelled north at weekends and got trashed. My ten pills a night phase was over but I couldn't stay in moping. I just did what people were doing. After a chatty afternoon at the Tsar's I drifted into the local Yates wine lodge. Next thing this little fella with a big bald head, a crazy look in his eye and sunglasses resting on a big ridge on his brow comes over. "Alright? I've pulled a fit bird and her mate wants you to come back to mine now. Come on, let's go".

"Is that an order?" "If you're not a faggot." I looked up and a decent enough looking bird waved at me across the room. He had a slightly better deal. I don't know why but I warmed to this rough looking dude. I went over and before I knew it I was in the back of an old Mini Cooper speeding towards more nookie that I didn't really want.

I found out exactly how much I didn't want to when I brought out the smallest whizz dick in the world. My new friend did not look impressed. She did her level best to budge it but she had been sold a complete dud. I felt for her as her mate called out shrieks of pleasure as Mad head filled his boots upstairs.

It was a long old night and he really had the horn. When he was eventually ready to drop me off he was very pleased with himself and

when the girl confirmed I was a faggot I thought he was gonna crash
the Mini. His laughing was a bit over the top. We wouldn't forget each
other in a hurry that was for sure.

Back in Navy world I moved back to a shore base. I hit it off with the
catering officer and I was put up for promotion. I passed the theory and
was advised to wear tight chef's pants for the practical exam as the
examining officer was gay. So I did. It was hilarious you prepped all
the ingredients needed for each of the six courses of the exam and then
hid them around the kitchen. All the chefs then sneaked the ready
made items in and I just pretended I was preparing things. It was a
complete farce really. One dish in the exam was Beef Bourguignon. It
was a stew cooked in a glass casserole dish. Everything in the exam
went to plan. My five other dishes were on display already. For some
reason I forgot the glass dish had been in an oven for two and a half
hours. I picked it up bare handed and my normally asbestos hands
stuck to it. I chose to walk about four yards to the display bench
holding the 180c dish. Mum's pain trick passed the supreme test. I
peeled my blistered hands off the dish garnished the plate and gave the
duty homosexual a cheeky wink. Promotion was secured.

Prison loomed. It was typical me. I'd passed for promotion at twenty
one. Way ahead of schedule and just in time to have it all taken away.
Never the less it was an achievement. The catering officer believed in
me and I always came through when someone showed an interest.

Chapter 32: Never in Doubt

Soundtrack: Status Quo - Down Down

My prayers intensified as the court case loomed. My dad
recommended the scruffiest solicitor in the universe. He had a greasy
Status Quo pony tail. His office looked like a squat. On the positive
side he looked cheap.

In court he seemed hell-bent on winding up the judge and the police.
He sniggered and mocked them. The prosecution produced a long line
of witnesses. There was the chap we rescued, three cops and the quack.
Not surprisingly they all said I was the friendliest criminal they'd ever
met. There was no doubt in any of their minds I was totally nutted.
They then wheeled out a professor of something from the University of
somewhere to tell the court my sample was off the scale. My solicitor
was laughing at them. I held my head in my hands. He was a nutbar
intent on doubling my sentence.

I looked up at Francis Rossi and the mad twat winked at me before he
launched into a rant telling the police and the doctor they had done it
all wrong. I didn't understand most of what he said. However when the
judge finally awoke from his coma four words registered loud and
clear. No case to answer!

Everyone started shuffling. I could see the police shaking their heads. I
looked at Mr Scruffbag. He was grinning. He shook my hand and said
"I don't want to see you again". My fuckin' prayers had been
answered. I could not fuckin' believe it.

The Navy got the truth. No case to answer. I was off the hook all
round. This was the first time I'd been involved in a miracle. For the
first time in my life I felt my prayers had been directly answered and I
was very, very grateful!

<h1 align="center">Chapter 33: A bit of fun</h1>

Soundtrack: KWS - Please Don't Go

Things were looking up at work. I was waiting on promotion and I'd just had my drafting papers through for the following year. I was going to go global on a twenty eight port jolly round the world on one of Her Majesty's aircraft carriers. Fuck me I could not believe my change in fortune. Magnificent!

I also had a result in the kitchen. A civilian girl chef asked me out. When we got it on I explained I liked her but I wasn't looking for anything serious as I was going away. She said that suited her fine. She was happy with just a bit of fun.

She had her own flat locally so I'd stay there about once a week or if we had a drink on the base she was happy to crash in my room with three other chefs pretending not to watch her getting banged. She was a bit of a minger in terms of after nookie hygiene as I had to encourage her to brush her teeth in the morning before she went off cooking innocent people's breakfasts. Obviously in the lob sided warped world that we live in the boys were impressed with my behaviour and she became known as the spunky monkey.

She was a civilian and therefore shouldn't have been staying on the campus. It was a matter of time before we got caught but it did make the working week quite exciting.

I was on duty over the weekend and I knew she was on a session drinking locally. I was cleaning down after the dinner service and she turned up a bit tiddly at the kitchen. She had her game face on so I told the baby chef I was working with he could go. I threw her on the meat prep bench and got my chopper out. The bench was a bit too high to engage properly so after a quick risk assessment I suggested we go either in the fridge and bend her over bags of potatoes or we go the chef's rest room which had armchairs and sofas. She chose the comfort of the chef's play room.

She stripped off ball arse naked and lay with her legs akimbo on the table where the chef's usually played cards at brew time. Ever the gentleman I carefully placed my oven gloves in under her bum, I stayed in full chefs kit and popped Percy out of my checked pants zipper. Job on!

The officer of the day and his entourage were rather surprised when the door flew open to reveal which duty the duty chef had prioritised. I was caught 'tatties deep!' The poor old fun seeker was left stitchless and fully exposed on the table. To be fair she just giggled as she confirmed she was not part of the M.O.D and I was not raping her. She was free to go. I was in the shit again. The skipper didn't crack a smile as he gave me fourteen days' extra duties.

A few days later I told the duty spunky monkey that I think we should call it a day. We'd had our fun and had taken it as far as we could. I was sick of being in trouble. I was surprised when she didn't take it very well. She acknowledged our initial agreement but said she couldn't believe I was finishing it. I was naive to think this sort of agreement would ever work out without someone getting hurt. I wished her all the best. Thanked her for what were fun times. We'd never had a crossed word. Disturbingly she had an unnerving and slightly deranged look in her eye. Oops!

Chapter 34: The lady in Blue

Soundtrack: Stevie Wonder - Isn't She Lovely

A fortnight or so later I went ashore with a baby chef on a Thursday night. He was a lovely young lad and we hit a few of the local boozers. We were in a night club having a boogie and a few cocktails. I never usually scored real women in nightclubs. I'd had the odd freak take me home early doors but apart from "Can I buy you a drink love?" I never had anything to say. To me I always sounded desperate. I usually just enjoyed the boogie. If a bird fancied me then she could come and talk to me. They rarely did.

That all changed when I spotted a gorgeous creature in what I can only describe as a modern clingy blue ball gown. I watched her for a while. She had brown bobbed shiny hair and huge luscious red lips. The split in her dress went high and exposed the outline of a very long leg. Her midriff was exposed. She had a lovely tanned belly with just a hint of abs. She looked very classy and miles out of my league. I ushered baby chef closer for a better look. She was all big lippy smiles and even though I'd never met her I could see she was full of life. We got close enough to overhear her saying to her tiny little pal something like "Sailors really are not for me." Oh bollocks!

Time and time again I'd heard sea dits where Jolly Jack the sailor had pretended to be a pilot or a secret agent or even an oyster fisherman in the hope of impressing a woman. I'd never tried these tactics but I wanted to talk to this bird and not just for a few minutes. I wanted to pick up my pension with her.

I explained to the young, daft and very tall baby chef in my company that he'd just been signed from Hastings to be Bournemouth's new Goalkeeper and I was their prolific striker. They were lovely and easy to talk to. They bought the football lines no probs and let us spend some of our hard earned footballer's wages on some drinks.

Before you could say "Come on you cherries" She let me taste those lips on the steps of the chippy outside. They tasted proper nice and my legs were a little bit wobbly woo as I got her number before putting her in a taxi home.

Baby chef was my new best pal. I explained to him that Miss Poshtotti worked in the telephone exchange on the base. The success of the bullshit operation in the club totally exceeded my expectations. I knew if I'd of come clean after her sweet kiss then her sailor inhibitions would have 99% k.o'd my chances of getting a date.

How to get that date was all I thought of for the next twenty-four hours. I decided to walk into the telephone exchange in full number one sailor suit. I took a card containing an apology for pulling the porky pie scam. I also took a real pork pie to smooth things over.

I stood outside her office sweating like a bubble coated chav in a sauna. Deep breath and in I marched in. She looked up in amazement and slowly mumbled "what have you got that uniform on for?" I nervously explained and handed over the pie.

She was lovely. Her big toothy smile radiated. She agreed to the date. I was soaking wet with sweat. Get in!

Chapter 35: YOB

Soundtrack: Edwyn Collins-A Girl Like You

I was really excited about this date. Love at first sight wasn't far off the mark. Edwyn Collins had a song in the charts at the time. I played it on repeat as I went through my pre-sesh beauty routine: "I've never met a girl like you before!" I had a very good feeling about this girl. She was classy.

She came to pick me up in the least classy motor I've ever seen. It was a turd brown coloured 1970s Renault rust bucket. She loved the heap of shit. I thought that was great. Whatever she did or said was great. I was putty in her hands.

We went for a beefeater style meal. In the restaurant I produced a colouring book and some crayons. I told her if we didn't get on then maybe we could do some colouring in. She looked at me like I was deranged. I hoped she'd get used to my crap sense of humour. This mini rejection put me slightly on edge.

She needed to visit the ladies' room. I dribbled into my prawn cocktail as I checked her out. She wore tight jeans and a crop top showing off her slender midriff. She was well out of my league. I congratulated myself on getting this far.

She drank beer and ate steak, she was ticking all the boxes. She told me about her love for horses and karate. She was easy to talk to although her beauty and classy demeanour did make me feel a little inadequate. There was a slight lull in conversation and I caught her eye. I panicked and felt I had do something. My balloon defence mechanism kicked in and before I could stop myself I'd picked up a Martini and lemonade off the table and poured it over my head. She gave me the 'what the fuck are you doing?' eyes. "Sorry I was hot." Her stone face let me know she was never gonna accept a balloon as a boyfriend. She was the first person to ever have set me a boundary outside school or work. I liked it.

We went into town and she seemed to know everyone. I liked the way she introduced me to everyone and kept me involved. We got stuck into a load of cocktails and got all touchy feely. I was proud to have her on my arm. It was all going rather well until the spunky monkey appeared out nowhere. She looked angry and she lunged at my date before anyone could react. The karate self defence technique wasn't up to much. Thankfully she only took one dig before I helped security escort Norman Bates' mum from the building.

The aftermath of our first date was mixed. Classy knickers looked less classy with a black eye. She travelled to London for a Virgin Atlantic interview. The eye helped her not secure the role. I was surprised how well she and her parents accepted the assault. They seemed excited by whole escapade. Somehow I was still in with half a chance. I explained the details of my split with the spunky monkey and told them I would speak to her.

I never got the chance because the next day the Navy police came to arrest me in the kitchen. I was sure I was drug free. What the fuck did they want me for now?

Norman Bates' mum was intent on causing me maximum damage. Somehow she had produced the scrap certificate of a vehicle we were supposed to have travelled to Manchester in some months ago. It was common practice in the Navy to make fraudulent travel expense claims in much the same way politicians all claimed for garden maintenance.

You got eight travel warrants a year. You could get rail tickets or claim a petrol mileage payment. Sailors of all grades including officers often claimed for unmade journeys and stayed on the base. I stayed the weekend in question with the monkey so I thought it was bulletproof.

At the time there was no mention of a car scrapping. She warmly accepted her half of the claim whilst coldly planning my demise. She had produced a grenade in the form of a scrap certificated dated the day before the supposed journey. My career was blown apart. Her prosecution case was bulletproof.

This betrayal didn't go down well with the chefs. She still had to work in the kitchen. She was ignored and spat on. I encouraged the lads to go easy on her. This mess was of my making. I shouldn't have got involved with someone I didn't want to be with and at the end of the day I had broken the rules. I vowed to accept my punishment and pick up the pieces.

The usual punishment for this offence was forty two days detention at her Majesty's pleasure (Colchester) and I would also lose my recent promotion. I explained it all to the classy chick and she agreed it was never dull in my world. I warned her I might be off to do some hardcore army bird. We didn't make any promises to each other. We just had a special kiss.

A week or so later I couldn't have timed it worse. A brand new skipper had just taken charge of the base. He decided to muster the whole base to witness my fate. I was to be a sacrificial lamb used to show he wasn't gonna take any shit in the future.

"Chef I have had a look at your record. In my opinion you are a YOB!" I couldn't argue with that. I started to drift into parade ground telepathy mode when the word discharge reverberated around the room. There were lots of gasps and some muttering before Captain Pugface went into his "let this be a lesson to you all!" speech. I was supposed to march out but as soon as the skipper fucked off lots of the lads crowded round to commiserate with me. The two coppers let everyone shake my hand before they explained I was to pack my civvies and get escorted to the main gates. From there I would be on my own.

My boss from the kitchen must have known my fate as they had arranged for a brand new bag of chef's whites to be made available to me for use in the civilian world. It was a lovely gesture. He also instructed the petty officer not to walk me to the gate but to drive me wherever I needed to go. Within half an hour a card and an envelope of cash was handed to me from the lads. It meant a lot. I had everyone's sympathy but I couldn't argue. I had taken the piss over the six years of my service.

I'd blown my trip round the world, my promotion and my easy life. More than anything it was embarrassing. Irresponsibility had done me again. My future was now uncertain in every way.

In typical Navy style I received a phone call some weeks later. One of the chefs who had spat at the spunky monkey in disgust had to ring me and confess he'd just shagged her. She was lying with him probably covered in you know what. He said "You don't mind do ya pal? She did say she was sorry."

Of course I didn't mind. It brought a wry smile to my face. Up the Andrew! It was a crazy old institution.

<h2 style="text-align:center">Chapter 36: Poshtotti</h2>

Soundtrack: Kaiser Chiefs - I Predict a Riot

I decided to hang around for the summer as my romance with Poshtotti was very sweet. She was the first girl who'd ever made me wait a period of time to engage in bedroom sports. Interestingly, six weeks in and I hadn't even asked. I know less than one percent of people will be thinking you shouldn't have nookie till your married anyway. In modern England six weeks is a long time and it makes your relationship that little bit more special.

So girlies, the worst relationship participant ever in the world has some advice for you. If you really like someone then make them wait. Even if you're gagging for it and you think they might move on to another more accommodating honey pot. Let them. If they are worth it then they will stick around to reap the following benefit, It's like smelling bacon before you get the full English. Your mind takes a recording of that waiting process and stores it in your soul. It's kept special and labeled precious.

When it came it was more like tea at the Ritz than breakfast at Weatherspoons. She was a class act in all departments. What she was hanging round with a broke smelly chef for I really do not know.

We lingered for the summer but work opportunities were limited by the seaside. We felt Manchester would have better career opportunities for us both. Her parents did what lovely parents do. They backed her decision, waved and cried.

Our first weekend in Manchester was a humdinger. Euro 96 was in full flow and the country was enjoying the sunshine. Excitement was building as Shearer and Sheringham were threatening to win us the trophy. Each victory was sparking great scenes of celebration around the country. In their last game England spanked Holland 4-1 creating a real sense of expectation across our green and pleasant land.

On our first day in Manchester coincided with England versus Spain. Everyone I knew was coming out for the match. Lads that is. As we were still very much in our honeymoon period I was very happy to have my new poshtotti by my side. She was pretty much the only girl in attendance.

There was a real cross section of people out for the match. My old raving associates, the Kavos crew and a selection of school and junior football chums all came together for the party.

I started to question if bringing the Missus was a good idea when pretty much straight away one of the borderline alcoholics amongst us told my new lady she was nice but he preferred the bird that liked getting beaten up in Kavos. She laughed it off and passed her first test without flinching.

Everyone was caning the ale and getting fired up for the match. We relocated to the local British legion. A normally barren venue which had been transformed for the day into a pretty passionate pit of testosterone.

The match was tense and end to end, chances came and went for both sides causing the sense of suspense to grow greater and greater within the room and around the country. The volume was creeping up and up. The only girl in the room cheerfully soaked up the atmosphere and all the free drinks, as lads can't help buying pretty girls drinks. I was proud of her spirit.

By the time extra time came to an end most people had about four hours' heavy beer intake in them. The shouts of encouragement at the screen were becoming more and more incoherent.

Penalties had been the nation's nemesis since Waddle and Pearce skied theirs at the 1990 World Cup. Shearer slotted, Spain rattled the bar and missed sparking a jubilant mini jump around. Platt and Gazza both did the business to match two equally effective Spanish strikes.

Then Stuart Pearce strutted up with a focus that gripped the country. He had the balls to try and avenge the 1990 miss. You could sense that if he scored he somehow had the power to turn England into a nation of winners. The room fell silent. He ran up and buried it. He'd waited six years for it and he looked like he was gonna come through the TV as he roared his celebration. The room erupted and a few pint pots of beer were launched. Moments later Seaman saved the Spanish penalty and England were through.

One lad couldn't contain his joy. He ripped the fire extinguisher off the wall and launched it through the T.V screen. That sparked scenes of sheer pandemonium. Chairs and tables were getting broken up, people were swinging off the fans until the fans brought down the ceiling.

I couldn't resist making my mark in a silly but non-violent manner. I wandered into a store room where I found a Christmas tree outfit which I slipped into. I stepped out into a wild west scene covered in tinsel and Christmas crackers. The Mrs looked strangely stimulated. I whipped off my fancy dress took her hand and led her down the stairs, crossing our names out of the signing in book at the entrance just in case the police put their thinking caps on.

As we stepped out into the road a Nissan Micra had already been rolled on to its side and there were four lads starting to give a Bedford Rascal the same treatment. The atmosphere was surreal and captivating. We watched the Rascal rollover before we stormed into Yate's wine lodge. No queuing for beer here. About five lads were already stood on the bar and others had barged past the bar staff and were pouring their own beer. The lunatics had taken over the asylum. We stayed for a minute or so to observe the scene then we legged it as the Black Maria's couldn't be too far away. As we dashed into a quieter road my girl and I grinned at each other. "Welcome to Manchester!" Imagine if they'd lost!

The lads involved in all that carnage were in the main good people. It was all very wrong. People's livelihoods, property and cars were trashed and the bar staff in Yate's were probably very frightened and that is clearly not acceptable.

Nobody that was there can say they weren't engrossed in the moment though. That sort of mob carnage resonates in the dark side of your soul. It releases an intense burst of adrenaline that is very stimulating. Once that spark ignites then people begin to disregard normal logic. They just listen to the first thing that comes into their heads. Those thoughts spring from the dark side in my opinion. It's why military mobs throughout time have committed atrocities and it's also why people are addicted to football violence. It's nasty good.

At this point in my life I thought my friends expected me to be at the forefront of any crazy business and my new Missus wanted me not to be. As for my own feelings I still hadn't sussed out that everything in life was a choice. I just did the first thing that came into my head. Usually the wrong thing!

Chapter 37: Back to the old routine

Soundtrack: The Beatles - Nowhere Man

I decided I wasn't a particularly good chef and the hours and pay were crap anyway. So I signed up with a load of agencies to do anything. My first mission was into the glamorous world of order picking.

It was a complete change from kitchen graft. It was different from the Navy because you got paid for the actual hours you worked. I liked that, I thought it was fair. I didn't mind grafting for cash.

About two hours into my first day I got asked to take out the rubbish with another angry looking little dude. As soon as we got outside he said with a big grin "I've just robbed a load of gear, it's in that bin. When we get to the bins I'll chuck the gear over the fence to pick up later. You just bin the rubbish as quick as you can."

I thought to myself "Why do I attract this sort of shit?" I just let him do his thing and he loved showing me what a scoundrel he was. I just laughed to myself. Risk of dismissal just seemed to follow me everywhere I went. At the end of the shift he gave me the thumbs up across the car park as he successfully scraped up his loot.

This wide boy was into everything. The trouble was he was a really nice fella. I couldn't stop myself warming to him. Very quickly we formed a bond. He was a grafter like me. We started working 6am to 6pm Monday to Friday plus 6am to 2pm on the weekend. We spent a lot of time together. We were fast pickers so we would do our graft then make dens amongst the stacks of electrical goods and chat shit while the rest caught up. He was a raver and apart from his missus and kid that's all he talked about. We would party together sooner or later It was inevitable.

Nearly all my northern friends were still partying hard I'd just turned 23 so I found it hard not to join in. The mrs bonded with most of my male friends pretty quickly. We went out clubbing most weekends for the first couple of months. She was totally drugs naive. In the

Hacienda everyone else in the place was pilled up apart from her. She was none the wiser, she just thought we were all really friendly. As long as she was having a good time there was no need to even discuss it.

Over a period of time she sussed it out herself and left the raving to the lads. Most of the Kavos crew got together at least once a month and it usually got messy.

Fairly quickly the missus started to get bored of my partying. She liked to go to bed quite early to go to sleep. I just didn't get it. I thought I was missing out. My demon didn't want me to find true happiness with this woman. So my dark side set out to convince me that the girl that I'd fallen in love with had actually been put on earth to make my life boring. It was self-destruction of the lowest intelligence.

A perfect example of this was the first time Mad Head and I had a pill together. We met our women after work at 10pm. We had a cheeky pill in the pub and had a nice chit chat with the girls. We had work in the morning so we decided to call it a day just after midnight.

I got back home and lay in bed absolutely wired. After 20 minutes fidgeting I told the missus my shoulder was hurting and it was stopping me sleeping. I was gonna go back to Mad Head's for a drink and go to work from there. I jumped on my push bike and rattled round there at the speed of light. He had built a bar in his lounge. We spent the night emptying the optics and chewing more pills. At 5.30am in the middle of winter we pitched up for work sucking ice lollies from the local 24 hour garage.

The general manager who had never before been seen of a weekend was sat in the locker room like a headmaster with his cane waiting for naughty students. As we came in talking shite and sucking our lollies the headmaster looked at us like we were naughty students caught talking about screwing his wife.

Mad Head was more twatted than me. We collected our order picking sheets and trolleys from the cabin. Mad Head was reading his sheet upside down. He looked putty grey and ready to puke. "Stick with me mate." The general manager started following us. I took a copy of Mad

Head's printed sheet and told him verbally which items to pick up. It was a very long eight hours. At clock off the manager told us we were his top grafters normally. He told us to sort our shit out and come to work in a half decent state in future.

This sort of deceit was harming my relationship with my woman. Every time I snuck out to party, a slightly bigger gap appeared between us. Somehow I was always creating something to feel guilty for. This was the story of my life thus far and I was doing it again. I didn't know how to do it differently.

One afternoon in the warehouse we had picked all the orders and were sat around talking shit. We started talking about some of the strange nights out of our past. Mad Head told a story about briefly taking Steve McDonald from Coronation Street hostage in a taxi. I told him about a little Mad Head in a mini who ordered me back to his flat four a foursome. We looked deep into each other's eyes; you have got to be joking! It was only fuckin' him! We had a hug and he told me his bird was that bird and his daughter was rustled up shortly after. How could I have not recognised him with that great big ridge on his forehead. Now the whole warehouse thought I had a tiny dysfunctional penis.

A few weeks' later we were all made redundant but 'Mad Head' and I would become lifelong friends. You don't question fate.

Chapter 38: Great Britain

Soundtrack: William Blake/Hubert Parry - Jerusalem

This book is about me but I would like to deviate a little and share Mad Head's inspirational story. It also ties in with my belief that a greater force guides us into and out of some life changing situations with coincidences that could only be arranged by that same great force.

He had a dysfunctional childhood moving between various council estates and schools around the northwest. His mum went from fella to fella and he and he and his siblings consequently tagged along.

You could tell he had to scrap for survival as a kid from the way he approached his adult life. He was always in people's faces attacking before he was attacked. If someone had a wart on their nose he would say "What's that fuckin' wart on your nose?" There was no need. I would get really embarrassed when he did it in my company. If someone looked hard he was straight over and in in their face saying "Who the fuck are you?" Luckily for him he had a cheeky face so the duty hard nut would usually end up embracing him. He just had to prove he wasn't scared of anyone or anything.

After my whizz dick experience. He and the howler upstairs had a whirlwind relationship. At the exact moment of release he knew he'd fired a live one off and she was impregnated almost immediately. They moved in together and had a gorgeous baby girl.

His Missus was a bit of a dreamer. She wanted to be a dance music vocalist. She could sing a bit and he supported her in that. She was only young and after she had the baby she went on the drift. Mad Head really loved her and as the relationship deteriorated he seemed to love her more and more.

They split up just before Valentines' and on the day he was fully tooled up with flowers, chocolates and saucy undies. She cold heartedly blew him out.

He called me to go in to town with him. He wanted to see if she was out in town. No way was I going out with him in this frame of mind. I advised him to stay in. "You're just gonna get in the shit pal!"

So he drank his way around town in search of his woman. There are 450 pubs in Manchester so he really was pissing in the wind. By now he was well worse for wear in terms of alcohol consumption. He stood outside a takeaway in the pissing rain, kebab in hand, sauce on chin. His quest had failed. He looked over to the taxi rank in the hope of getting a ride and there she was getting hers. His Valentine stepped into a taxi with two lads.

The food hit the floor and he jumped in the cab behind his child's mum and her new friends. He followed them back to the house they shared. The three of them went in. The curtains were drawn so he couldn't see in and loud music started to make the windows shake. The door was bolted so he couldn't gain access in the traditional way.

In the back garden the rain deluge continued. He had by now totally lost the plot. He shimmied up the drainpipe and onto the roof. He started pulling the tiles off. Pretty soon the hole was big enough to drop into. He plummeted straight in and crashed through the bedroom ceiling bringing a large part of it down with him. The pounding music left the downstairs guests totally unaware that they had a guest.

He was covered in soot and blood from the light scratches incurred in the fall. He must have looked like a wild animal. I would rather have faced John Rambo than Mad Head. He was ready to kill.

As he stumbled down the stairs and into the business section of the house, he spotted his baby crying in her cot. The poor mite had been left home alone.

The poor guy then had to take in the sexual scene in the next room. I don't know the details of what went on in that room but I think it's fair to say the visitors were asked to leave.

After the fracas he escaped and went to his mum's. He was delirious. Indescribable pain coursed through his veins. He wanted it ended and he ate every tablet in her house.

When he came round he was being made to drink a thick charcoal solution. They had saved him. He was sectioned whilst he explained his actions.

I met him the day he got out. He was a bit shaky but glad to be alive. He was off to spend some time with his sister in Germany. When he came back he had a plan.

He had a decent well paid warehouse job on nights. The most important thing though was to get custody of his little girl. To do this he wouldn't be able to work. He would have to take any flat that came available from the council and try and get by on benefits until baba was of school age.

The mother handed over the child. She was not equipped for motherhood, she was out for herself. I'm sure she loved her baby but she couldn't look after her. He hit charity shops for wallpaper and did his best to make his new home livable. He gave his baby the home and the love she deserved. You had to respect that.

Between him and his brother they managed to scrape enough money together to buy a pallet of broken electrical goods from his old warehouse. He spent his spare time fixing all the components best he could. A month later they went to market and turned £200 into a £1000.

Little 'un started school and his business was born. He's now a very successful fella and family man blessed with a lovely missus and two more kids. He's still got a little edge but he's soft as shit really.

This story shows you why this island is such a special place to live. His life was saved by the NHLess, the government provided emergency housing and money to survive. Then he used this opportunity to give his daughter free education. This great country gave him a springboard to use his brain and make something of himself.

Now he pays lots of tax back into the system. I wonder if he thinks the next recipient of that money will use it as wisely.

Chapter 39: Thai Fish Food

Soundtrack: Enter the Dragon - Lalo Schifrin

Bangkok was a vibrant eye-opener. The missus and I loved this sort of buzz. We sampled the nightlife down Patpong Road. My girl and I sat at a bar facing a typically enthusiastic crazy barman. Behind him ten young ladies in bikinis were dancing around looking fairly uninterested. All the girls were sporting black bikinis apart from one that wore white. The Missus asked the barman "Why does only one girl have a white bikini on?" "Because she's a superfuck of course!" Obviously! We pondered what merits a superfuck as we moved down the road into Gaysville.

The stage in the next club was full of men in bikinis. We were befriended by a lovely little fella who was not in a bikini. He wore a loud red flowered Hawaiian shirt and had an orchid in his hair. At chucking out time he insisted we share a brandy with him outside. Just as we took our seats a giant elephant turned the corner and started mooching through the traffic. It was about 3am and the street was a fruit basket of colour. My little friend sat down and nonchalantly drew a gun out of the back of his pants and placed it on the table. He had a long pink balloon that had been twisted into the shape of a cock with balls. He wiggled it and gave me a wink. We made our excuses.

Phuket was equally as interesting. The place was a total Ying Yang experience. There were temples next to brothels, classical music recitals at premiership football screenings and five star food establishments next to Burger King. The beaches and the fish laden sea were magnificent.

From Phuket we made for the Phi Phi Islands which were truly breathtaking. We arrived by boat. The town was off to the right and to the left of the jetty was a bamboo path with a sign pointing to the jungle bar. The sign gave no clue what lay beyond the bushes. As you stepped through the cultivated secret entrance it was like walking into the Garden of Eden. Huge smiles adorned our faces as we took in the most amazing view. The bar overlooked a huge bay and natural harbour. To each side of the harbour entrance were giant towers of limestone. It was close to sunset and the sunlight flooded through the two giant pillars to flood the bay in a truly magical way. Both sides of the limestone entrance were lit up electric purple as the sun beat into them. Just to top it off they had sour cream pringles to go with your cocktails. The missus looked stunning. It didn't get much better than this.

Sharing the experience was a Swedish family who were equally blown away with this epic pub. The dad owned the biggest and best herring business in Scandinavia. This guy loved herrings. He loved them so much he brought his own bar snacks. Yes tinned herrings. I don't know what was more impressive, the view or one mans love for tinned seafood. We spent the next day in their company and it was a real pleasure to be around a really happy family in such a beautiful place.

The next day was a relaxing beach day and the missus was pleased to be in the company of three young handsome Swedish party fellas. By tea time her enthusiasm was on the wane. It was a carnival atmosphere and I was leading the parade. When I got in that sort of flow she might as well have not been there. I don't remember too much about the evening but it went something like, beer, volleyball, Sang Thip whiskey, fire-eaters, curry, running and jumping bonfires, big fight with young boy being glassed by ruthless locals. I wasn't involved but it shut the place down.

After maybe two hours' kip. I crawled to the shower room. It had everything I needed, a hole in the floor. I'd lost control of my organs and was exploding at both ends. I heard my life partner mid insult mutter she was off for breakfast. Once I was empty I slithered down to brekkie. I sat down and watched her eggs arrive. Oh no, in a flash I was over to the street side gutter retching for England. Nobody was impressed least of all the missus. I waved an apology and stumbled back to bed. My slumber was short-lived, she let me know I was a wanker for going out on my own the previous evening as she was left scared and home alone. I was too ill to acknowledge her completely valid point of view. She looked on in disgust as I revisited the hole in the bathroom. There was further bad news as our ferry off the island left in thirty minutes. I was in no fit state to travel but we were flying onto Chang Mai so the two and a half hour ferry trip was unavoidable. I was dog rough and carrying our bags down to join the boat was a real tester. It was a test I was never going to pass. Without warning my body decided it needed to discharge. Panic stricken I sprinted into the Andaman sea and let it all go. It was like a scene from Piranha. Every fish in the sea came to lunch I could feel them pecking at my waste rimmed orifice. I opened my eyes and was shocked to find myself in a BBC wildlife documentary. The disgusting sight of the fish feeding on last nights green curry triggered more fish treats and vomit was introduced to the eco system. I quickly rinsed my pants out amidst the attack and ran out of the sea twice as fast as I'd run in. My partner had sensibly already boarded the boat. I stayed on the sun baked deck and wished I was dead.

Overnight I recovered my composure. Lady love didn't let me ruin her holiday by bearing a grudge. She knew I knew I was a disgrace. By the time we got to Chang Mai thoughts of shopping, food and adventure had fortunately rejuvenated her.

Trekking in the hills of northern Thailand was exhilarating. Our touring party of ten was an intriguing mix of people. Two oversized German Rock Gods complete with Axl Rose hair were the entertainment. At our first meal together the two of them were blowing whole boiled eggs out of their shells and competing to see which one of them could eat the most. The missus sensed we might get on.

They were text book Germans in relation to not doing queues or showing any consideration for other holidaymakers. I had to chuckle they were always last to bed. We were sharing the local villagers huts so you could hear them laughing and joking round the camp fire. When they came to bed they used their torches, spoke really loud and tripped over everyone. This went on for three nights before they were told to start respecting the other guests at bed time. At 2am they rolled in doing the loudest comedy whispering act ever. I loved these guys.

The trip was a real life enhancer. The multi-nationality trek team, the locals, and the scenery combined with great elephant and raft experiences made it an unforgettable trip. The only downside was the food. An unchanging menu of cold rice and vegetables seemed almost cruel in a country blessed with such great food. By the time we arrived back in Chang Mai everybody craved junk food after five days on the veggies. The Krauts suggested Pizza Hut and we all got some junk and beer in. Five beers in and the team started to thin out. The Germans suggested checking out the Thai Boxing. The missus wasn't keen but I loved these oversized Bavarians and I knocked back her request for an early bath.

As we approached the Boxing Centre a vendor was selling Thai boxing shorts. I fancied a photo in them. Sold. The ring was in an entertainment centre surrounded by pool tables, ping pong and video games. It had about four rows of seats around the ring. As we arrived the compare was announcing a match. We got some beers and watched a pretty brutal tear up.

Once the match finished the compere came back in the ring to congratulate the winner. There were only about twenty people sat watching and it seemed pretty laid back so I went ringside and shouted to the compere. "Excuse me, is there any chance of getting my picture taken in the ring in my new shorts?" he explained I was welcome in the ring but only to fight.

Eyes wide open I looked to the Mrs. "No fuckin' way" she said. Of course I accepted the challenge. I didn't have any kung fu in me, I was the least flexible man in the place and I just couldn't knock back this sort of experience opportunity.

The compere announced an Englishman was going to fight and the place filled up immediately. Fee fi fo fum and all that. The missuss was frantic. As the Germans celebrated their promotion from spectators to bucket men she laid in to them saying if he was your friend you wouldn't let him do this. Two Americans with oversized cameras advised me I could get beaten to death.

I was told to go and get changed and gloved up and wait for the announcement. I was buzzing my tits off. As he announced me I came out like a mad man shadow boxing and growling at everyone. I decided to try and execute a Prince Naseem style flip into the ring. I succeeded in briefly dislocating my shoulder. The missus clocked it but she knew I wouldn't back out now. I started playing the crowd again but the shoulder movement put big doubts in my head about my decision to fight. Never the less I decided to try and enjoy the experience. I started silently repeating the mantra "Nok su kow!, Nok su kow!"

The local assassin didn't look too threatening; he just had a normal man body. They made us both wear a head dress thing and pray in each corner. I plugged into that and asked for divine intervention. I winked at my bird, ding, ding round one.

Traditional Thai boxing methods didn't really suit my style. I took one painful kick to the shin and jumped on him. I got him in a head lock and gave him a few digs. They pulled me off him and he looked a bit flustered. He wasn't that flustered though because he spent a very long two minutes giving me a Muay Thai lesson. He kept drawing me in then stepping back just enough to deliver a powerful kick to my lower leg. Then he'd knee me in the ribs and move back out before I got near him.

At the bell the missus chucked the towel in. Bucket kraut threw it back out and congratulated me. She opened up on him saying "Why don't you fuckin' fight him?" She was starting to get upset and much to my and their dismay I agreed to concede the match. I was touched she cared enough to look so concerned. I got booed as they announced the result. I wasn't bothered, I'd had my fun.

The next morning, I was a bag of shit. My shoulder was really fucked and I could barely walk. My girl had to drag two rucksacks through the airport as I hobbled behind.

This chapter more than any shows how my zest for life could turn great experiences for me into embarrassing nightmares for her.

Two weeks later tinned herrings arrived in the post from Sweden. They were fuckin' horrible.

Chapter 40: Chicken Tikka Balloon

Soundtrack: Inspiral Carpets - This is How it Feels

By now we had bought a house. The missus' career was taking off nicely in the property game. I worked hard and brought in decent dough but I thought of my self as an unskilled grafter. I spent a year and £4000 learning COBOL computer programming. When I got the certificate they told me COBOL was out of date and they wanted another £5000 for me to learn the next language up. I only really started on the programming trail because once the missus started doing well she said she didn't want to leave me behind. That meant pull your finger out. It didn't really excite me though. Wasting the time and money on picking the wrong course led to more guilt and self-disrespect.

We started to go out partying separately. I felt inadequate around her property friends. I couldn't look them in the eye. I went out with the lads and the shit kept coming my way.

A trip to Bolton went very wrong. We had a good pre-rave booze around the town before being denied access to the local rave establishment, the Temple Club. We should have just gone home then but we ended up in the local beer heads' club. It was rammed busy and full of stag type mobs of blokes. Pretty much straight away there was a fracas.

Someone cracked my pal, I cracked him. Everyone jumped in blazing saddles style and some prick bottled a youth. Whoever it was never owned up to it. I got nicked and charged with a section 18, wounding with intent.

They took my clothes off me for forensics and gave me a paper suit to wear instead. It was fuckin' freezing. They said "You can go when you've sobered up." I wasn't even pissed. It was a chilly, shivery night and my penis and testicles took refuge inside my body. By the time I was released it was hard to decipher my sex through the silhouette of my soul destroying suit.

The missus picked me up and told me she'd had enough, "Look at the fuckin' state of you!" She was right, I was messing my life up. I hadn't even tried to break the cycle. I just drifted from one fuck up to another.

Even so I was shocked that the police were intent on pinning this on me. They re-arrested me at work for further questioning. They asked me to identify people off CCTV. I fucked them off and the charge was eventually dropped. I hoped whoever got potted was okay. The whole thing was totally unnecessary. I needed to stop brawling whatever the circumstances. Nobody ever wins a fight.

I became more of a loser when the missus told me we were splitting up. It had been coming for a while. When you stop socialising together it's only gonna go one way. She was on the up I was in freefall. She moved into the other room and I had to watch her go out glammed up every night. It was harrowing.

I was not equipped to act right and cherish the relationship but deep inside I knew she was right for me. It hurt and the demons were sharpening their forks. My immediate plan of action was to party my way out of the situation.

The self-destruction button had been pressed. It's weird how the process of destruction manifests. All the thoughts that come into your head encourage you to go out and enjoy yourself. It's just a smokescreen. If I had an ounce of wisdom in me I would have understood that below the surface was an undercurrent of pain just waiting for the opportunity to fuck me up. Going on the piss was never gonna make me feel better. Alcohol on top of pain just makes worse pain.

Here's how my first piss up since her decision to terminate our romance went. I met friends in Castlefield, Manchester and got stuck into a load of Stella. Pretty soon I was ballooning. First it was a break dancing challenge, then it was rolling past the Barca bar in a wheelie bin. I followed that with a dip in the Bridgewater canal. Amazingly a bird thought I was funny and gave me her number. Just to add to the madness of the day she was deaf and dumb.

Ballooning is doing silly things for the benefit of the crowd often to your own detriment. Ballooning is a very British defect. Nobody ever stops the balloonist. It's often too cringey good. I don't know if it's the mad dogs and Englishman thing but people love to observe the loon.

From my personal loon perspective it was obviously a symptom of pain, an outpouring of self-loathing. Most of the time those feelings were in the subconscious but there were occasions when I chose to hurt myself. I once got into a comedy brawl with a close pal of mine who had a few issues of his own. We were scrapping for over an hour with all our pals balloon-watching over us. I was letting him punch me cos I wanted that pain. I needed it.

Once the crowd lost interest I climbed out of the canal and bailed. I walked up to a bar the missus sometimes frequented. I suppose I would have mutilated her new fella had I caught them enjoying a normal time.

I walked into the kebab shop a disheveled mess. I was about to get messier. The place was a good eatery and I joined the queue for quality marinated barbecued meat products. I must have waited ten minutes before this fella bursts into the shop walks past me and places his order. I was in no mood for German queuing etiquette. He looked about nineteen. Instantly I said "Hey what's the crack? I've been waiting ten minutes" he said "fuck off I'm with the Gooch." I hit him very hard on the chin. He crashed into the window. Ten seconds later he scraped himself up and through the embarrassment he started making "Your gonna get shot!" threats. I just ignored him and placed my order. He jumped on his BMX and shot off. The fella behind the counter said "That was brilliant but you'd better fuck off I don't think he was messing." "I'll risk it I'm fuckin' starving." The devil in me wanted him to come back and I wasn't to be disappointed. Two knobs on bikes this time. I managed one big bite of a large chicken tikka naan before I shoved it in Gobshite's face as he came at me. I gave him a good flurry of digs and his mate didn't fancy it and got back on his BMX and fucked off. I'd lost it. I dragged him and his bike over to the taxi rank and forced him and his silver Mongoose into a black cab. "Take me to the Gooch" I said as we grappled in the back. I had lost my mind and decided I was gonna drive him to his patch and post his head on a stake or something. He got a bit of a wriggle on and let a few digs go. The door opened fully and we got in a tug of war for the bike. He lost and fell to the floor. The door shut and we pulled away. Fifty yards away I stopped the cab and threw out the bike to make a point. Gooch my arse!

My demon had justified my behaviour because he was a gang baddy. What really happened was I'd bullied a little kid. A little kid who could have shot me.

I arrived home with one shoe on. Blood and chili sauce splattered wet clothes. The house was desolate. I really was all alone.

Chapter 41: Black Out

Soundtrack: The Wanted - All time Low

Staying in was as painful as going out. I watched the woman I wanted to be with leave the house in a killer outfit. She'd moved on. I had to try too. I decided to ring the deaf bird. It was an automated system and a computerised voice told me her address and informed me that I was welcome to call round.

I buzzed up illuminating a flashing light in her nice posh flat in unposh Salford. My canal swim memory recall was a bit out. I knew she was pretty but I missed the long blonde hair. She was charming. She was well educated and raised in Namibia. You had to respect her she came over friend and family less and worked two jobs. I kept my resume brief. I was separated and child free. That was as good as it got really.

Her lip reading was shit hot. Her speaking wasn't normal but seeing as she'd never heard speech it was very good. I thought she was very impressive.

I was a bit surprised because straight after our brew she moved in for a snog. It was a really horny experience. She couldn't hear herself breath or murmur. She did both and you could tell she was getting really turned on. That is a good noise. I left with a right rock on. We arranged to go out for dinner.

She looked really nice as we shared a lovely meal in Manchester. We knocked back a couple of bottles of vino and the only negative was I kept whispering in her ear. It's hard for a deaf bird to hear whispers or lip read through her ears.

We walked hand in hand up Market Street. She had surprised me when she suggested taking in a club. She explained she picked up the vibe of really loud music and she liked to dance.

I decided not to scare her in a drug-rife environment and selected 'Saturdays', a grab a granny style haunt on Piccadilly. I paid a fiver each at the hatched window on the stairs. Two massive bouncers were looking threatening at the bottom of the stairs.

As I stepped off the bottom tread of the staircase onto the club floor bouncer number one hit me with a big right hand. I was knocked down and pretty sparkled. I got to my knees Claret was running down my chin and my front tooth crown had been knocked out. I asked bouncer number two "What the fuck was that for?" He replied "I bet him fifty quid he wouldn't knock the next person down the stairs out, I didn't think he'd do it." He gave me a tenner and told me to fuck off. She was long gone.

I had a quick scout around the bus station for her but she must have jumped a cab. I wasn't really angry, just a bit shocked. This was my karma for my recent 'Gooch' fight. I accepted that. I took it on the chin. Right in the gob to be more accurate.

I tried to ring the deaf white African. No answer. She rang me back in the morning. She didn't know what I was mixed up in but she didn't like gangsters. I told the truth, she wouldn't have it. An automated computerised voice explained to me that date number three wasn't going to happen. I told Metal Mickey "It was nice to meet you and good luck."

If this experience was sent to teach me a lesson and stop me fighting it didn't work. If anything it annoyed my demonic subconscious. The following week I had one of the worst experiences of my life; total black out. I went for a good drink with my dad on Saturday lunchtime. I was pissed when I called in at my friends not too far from the pub. I got into some vodka and that is the last I knew about it. I woke up at my dad's the next day. I couldn't remember fuck all of the previous evening. At lunchtime we went back to the same boozer to get back on it. The landlord said "Are you taking the piss? You're barred." "What for?" " Do one, before I send out your friends in the vault!"

My dad asked me what the fuck had I done. I had no idea. It was a horrible feeling. We made enquiries and the story unfolded. After the vodka I went back into the pub on my own. I was minging. A guy who was known for stabbing people started taking the piss out of me. It was a bad decision for all parties as I took the bait and cracked him one.

His friends confirmed he wasn't hurt but he was embarrassed and he'd probably try and carve me up sooner or later. To this day that story haunts me. I could have woken up on a murder charge; I had no recollection of the dust up. I could only think I was playing the vigilante again. Filling in the bad guy. My dad was in danger now. I'd hit a new all time low. I had become the bad guy. It was an awful feeling. I'd been a balloon for many years but never evil. This was not nice.

I prayed for forgiveness. I prayed for my victim. I prayed for help.

Chapter 42: The Plane, The Plane

Soundtrack: Frank Sinatra - Come Fly With Me

My old man took me off to Ibiza to take my mind off things. It was all
a bit tragic. I just wanted to be back with my missus. Autopilot bagged
me a bird from Grimsby. I didn't hold that against her but she could tell
my heart wasn't in it. I felt for her as we got back to my dad's digs. I
knew I wouldn't get a hard on. I just went through the motions of
copping off, a complete waste of time.

On return the ex unexpectedly called me at work. "If you're still
interested I'd like to give it another go. I'm at home now." She was
honest. She told me how a really good looking guy that she was proud
to have as her fella had turned out to be a bit of a fraud. He too had
pulled the 'I'm a footballer' scam. He never produced a pork pie
though and had let it roll on. He was Macclesfield's number one
hitman, at least with the ladies.

I understood that if he had have been genuine I would have been
history. I couldn't argue with that I was just glad she was back. My life
was barren without her. Fate was back on my side.

My first weekend visit to her parents place after the reconciliation
wasn't too encouraging. Mother in law still had a team photo on the
wall featuring Macclesfield's finest cracking his footballer's smile with
an arm around both his new girls. If that felt awkward I also didn't like
being in the bed he'd recently been entertained in. It was a very weird
weekend but I'd nearly just been to Grimsby docks and back so I had to
keep it real.

Never-the-less I felt blessed to have her back. We enjoyed another
honeymoon period of our relationship when we were just pleased to be
together. I felt I was ready to sort my shit out. I really wanted to be
with this girl and I set about letting her know how special I thought she
was. I decided to hire a bi plane to pull a banner behind it asking her to
marry me. I'd never really bought her any jewellery so I put some real
effort into sourcing a big diamond and designing a ring fit for a
princess.

I rang her dad and nervously asked for his blessing. He was cool and said get stuck in. I invited them up as part of the surprise.

She went out with her pal the night before on a heavy drinking session. We had to be near Sheffield for 11am. She flatly refused to get out of bed. "Come on, it's a gorgeous day. I want to take you out for a nice walk." "Fuck off!" That was out of character but being stubborn wasn't. Her family had travelled north for this. The plane cost a fortune. I needed to get things moving. I whipped the duvet off "Cup of tea here love!" "What are you fuckin' doing?"

Further expletives followed as I rumbled her into the car. It was a glorious autumnal day. She wasn't plugged into appreciating nature in this mood. My normally gorgeous lady was a pretty minging putty shade of grey. She didn't look well.

The fly-by was scheduled to take place at Ladybower Reservoir in Derbyshire. It was the location for the bouncing bomb tests of the Second World War. As I guided the walking wounded down to the dam bridge. I hoped my plan would go off with a bang and not a costly misfire.

The weather and the setting were beautiful and dramatic. Unfortunately the mood of my beloved was not in keeping with the surroundings. My phone went off. It was airplane control. Due to the good weather the air strip was busy and the fly by was about forty minutes behind schedule. I now turned hostage negotiator. She was calling me all the names under the sun. I was comedy restraining her as she tried to leave the bridge. Eventually I could see a spot in the sky and I started trying to get her to focus on it. She'd had enough and was adamant she wasn't going to look. As it got closer my strategy intensified. I got her in a head lock and twisted her head upwards to see the banner. The romance of the moment was starting to drift away. I decided to release her and spell it out. "Just stop. Focus on that it's for you!" She looked up read the sign and started crying. I dropped to my knees and asked her to marry me. "Yes, you Knob!" We were applauded into the Ladybower pub by both of our families. We both had tears in our eyes.

A fantastic day followed. Lunch at the pub then back home to glam up before a limo out for dinner at the Midland Hotel. I was proud. She was completely rejuvenated now. She has the most beautiful smile.

Chapter 43: Too much Thinking

Soundtrack : Madness-It must be love

We were engaged for less than a year. During that time my inner monster started to fight back. Not through violence or over indulgence. The darker side of my subconscious kept throwing in the same negative thoughts about the relationship that had plagued me all along. Half of me craved some sort of pure love and a soul mate connection. The other half of me knew it was only myself or another force within me that stopped me giving myself completely to a woman I respected in every way. It was a horrible mental situation and it drove me potty. I just didn't know how to break through it.

My darker thoughts would obsess about alternative women that could fit the pure love/soul mate criteria. I'd be bombarded and consumed with such ideas. Self-destructive thoughts are a test. Unfortunately at the time I still just accepted those negative thought processes as rational parts of my personality.

The closer we got to the wedding the louder the dark call to wreck the relationship became.

It embarrasses me to admit I could be feeling like that running up to my wedding but that's the twisted chemistry that plagued my mind.

Our friends were married just prior to our wedding. I got emotional watching them exchange their vows. I was really happy for them but also sad for me. I was still a selfish self-pitying pig. I didn't want to be. I was just consumed by a force that wanted to deny me love and happiness.

I thought about this more than anything. Had I settled for the wrong bird? Was I corrupted or simply mental?

I decided that maybe I just thought too much. This woman was for me I knew that at core. I hoped the wedding would bring mental peace, let me love and bring us both happiness.

Chapter 44: More Fish Food

Soundtrack: Justice vs Simian - We are your friends

I was humbled by the turn out for my stag do weekend. Thirty or so family and friends made the trip to Ibiza. It was my third visit to the party island. It was the first time I wasn't on the shagging or drug trail. That felt good as there was no pressure. I was just looking forward to lapping up the sun and enjoying a few beers in the company of my people.

I'd invited my future dad and brother-in-law and was chuffed they'd come along. The party had a good mix of characters and would give them an idea of the stock I came from.

There were at least four prize balloons on the trip but the ultra-balloon was probably my dad's pal who was in his late forties. SAS was an ex-services bloke who looked like a German porn star. He had major snags. On arrival he said "I've got to ring the missus." We were all sat around having a beer watching as he instructed his girlfriend to speak dirty to him on the phone. She obliged and he started rubbing his cock and getting all excited. Everyone was thinking "Who the fuck is this nutcase?" The fact he was older made him more shocking and funny.

He didn't last long out on town. Dancing wasn't his thing. Five hours later when we were dragging our sorry arses back to the digs we spotted SAS opposite the hotel. He was still on the phone sex buzz. He'd taken it up a notch or two though, he was having a proper open air wank on a public phone. When he spotted us he was dead chuffed. He shouted over "It's the Mrs she's just helping me have a wank." He had a wig with blond pig tails on and not a lot else. He looked even more like a German porn star now. He moved straight to the top of the balloon league.

In the morning my dad found out how wrong this fella was when he awoke to find an SAS shit on his pillow. Pops was shocked that he'd been logged and told him to get a life and sort the shitty mess out. SAS said "No problem bud." Then he proceeded to flippantly chuck Dad's mattress off the third floor balcony. "Sorted!" he said with a big cheeky smile. You couldn't help but like him.

My balloon in pain symptom theory seemed to add up with SAS. His wife had died of cancer and whatever was going on his head seemed to manifest in extreme silliness.

SAS's best pal was a Cockney Red pal of my dads that he'd known for over thirty years. Tragically his twenty year old son drowned in the River Medway after jumping into the drink for a second time while partying with friends. His old man was crushed. He and SAS were close and part of their coping strategy was getting smashed together. They often got the supporters club bus from London to Old Trafford and caused mayhem for five hours each way. They constantly puffed weed and were offensive in every way. At heart they were really lovely, nice fellas. In America they would have got counselling to help cope. In England we do it very differently.

Another mad man known as 'Pooly' brought a stash of E's with him. Most of us were abstaining now as the majority of us were now twenty seven years old. He was about thirty five and was having his own stag do. He got pissed on the way over and ending up crumbling early on the first night. So when we came in at 5an he woke up popped a few pills and had a great old time annoying the shit out of everyone that was trying to get some sleep. He's a very funny lad who was of course shattered by tea time and back in bed craving pot noodles when we were all getting ready to go out again.

On the second morning I started the day in the traditional way, I woke with a good old fashioned boner. I walked into the room with the most lads in and picked up the 28" TV and started smashing it down on my boner. Then when I had everyone's attention I slammed it in various drawers and sliding doors. People find that sort of thing funny or at least I think thought they did.

Fired up after a spot of willy banging I went and explained to the hotel proprietor that it was my stag do. Would he object if some of our party spent a naked day round the pool? Surprisingly he said "Yeah just stay away from the kids." My plan was to spend the day naked so that when the time came to be forcibly stripped and handcuffed to a lamppost there would be no point. I told the gang that we had the naturist green light and challenged them to join me in the buff. The only taker was the brother-in-law to be. Bless him. he's laid back and lovely. We spent the day arm in arm naked and nobody took offence. His penis was three times the size of mine but it wasn't embarrassing. A small pecker added to the funny factor.

Things still got a little messy around tea time. Some cockneys were buzzing off us around the pool. About ten of us ended up in their room for beers. The temperature was dropping and my knob was starting to retract. They thought it would be funny to lock me out on the balcony. It was funny for five minutes as I squeezed my genitals against the glass but it soon became boring and cold. The music system that was generating the disco sounds inside the apartment was outside on the balcony. I caught their attention and dangled it over the balcony as a threat to let me in. They just gave me a nod like yeah as if you would. I did and four or five angry cockneys darted towards the balcony. The cockneys swore down at me as I did a naked spiderman down the side of the hotel. It was a dangerous descent and one or two residents looked a bit confused as a naked window cleaner using his nuts for a chamois leather shimmied down their apartment exterior.

I turned back into Peter Parker for the planned highlight of the weekend. Religious fancy dress was the Saturday night crack. Everyone had made the effort. We walked round the bay at dusk. A candlelit procession of vicars, nuns, monks, Muslim ladies and Hare Krishnas making our way into town. It was indeed a blessed evening. We met a naked female leaflet distributor from Doncaster. She obviously had snags. Surely being in the buff wasn't in her job description. She was very confident and endured about ten minutes of holy shit treatment before the senior monks in the party scared her off.

When we got home 'Pooly' was just getting his Hacienda head on. He had us in stitches as he berated us for going out without him. He must have only spent twenty quid all weekend the mad fucker.

Sunday was the last day and by now there was a tremendous spirit of friendship amongst the group. We went on an all out bender and some of the beachside buffoonery was comedy gold. The boys had thought long and hard on how to stag punish me. The other ex-Navy chef on the trip explained to the lads I wasn't into fish. So they went around all the restaurants with a dust bin collecting a disgusting concoction of rotting fish.

Pretty much the whole party was sat on the promenade wall looking out at the beach. We were well sauced. I was drinking pints of vodka Red Bull. We were only an hour away from a taxi ride to the airport. I just about thought I'd got away with it when the tsunami of fish sludge hit. It stank. I was half blinded by the putrid muck. I could just about see my pint. it was about 30% fish matter. I toughed it out and glugged it in one. This triggered a mass puke off. I puked my broth straight back into my pot. I examined it and it didn't look too offensive so I swigged it down again. That was too much for most of the team. My best man had a weak stomach puke history and he trebled my spew output immediately. I finally emptied my stomach completely and set about cuddling everyone to share the moment. Setting off more comedy retching. Hat's off to the lads. They truly got me.

Luckily there were showers on the beach to help us de-fish. The cabin crew on the plane took one sniff de poisson and bullied us into an undeserved beer ban. Pooley didn't mind too much because as we descended into the realm of normality he was just coming up on his daily ration of badly timed Ecstasy.

I'd felt almost in control of the monster this weekend. A fitting testimonial to my ballooning career?

Chapter 45: The Band of Gold

Soundtrack: Perry Como - And I love her so

Our wedding was quite a lavish affair. We decided on a Christmas wedding not just because we loved Christmas but because prices were 50% off the summer piss take. Wifey's dad was cool with that as he covered a large chunk of the funds to fund his gorgeous daughter's big day.

In the main I'd managed to disperse the negativity that had haunted me in the run up. When the day came we were humbled that all our friends from around the country had given up their very last weekend before Christmas to travel to the Southwest. The venue was a fifteenth century house which looked spookily resplendent on a foggily atmospheric winter's day in the West Country.

Unfortunately the bride missed out on the mulled wine, the Sally Army Band and the Christmas Carols. When she did join the party she looked stunning and I was proud to take her hand. All the good will in the room couldn't stop my dark side casting shadows over the day though. I felt not worthy of all this goodness. We exchanged our vows and I kissed my beautiful wife. I didn't just feel lucky, I felt totally unworthy.

I was very close to my grandad He was a great man. He did us the honour of singing Perry Como 'And I Love You So.' This is verse two and the words signify all that I hoped for:

I guess they understand
How lonely life has been
But life began again
The day you took my hand

And I love you so...

My Best Man blew me away with the love and thought he put into his speech. I wish I'd listened closer to his observations as he identified my strengths at a time when I had little self-respect.

My speech was supposed to be both funny ha ha and serious at the same time. I cracked a few funnies including the disposal of the shitty stick I used to beat of lady admirers off with. I then brought out a knackered old guitar which I had no idea how to play.

I struck a chord I think and sang my love song to the wifage. In a cranky Mediterranean style I belted out a very drawn out "I laaaaaaaaaaaarv you....!" Then "I do laaaaaaaaaaaarv you..!" Then finally "I really do laaaaaaaaaaaaaaaaaaaarv you...!" This turned into Bad Manners' "I love you, Yes I do, and I know that your Loving me too." I meant it. I think most people in the room knew I meant it. Wifage didn't really get it.

This was the sort of stuff my demon fed on. That connection wasn't there. In the real world maybe a simple heartfelt delivery would have done the trick. My destructive self just loved to agonise over such points. She didn't get <u>you</u> was the repeated message.

The wedding was awesome. We both partied hard. I rocked the dance floor too much and produced way too much sweat. I didn't spend enough time holding my new wife's hand.

We should have been more together that day. I hoped one day soon we would be.

Chapter 46: The Wedding Crasher

Soundtrack: Dean Martin - That's Amore

I would like to say Grandad's prophecy immediately came to fruition but I have to be honest and admit after we got married all the issues that I had didn't go away.

All the same doubts and insecurities still haunted me. I worked hard to help build us a decent home but even after discovering the news that we were expecting our first child I still didn't feel worthy.

Every now and again I would disintegrate and outwardly combust. It kept happening and every morning after I felt spiritually dead.

I managed to turn one joyous occasion for my now pregnant wife into a complete nightmare. We were both guests at her best pal's wedding in Sorrento. They held their wedding reception aboard a plush yacht on a trip to the Isle of Capri. The plan was to enjoy afternoon tea on the island and take in the sunset on the trip home.

The fizz was flowing and the bridegroom's brothers were enjoying the balloon show. I got one of my urges to jump. Not for one second did I stop to consider the consequences of attempting the stunt. I got the Evel Knievel bit all wrong and smashed through all the equipment holding a dinghy to the vessel. I was very lucky not to break my back. On arrival in Capri the boat owners stopped the wedding while the police came and fined the human cannonball one thousand Euro. I just wanted to pay and resume the party but the bridegroom decided they were ripping us off and entered into a long drawn out unsuccessful heated negotiation. The longer it went on the more the wife and I cringed. I was stupid, selfish and irresponsible. The missus hated me. I certainly hated myself.

Over the next few months the self hate intensified and I started to become withdrawn. I started wearing an earpiece at work as I became obsessed with melancholic music and escaped into it whenever I could. It was a sense of despair that my dark side enjoyed. Every morning just as I arrived at work I sensed something dark. I was on the edge of mental illness or under attack from the dark side. I didn't understand it. I just knew something was happening to me.

Chapter 47: That Person Isn't Me

Soundtrack: Nelly - Hot In Here

I came round with a white wine head and the cold shoulder from the wife. I had embarrassed her the night before by getting overexcited at a Neil Diamond concert. I was doing headstands on my seat and putting the fear of God into all the Jewish grannies that were sat roundabout us.

I always felt worthless the day after such an outburst. I would either blame the method of intoxication: "White Wine doesn't agree with me" or decide I just can't handle booze and go through a period of abstinence. Neither method worked. It wasn't the type of grog that was wrong. It was my state of mind and periods of   non-binging always ended in relapse. The benefits of not getting into trouble seemed to be outweighed by feelings of insignificance. I always felt boring not drinking so I'd risk disgracing myself again and then feel bad about that. It was a vicious cycle that felt impossible to break.

The arrival of our first child was a big deal. Thankfully love for my son came easily. Nothing felt more natural to me. It should have fully cemented our marriage but the same negative thoughts towards our relationship still dogged me. I was still unable to give myself fully to the woman who had just given me a son. With that came even more guilt.

I was two months into a self-imposed alcohol ban when a logistical nightmare and bad weather forced my catering team which travelled around the country doing corporate hospitality to get pulled off a job. We were unable to work from lunchtime and were transferred to an all-expenses paid hotel for an overnight stay.

My lady boss was approaching retirement and announced this opportunity was to be her improvised complimentary leaving celebration. I got roomed with a quiet little homosexual fella. We shared a cup of tea and a biscuit in the room before joining our colleagues in the dining room.

Boss was a legend in the catering industry. She was a complete dragon. She terrified chefs and waiters of all levels. At work she was selfish, racist, mean and false. She had a posh voice for speaking to the public and a rough arse fire breathing bad mouth for staff. Sometimes she'd defend her team at all costs; sometimes she'd sell us down the river. She would have made a good Nazi. At all times she knew exactly where her team were and exactly what they should be doing. I felt she's missed her vocation she could have been a great evil dictator. Surprisingly Out of work she was a totally different character; Caring, polite and funny. She'd botched her private life shagging bad married men on the job. She'd lived a bit. You couldn't dispute that.

At lunch she was taking the piss good style using her finest lah-di-dah voice to order the hotel's most expensive wines to go with their most expensive steaks and seafood. I watched the party develop and was surprised how quickly everyone got twatted. I lasted about three hours before I rang the wife to explain the situation. She gave me her blessing and said "Just be responsible."

I did the complete opposite. It was like I did a Worzel Gummidge style pit stop and screwed off my sensible head and replaced it with my balloon head.

I went over to the Boss. My wicked smile said it all. She thanked me with a bottle of the hotel's finest Vin Rouge. I told her my plans for the evening.
"Boss I've often thought I'd like to stand with you, arm in arm, naked and glorious and toast our blessed kitchen union." "You want to give me one?" "No dear I would like to mark your retirement with a naked wine and cheeseboard experience."

I decided to decant my Shiraz into a pint pot and let out the Yob. It didn't take long for me to get loud and lairy. A business man started a bit of banter with me. I dipped my nuts in his pint then into a bowl of complimentary Bombay mix. Then back into his pint. He was speechless. Each time there was a break in play I reminded Boss about the naked cheeseboard.

Dinner at this hotel was supposed to be a fine dining experience. We managed to turn it into a wankered chimps tea party. Food war broke out and bread rolls and asparagus spears were being launched around the dining room until Graham the Hotel Manager came over to reprimand us. Boss struck a deal with him. We'd clear the restaurant if we could have some drinks up to take up to our rooms.

Five of us made it up to Boss's room: Boss, two waitresses, myself and my little gay pal. As soon as I got through the door I was naked. MTV went on the tele. My dance portfolio included The Running Man, The Crazy legs shuffle and most offensive of all, Shaking the Tail feathers complete with full bollock swinging.

The other four were wetting themselves. In my mind they were having as much fun as you can with your clothes on. The adverts came on and I took the opportunity to pause for air and wine. With a big smile on my face I asked her again: "Come on, get your kit off love!"

Once she'd made her mind up she didn't mess around. She put her thumbs in her waistband and dropped her elastic slacks and knickers in one. A big grey muff joined the party. She quickly unbuttoned her blouse, pinged off her brassier and exposed a giant pair of blue veined norks. I was proud of her. I gave her a congratulatory hug before guiding her to the shower room. I told her I had thought of an acceptable way for us to enjoy our nakedness without contravening married man law and all that. I was to gyrate from the inside of the shower cubicle while she embraced the other side of the glass. Watching my sixty year old boss's privates being squeezed against the glass was a surreal experience. It didn't last long though. Graham the hotel manager was at the door.

We decided honesty was the best policy so one of the girls flung the door open and we busted a few moves. "Oh my god!" That was all he had to say as he retreated down the hall. I shouted after him, "Can we order a Cheeseboard?"

The next thing I can remember was being woken up by the cold. I was duvet less and fully exposed. My homosexual colleague had a grin on his face as he asked "Would you like one of my quilts?" I was that bolloxed I chose not to think that through. I took the duvet and nodded off.

One of the girls came to wake us up for breakfast. My roomie let her in and she made us a cup of tea. The two of them started talking about what a fantastic night it was. My head was banging. I focused my mind and all the madness started coming back.

I sat up and the young waitress said "Hey you mad bastard you'd better check this out!" She'd made a mobile phone video of the whole naked Boss room escapade.

I'd never seen myself in that sort of state before. My eyes were devil red and there was a really, really crazy look in them. That person was not me.

I also found it difficult to watch footage of the Boss squeezing her bits up against the shower glass. I never intended to embarrass her but watching the video I felt It was very wrong to have manipulated a sixty year old lady into that. The waitress told me it was my lucky day, she thought the Boss was ace for playing along with me and as her friend she had to delete it. As funny as the footage was it was harmful to our Boss. She binned it on the spot.

I put on a dressing gown and headed back to the Boss's room to get my clobber. She looked frightening bless her. "Happy retirement love!" She smirked back: "You mad bastard!"

She told me to follow her to reception as we needed to smooth things over with Graham. As we approached the hatch she went into full Hyacinth Bucket mode. "Excuse me Graham, if I could please take this opportunity to apologise for last nights over exuberance. Long day, high spirits!" His reply was not what she wanted to hear, "I've already emailed your superiors. You're lucky I didn't call the police." She dropped the posh voice, "Graham your a fucking wanker!"

Chapter 48: Light at the end of the tunnel

Soundtrack: Massive Attack - Teardrop

On the trip home the team discussed a historic night. I was in shock.
Even though I always felt like shit after a binge, I had always been
under the impression that whatever crazy shit I did I was still a good
man. The man I saw on the film wasn't close to good. He had devil
eyes. He looked possessed. I can honestly say I looked at that video
and I was shocked by the darkness of what I saw. Over the next few
hours I started to come to terms with the fact that the man on the film
was me. I had become that beast. It was a lot to take in but as low as I
felt my main emotion was one of relief. The time for real change had
come. I had no desire to bat for Satan's team and if the truth be known
all that stuff scared me to death.

I wasn't brought up with religion and I hadn't studied the Bible. I think
I just came to a point in my life where both good and evil just
presented itself. I'd spent years not recognising I had a choice but now
it was a crystal clear no brainer.

First of all I spoke to the wifage. She'd heard it all before. She took my
latest shame story about the old lady in the nude in her stride. Not a lot
surprised her by now. I was just grateful she never mentioned divorce.

I decided to write to all my friends and family and apologise for my
crazy behaviour down the years. If I screwed up again I'd have
nowhere to turn. Few people replied and the ones that did, didn't
disagree with my thoughts. That said it all really. Nobody said "You're
great just keep doing what you're doing." or anything like that.

Initially I didn't have a plan but I prayed more and asked for
forgiveness and direction. As soon as I decided to make a change my
thoughts became a lot clearer. I was intrigued by the spiritual side of
my crossroads and I start reading about different faiths. Looking for
answers I suppose. I decided to change everything to try and reclaim

my soul.

Obviously the ale went. I didn't feel I was an alcoholic but I clearly wasn't settled enough in soul and spirit to do booze.

My next decision was to quit wanking. Over the years I'd convinced myself that if I didn't spank out five wanks a day I'd be like a tensed up, boiled dry pressure cooker that had been left on the gas to ready to explode. So to avoid such catastrophes even on a quiet day I'd crack out 3 of my 5-a-day. It wasn't a secret. I'd made a joke out of this habit since the days of my naval wankathons at sea. I didn't have a massive stash of porn but I suppose I did have deep emotional ties to some of the ladies in the films. Handing them over to another pressure cooker was like getting divorced. It had helped control my mind for a long time. I wanted my mind back. I picked up a Buddhist book maybe a week after I said goodbye to Courtney Cummings and friends. The book said "it's fine to let a bird land on your head as long as you don't let it build a nest." I had to agree. If I could learn to let porno thoughts pass. I'd be left with a clearer mind, and most definitely cleaner bed sheets.

I found the Buddhist methods of controlling your thought processes an interesting fit and I set about trying to retrain my mind. I started dismissing all wrong thoughts. I wasn't looking to convert or join any particular faith and I didn't really see this as a religious move. It was just the first book I picked up and it had a guide to thinking right. That's what I needed. It made sense. It was meant to find me.

I managed to start the process but my darker side was in utter turmoil. It was as if the devil in me decided you don't get away this easy. My nerves started to go. I felt as worthless as I ever had. I resisted and started dismissing those negative thoughts as well replacing them with positive ones. This seemed to anger my inner beast further.

Each morning as I arrived at work I felt a darkness engulf me. I lost a lot of weight through the stress. The wife was brilliant. She did her best to understand me. Trying to explain you can't love properly to the woman you love is a tricky one. She accepted it remarkably well and vowed to help me find myself. Even so she couldn't take my meditating seriously. She took the piss. Until you come under attack and face nervous system issues you have no idea what people are facing.

As my nerves started to go meditation was the perfect antidote. It calmed everything down. Listening to yourself breathe reminds you you're alive. I constantly prayed thanks for that. I liked to sit in the garden and do it the most. When you finally open your eyes the flowers jump out at you. The wife thought I was back on the drugs when I tried explaining that particular phenomenon.

I tried joining a bunch of lentil munchers in Chorlton for a group meditation session. I walked into a hushed room and the lady who must have been running the show savaged me for not removing my shoes. It took all my new powers of right thought to not inform her that if she was a good hippy she wouldn't talk to people like that. Group peace wasn't for me. I found the false silence unnervingly noisy.

My lifestyle completely changed, Instead of all night benders I took to early nights. I was amazed wife wanted another baby with me so bedtime meant nookie and or reading a mixture of religion or cookery based books.

This totally different sort of pre-sleep routine antagonised my 'need to be naughty' innards further. My dreams were all over the place. A battle raged in my subconscious. I often woke to a pounding heart and chest pains. Walking into the light was not going down well with the grim reaper dude.

Chapter 49: The search for the unbroken boy

Soundtrack: Primal Scream - Moving on up

The more I focused on the mess of my past the more my nerves deteriorated and the shakier I became. Nobody really noticed as I was renowned as a clumsy twat.

It's a frightening experience to have such a powerful force take over your body. Funnily enough although it scared me I felt I needed to feel that way. Not only as part of my punishment but also as part of my spiritual education. It felt to me as if I was in close proximity to the good and bad forces that control this world. I felt blessed to be aware of that.

Mornings were rough. I felt like I'd been beaten up in the night. So much stuff was going on inside of me. It left me wiped out and nervy each morning. In one of my dreams I kept seeing myself as a child. So the next day I dug out a photograph of myself as a four year old. It's the photo I've tinkered with on the front of this book. I wanted to reclaim the spirit of that unbroken boy. Every day from then on I looked into that photo. That was the real me and I wanted to reclaim that goodness. I also started looking into a mirror, right into my eyes I wanted to accept myself at last.

The more I started to pray and connect with my good side, the more the thoughts that came back sounded like good advice. The buzz I'd chased all my life was surprisingly there for me too. For the first time in my life the prayers I said were aimed inwardly as I came to the realisation that my God was in me. When I made a connection through prayer that way, then good decisions and realisations were rewarded with a rush of adrenaline that matched any sensation from my chemical past. It was a pure buzz. Once I'd experienced that connection I knew all the depression related symptoms I was experiencing would pass. I suppose I was developing what people call a faith.

I certainly never visited a doctor. I'd seen plenty of people lose themselves on medication. I was out to find myself, not switch myself off. Within six months the wife knew the change was genuine. Our relationship was improving all the time. She'd stood by me when I was a wretched individual. That gift to me was starting to pay dividends. As my self-esteem started to grow I was able to be genuinely more affectionate. I couldn't agree more with the old saying: 'You can't love anyone until you love yourself.'

I was humbled by the wife. Looking back I still couldn't understand why she'd stuck with me through the crazy years. I didn't hide my gratitude. I loved her and everything she stood for and for the first time ever I could say it from the heart. She rewarded me with the most amazing news: She was expecting twin girls. Truly amazing!

Chapter 50: There's Only One Graeme Souness

Soundtrack: Mika - Big girl (You are Beautiful)

Very quickly my life had turned around. Home life was sweet. Our two year old boy was special and the wife loved carrying the twins. Out of the blue the nice couple over the road knocked on our door and asked us if we would like to buy the house next door to them. It was their father's house and he had recently expired. We asked them in and gave them too much wine. They said we were nice people and they told us that they didn't want crap neighbours. They would like us to move in next door to them. We sold our house quickly for a good price, bought theirs cheap and spent the difference on turning our new place into a palatial family home. It came out of the blue as we hardly knew them. As a double bonus they were lovely. So we got new friends, neighbours and a house upgrade all off the back of an unexpected knock on the door. I'm convinced that good stuff like that doesn't happen by accident. As I write this I'm still praying thanks.

In the day job I had started to get really passionate about my cooking. Everything seemed easier in the kitchen now. My mind was freer and sharper. Such was my progression and passion that many of my work colleagues and friends kept telling me I should have my own restaurant. When you put passion into food it's amazing the reaction you can get from people. I could whip people into a frenzy with a simple plate of scrambled eggs. Loveless eggs are a million miles away from loved eggs and my eggs were fully romanced. I decided to go back to college and sharpen up my skills further with a possible business venture in mind.

Meanwhile wifage was on a measly part time wage. So I now worked full time and overtime between Monday and Friday. I also ran a different kitchen at weekends and squeezed college in around all that. We British are a nation of grafters and whatever the financial climate I think if you really want to work you'll find some. I did and I grafted my little cock off to stash some cash ready for the arrival of the twins and with my new vibrant 'what's he so fuckin' happy about?' approach to life. Everything I did, I did with enthusiasm and as corny as it fuckin' sounds, if you smile at the world the world smiles back at you.

People started buzzing off me.

Back at the ranch pregnant women are funny. All that cluck, cluck, clucking. Carrying twins makes everything twice as hard for the wife and twice as humorous for the husband. Bless her, carrying twins is serious shit. First she got hit with a double dose of morning sickness. Everything she laid eyes on she wanted to yak on. Our new neighbours thought she was bulimic before we announced the pregnancy as she kept running out of the kitchen door to share her breakfast with them.

She didn't have it easy. Pretty much straight away she suffered with sciatica. The hospital gave her crutches. She looked a right case trying to take charge of a two year old in that state.

Her hormones were all over and she suffered from cloasma which is a skin complaint that can afflict pregnant ladies. Unfortunately wifage's temporary affliction looked very much like a Graeme Souness moustache. She accepted it with grace and we exchanged some excellent lip warming banter.

She also had insomnia from a mixture of the sciatica, the movement of the babies and excitement about meeting the twins. She walked the house at night eating stuff and performing a strange kind of a Maori Haka yoga waddle. It was meant to move the babies off her sciatic nerve. Whenever I saw it I found it tragically horny. I was in awe of her. She was knackered, she looked like shit. Her body was getting stretched all over like pizza dough and she still claimed to be enjoying it. For her all this shit made the motherly connection with her kids more deep and meaningful. I was glad to have been born with a penis.

I caught her one morning playing Russian roulette with a pair of scissors. She was trying to trim her now Amazonian bush. She couldn't quite get there so she was taking pot shots. With all the extra pressure down there I was concerned she might snip off something she needed so I got involved and we had as much fun as you can have with a huge belly, a pair of scissors and a tube of immac. The strip was fully prepared and ready for landing!

To other people she may have looked like a run down, pale and bloated Willie Thorn fat lookalike with hair on crutches but to me she was perfectly in bloom. She'd given herself to us. She was a truly magnificent creature.

Chapter 51: The Girls

Soundtrack: Dies Irae from Verdi's Requiem

As the big day loomed the Yoga Haka got funnier. She was Gigantasaurus by now and at thirty five weeks it was show time. She felt her waters go while I was at work and made her way to our local hospital. They did a swab to prove that her waters had gone. It was inconclusive. So they monitored her overnight. She was sent home in the morning only to receive a telephone call informing her that the swab showed she had Group B Strep which is a harmful bacteria that can cause fatal infections in new born babies. They said "You don't have to worry about it unless your waters go." The wife said "It was inconclusive that my waters haven't gone."

So they suggested that she came back in then for further analysis. On arrival one of the babies' heartbeat was erratic so they whizzed her down to theatre: 'If in doubt, whip them out' was the midwifes mantra. In theatre that wasn't the registrar's view. He said "This is nothing to worry about just take her back and monitor her further." These heart monitors can give you a heart attack yourself. When the twins move around they can stop each other registering a heartbeat. So every time one went missing. It was squeaky bum time until the flat line went wiggly again. After an hour or so of heart monitor torture, it was still inconclusive.

The registrar told us that her waters were still intact. Once a woman has experienced giving birth once they know what a gush of fluid between the legs means. We were very surprised. The wife explained she knew the difference between a swamp and a sack burst but they were adamant.

He said "Please sit on the bed for two hours if you don't lose more waters pooling then we'll send you home." They gave her a steroid injection to bring the babies lungs on and said "You can always come back if anything else happens." We weren't happy but she didn't leak over the next two hours so we took their advice and went home. The next week was spent in a state anxious discomfort. On the Saturday I rose early to find the wife feeling rough. She had no temperature or contractions so she sent me off to work.

Just as the lunchtime service was kicking off I got the call. I rang a cab and gave the baby chefs their 'hold the fort' instructions. The taxi took ages to come. I received another call from the wife's best pal. I heard her screaming from the contractions in the back ground. I fucked the taxi off and ran the three miles to the hospital in less than twenty minutes. I felt very excited on the run as if I was about to experience something amazing.

I burst in panting like a bulldog and tried to look unflustered. They had just had both of the babies heartbeats confirmed and were preparing to go to theatre. Wifage seemed fairly calm considering she'd had to wait so long for the registrar and the anaesthetist to come and examine her and issue antibiotics for the Strep B. All in all it took about one hour forty minutes for them to inform her she was 8mm dilated and too far gone to go for the standard practice cesarean section for twins.

The first baby would have to be delivered breach. Wife was strong and just accepted that news. The Registrar that had the opportunity to deliver the girls a week earlier was in charge again. I felt a bad vibe off him. I hope she couldn't.

Finally we were rushed down to theatre. Lots of staff appeared out of nowhere and very quickly it turned into a very distressing scene as the wife was unable to get any pain relieving drugs because it was left so late. She'd had our boy without pain relief. She was so brave back then but he came out head first. This was going to be a very different experience.

A bottom first breach delivery is incomprehensible. The baby is bent in half in a head to toe fashion. So the circumference of the babies bum, hips and back is massive. Her desire to have the babies was monstrous. How she controlled her reactions to the amateurish efforts to remove them I will never know.

Hands, forceps and a vacuum extractor were all used to totally brutalise her before the Registrar finally took the decision to cut through her undercarriage to get the first baby out. The wife didn't scream. She let out deep defiant growls. She was hell bent on having these babies. I was shocked and amazed by the graphic horror of the procedure and the heroic strength of my wife.

When the baby came out they put her straight onto mums chest. She briefly let out a smile but we noticed before the staff did that the baby wasn't breathing. They took her over to a heated cot and a team started working on her. The room was in panic and soon the defibrillator was being used.

I held on to my wife's hand and prayed. What came next will haunt me forever. The Registrar told us baby two was also breach. The best thing to do was to turn it through the stomach. He pushed hard into my wife's stomach and grabbed the baby, viciously twisting everything inside of her. This assault was wrong. She fought him off. It was never gonna work. This guy had lost it.

They told me I couldn't stay as they started to prepare for a caesarean section. I kissed her and told her I loved her before I was made to sit outside the theatre door.

I tried to connect with my God. I asked for forgiveness and for the sparing of the lives of the girls and my wife. If I'm totally honest my main concern was my wife. I really thought her life was in danger. It felt like an eternal fifteen minutes. I had a vision off two blonde girls doing 'ring a ring a roses' in a summer garden. I could hear more panic in theatre and I went in briefly to enquire. I was ushered out and a nurse sat with me for a few minutes. She didn't know what to say so she said nothing.

It all went quiet and very quickly a lady came out to tell me the news. Both babies were delivered still born. My wife had been butchered in vain. My thoughts were only for her. I wished, willed and prayed for her safety. She was made for this moment and it had been taken from her. I just felt love for her. Love and sadness.

I called the parents. Her folks said they would drive up immediately from the South West. My mum came to see me and my dad was shattered on the phone too.

It was confirmed Wifage would be okay and I had a two hour wait to see her. It was great to touch her face. She was understandably in shock. Almost immediately they asked us if we wanted to see our still born babies. We agreed and two perfectly formed girls were handed over. They were stunning. Nobody could ever be prepared for that. It was the most bizarre scene. We sat there kissing and cuddling our dead babies. They were beautiful. We'd been robbed. Thoughts for the lost gift of life for the twins would come later. I was angry my wife got no reward for her bravery. It was wrong.

Chapter 52: Never Forget

Soundtrack: The Stargazers - Twenty Tiny Fingers

For the next two days we played dollies with our perfect little girls. We were both nervous to meet them but we agreed it was a non-decision. We had to bond with them and see what should have been.

Sadly their nappies would never need changing. We couldn't help wrapping them up and keeping them warm though. They were adorable little babas. Their perfect condition made it much harder to accept they were lifeless. That opportunity to fall in love with them was invaluable as it gave us real memories of them to treasure forever.

We had a big decision to make as our boy had just turned three years old and he was adamant that he wanted to meet the girls and claim his treasure too. I explained to him that seeing them might affect him in later life. "You were supposed to see them alive son." He said "Dad if you don't let me see them, then I'll never see them." The gorgeous little fella was right of course. I'm still not sure it was the right thing to do but we kept him away. He's seven now and he still holds it against me. He's a special sort of a kid who could have probably handled it but it was a risk that we weren't prepared to take.

The time with the girls was precious. The three days we spent with them was 'Pink time' as we were fully aware that we may never be able to have girls again.

My new found faith helped me a lot. Instead of looking at the girls in a melancholic self pitying daze, I just radiated love towards them and their spirit. Fairly soon my darker side would start heaping the blame of it all onto me but initially I just felt love for my wife, my son and the girls.

The hospital had a double room for people in our position, so I could support the wife. She was in a right mess as the baby twistage followed by a caesarean had totally smashed her stomach muscles.

Down below was messy too. After a week she had to start using the toilet naturally. I couldn't resist taking the piss as I walked her to the bog because she looked like my pet chimp walking bow legged and wearing support stockings. Her stomach muscles were in no state for laughing but it was worth it.

That week was certainly a special one for our marriage. As a man I cringed every time she used the toilet. I really wished I could share some of her physical pain. I was totally useless but I knew she liked having me there. I knew there and then that sharing this tragedy would make us forever inseparable. We were one now.

Feelings of loss and sadness for the girls took longer to manifest than you might imagine. After a week the wife asked a nurse why she wasn't grieving. "Everyone's different, it will come." Two days later it did come. She was crushed. It was hard to watch but necessary to see her start to digest what had happened. Through the tears she told me we were gonna have another baby. She was a fuckin' rock.

I never went through a real grieving process as I felt the girls' spirit just became part of me, of us as a family. Their souls were pure, no pain would ever come to them. That doesn't mean I wasn't sad that we all had unnecessarily missed out on having a mad house full of gorgeous kids. I was sad for sure but the only thing that made me cry was seeing the wife and the boy upset.

The hospital had an extraordinary nurse in charge of all things baby. She was called Nora. She was the top maternity guru in the place. The passion she put into the anti-natal classes enamoured us towards her immediately. She was an Irish angel. She radiated love. Afterwards she hugged us, cried with us, joked with us and prayed for us. More than anything she helped me accept the decisions the Registrar made the week before the delivery and in the heat of battle in the delivery theatre. Those decisions that seemed to be so misguided and inadequate. She said "Whatever he did wrong, he didn't want to kill your babies." I thought about it and she was right the poor bastard had to live with his decisions. Whatever you do in life you have to learn from your mistakes and I really hope that he did. He needed love not vitriol. Wife spoke to him briefly, she asked if he'd do anything differently. He said no. We just left it at that.

Our friends and family swamped us. It was humbling and we felt their love. In the age of technology and smart phones we needed a PA to keep up with the messages of good will and in the end we just craved a bit of peace.

After a week in the honeymoon suite we were released to prepare for the funeral and before we knew it I was carrying a double white coffin into the crem.

We didn't want the funeral to be a circus either so we just invited our immediate family. Our boy also missed out again much to his annoyance.

The young vicar who did the service was scared to death. When he came to see us at home prior to the service he was shaking but he gave a lovely sermon and did us proud. After my speech I had to console the vicar. It was all too much for him.

I paid tribute to the Rock and to my boy and everyone in our lives including Nora who came. I said the wife had always been a good person. If anyone had brought this bad karma on us it was me. I addressed Satan and acknowledged he was after me. I challenged him to throw cancer, whatever he wanted at me. I was ready he couldn't break me and my family.

Wife still wasn't healthy. This was confirmed on a trip to the toilet as she passed a piece of placenta. They hadn't removed it all. This was not only dangerous but increased the possibility of her requiring a hysterectomy. She reluctantly went back to the scene of the crime.

Worryingly it took a week after the procedure for her temperature to come down I started to regret issuing the Satan challenge but she came through. She always did.

They said it would take six months to see if she could still have kids but we knew that the spirit of the girls would live on in another child. It was just a matter of time.

Chapter 53: Giving it all away

Soundtrack: Pink Floyd - Money

After the funeral the slow burning idea of buying a business back in the South West set on fire. We made a series of life changing decisions very quickly. Even though I'd been back to school to brush up on my culinary skills I had zero business experience. It showed as we paid 50k for a twelve year lease on a harbour side eatery back in Wifage's home town.

Next door took the news well. Their nice neighbour plan had slumped but they understood we didn't plan it. We just felt we should be near Wifage's family and I should stop reading cookery books in bed.

We sold the house that we had just spent six months renovating at a give-away price. We gave our notice at work and we were just about ready for the off. I decided to give everything I owned away to make a complete new start. So my clothes went to charity and my vast music collection to a good friend. I wrote thank you letters to everyone I loved in Manchester and we were off.

I drove the family down then made the trip back to pick up the rest of our belongings. On the second run I had just come off the M5 in Somerset, I was driving along a dual carriageway when my peripheral vision caught sight of a deer in full flight two fields away. I knew it was coming for me. I started to pray for protection. Thirty seconds later it burst through the bushes and bounced off the front left headlight area of the car and flipped into the air straight over the roof. I held the car straight and pulled over.

I got my head together and walked back up the side of the busy carriageway to check out Satan's missile. The deer was lying motionless just off the road. Next I inspected the car damage. The only evidence of any impact was some deer fur stuck in between the seams around the headlights.

On the last leg of the drive south I prayed thanks but I also wondered if it was a sign to not move south. On arrival I told the story to the family and they just laughed it off.

We had exchanged our posh gaff for a tiny rented two up, two down semi but I had big plans and didn't expect to be living in a shoe box for too long.

We opened a posh tea rooms doing a bit of fresh fish from the family fishing boat. Fresh crab, dobber quiches, homemade burgers and loads of freshly baked cakes, scones and pastries.

My enthusiasm and output was phenomenal. I was up at 4am to buy groceries then I knocked out about two hundred portions of sweet things before serving breakfast and lunch and afternoon tea.

My plan was to gather the family each evening around our nice outside tables on the harbour. Wifage was not cut out for catering, she had zero passion for it. By the end of the first day she told me she couldn't hack my attitude as a boss and she didn't want to work with me. She also decided the harbour side traffic was too dangerous for kids.

I'd lost my natural restaurant manager and my family time on the first day. I took it on the chin but my concern was it wasn't family concern anymore and it put me in a sorry situation. My vision of an idyllic daily family gathering on the harbour had been kiboshed and it all felt a bit pointless.

I understood I was a perfectionist knob and I'd obviously watched too many Gordon Ramsey programmes. I was convinced my way was the right way. We were running a fuckin' cake shop but I had a Michelin starred mentality and I obsessed about everything. The table cloths had to be Nazi clean, the food completely fresh and the tea blend had to taste just right.

There were a lot of birds on the harbour and from day one a group of pigeons decided to torment me. They walked in uninvited through the kitchen door a few times a day. I bought a chainmail curtain but they simply walked through it. Little fuckers they were.

The place got busy quickly. My plan was to work like a prisoner in a concentration camp from April to September leaving the rest of the year for family time. Hard labour didn't faze me but I got it all wrong. Seven fourteen hour days a week was crazy and the guy in the ice cream parlour next door kept telling me I was doing too much. "Your gonna make yourself ill." he kept telling me.

As the season went on the place got busier and staffing the place became a major headache. I put a notice in the window for a pot washer wanting to learn about food. Minutes later Radar walked in to offer his services. His ears earned him his nickname and I took to him straight away. He'd never set foot in a kitchen before but if you showed him something once the next time he tried it he would perfect it. Unfortunately he had a few snags. Post traumatic stress disorder from the Gulf being the major one. He needed a fag every few minutes to calm his nerves. I tried to empower him and give him responsibility but he was a liability. After a twelve hour day in the shop I was twice dragged up the hospital because he'd tried to kill himself. He was rubbish at it. He kept trying to overdose on non-fatal tablets. He took eighty Ibuprofen. It sorted his bad back out but they laughed him out of hospital. He was tragic.

My recruitment policy wasn't the greatest. My sister-in-law worked with special needs adults and I agreed to give one such fella a try out. He was a gorgeous bloke but if you gave him an onion to chop he would chop it then freeze in the position of the last chop. In a busy service I would often forget him and he'd be stuck statuesque until I got time to re-task him.

Finally I had a big and daft 'un, Very helpful but pretty skill-less. I loved them all but as a catering force they were shite and I paid them all to watch me do everything.

Half way through the season we studied the books and it seemed I'd done it all wrong. We hadn't made a bean. Somehow £2500 take a week wasn't enough. I was flattened. We got the accountant to look at it and he told me I was a busy fool. He told me to stop curing salmon. Stop doing my cake counter out like a Parisian Patisserie. He said"You can serve shite in the six weeks holidays, nobody cares, you'll never see them again."

Serve shite, nobody cares. It was all too much for my perfecto brain. I was reduced to tears. The accountant was a family friend and he looked distressed at my state. I'd lost three stone in the concentration camp. I didn't make time to eat. As I looked up from my tearful palms two pigeons stood and stared at me, they had walked through the kitchen and into the restaurant. I chased the fuckers out so they could tell their friends I was losing it.

The next morning the pigeons were back. They were getting to me, everything was now. For some reason the veins above my wrists became tender and everytime I did some choppety chop thoughts of debilitation festered in my mind.

Knocking out my two hundred cake portions became tougher and tougher. My brain started to buckle. My short term memory started to fail as I began to become consumed by suicidal thoughts. I had been too busy to eat and too busy to pray. The faith that had helped me so much of late was neglected. I felt very alone. I made a couple of limp efforts to do myself in. The dark thoughts I listened to kept telling me to free the family from the lease and from debt by taking my life. I tried to secure a brush on the gas knob on the cooker but it kept coming loose. I also tried to run into a wall and drive a big cooks knife into my gut. I'd got to a point when I couldn't execute an omelette never mind myself. I was broken.

The six weeks' holidays loomed like an army of tooled up debt collectors and my brain simply came to a halt. My father-in- law was following me around counting my eggs out for me as I lost the ability to count. I couldn't remember if I'd put one or three eggs in a bowl. I couldn't make a decision on anything. It was heart breaking for the family to see me wilt and watch my dream die. Dad-in- law made me stop. He said "Walk away before it kills you!"

I closed the restaurant and spoke to the wife. She suggested asking the landlord to let us relinquish the lease. To our surprise they agreed and we handed in the keys and walked away having lost about eighty grand in six months.

I gathered my special team together and informed them of our decision. Big and daft said he'd work for me for free. He meant it and I cried. Special needs hugged me until I had to tell him it was time to let go.

Chapter 54: The Black Claw

Soundtrack: The Boomtown Rats - I Don't Like Mondays

Wifage was great as usual. She said it was a blessing. She didn't want
us to spend one minute more in catering prison.

My mind had come to a grinding halt. We went to the supermarket and
I couldn't make any decisions at all. I was locked in a frightening
mental battle. Buy a can of beans or don't buy a can of beans. It
seemed impossible and I changed my mind at least ten times, walking
back and forward. When your decision computer goes down
everything becomes difficult.

Wifage made light of my plight. She didn't pretend I didn't look like a
lunatic. I was under ten stone and my hair hadn't been cut for six
months. She took me to the doctors and explained my brain was
broken. What could they do for me? He listened to our story and said it
was completely normal for your brain to give up under this amount of
stress. He gave me a rhino stopper sleeping tablet and said have a big
sleep.

I'd felt depression before but over the next few weeks I felt the full grip
of the Black Claw. Guilt was again the trigger. My dark side wanted to
punish me. It was easy as the ammunition was plentiful. I took
responsibility for the loss of the babies, our house, our jobs and our life
savings. I had stupidly challenged the devil to attack me and I was
learning the hard way that man should never invite such an attack. The
icing on the cake was my crap suicide attempts. I felt awful for
considering that.

I'd witnessed suicide attempts by both my father and my brother in my
youth. At the time I'd thought them weak and selfish. Now I was in
their club and it hit me hard. What I didn't understand back then was
that considering suicide could be a selfless act. I saw it as a help to my
family certainly not an escape for me. As I thought it through I
certainly didn't want to be dead. I just couldn't see any joy for my
family with me around.

Over the next two weeks the depression intensified. Each morning the Black Claw held me in my bed. It felt sickening to lie there wallowing but the thought of getting up seemed equally as putrid. That's the frightening proposition thousands of British depressives wake up to each day. I thought about the people with depression that I knew. I had no idea they had to face such severe symptoms. Depression is a vile and poisonous curse. By the time I went to bed each day I felt normal-ish but in the night Satan returned and stuck a hoover in my arse and sucked the life back out of me. It was terrifying.

My family and my faith were all I had left. I trusted in both. I kept the unbroken boy in mind and tried to calm things down again through meditation.

I tried to go for a run along the sea front in the rain to try and get some adrenaline back in me. It didn't work as I had to fight the urges to jump in front of the oncoming buses coming in the opposite direction. Each and every one of them looked like a solution. I was consumed by doom.

The fact I'd left us penniless hit hard. I'd never been driven by money but now I'd frittered away so much, so quickly I'd learned my lesson in life. Proper dosh management was something to be admired. Money did matter it gave your kids opportunities. If we ever got back on our feet I vowed to guard the family nest egg and educate future generations of our family in that vein too.

I felt ashamed about the business crumble. It was hard to be around neighbours that had just seen me fail so spectacularly. Even so we looked into staying local. I had an interview and secured a job as second chef at the local college. The wage was pitiful. There was no way we could get by on it. We searched some more but the job opportunities in the South West were poor.

I decided to write to my former Mancunian employers. It was a privileged position that I had left to open the business and the unwritten law of the company was that if you gave up that privilege there was no way back. I decided to ask anyway. I left on good terms on the back of a situation not completely of my own making. It was worth a try.

My southern in-laws were devastated that we decided to head back north but silly southern house prices and lack of job opportunities justified our thinking. I promised to reclaim my brain soon and make their daughters life a worthy one. We thanked them for all their help. They were amazing, they'd done everything they could to make our move a success and they tearfully waved off their beloved daughter again.

My mum agreed to take us in short term until we got back on our feet. It was an opportunity for her to really help me and the unbroken boy deep within liked that.

Bringing back the real me wasn't going to be easy. Each morning a deathly emptiness engulfed me. I knew I had to get out and succeed for the family but the depression wanted me to stay home and die. Physical barriers to re-entering the job market emerged. My recent inability to think straight and make decisions was my primary concern but more and more sinister symptoms were sent to test my resolve. My nervous system was under attack. Adrenaline started to pulsate around my body. What started off as a chopping tenderness in my forearms now looked freakish. The whole if my lower arms were covered in big bulging veins that were tender to the touch. I tingled all over as each and every nerve ending seemed to have an electric current surging to and from it. My heart constantly raced and pounded and mini heart attacks threatened to do me in.

I refused to panic. I didn't understand all this shit. I prayed and meditated and both disciplines gave me hope and respite from the nerves but still my condition declined. I went to the hospital and they stuck me on a running machine and monitored me. Whilst I was on the ECG machine I felt like I was going to die from a heart attack. I explained to the nurse I could feel my heart being squeezed. I had the left arm tingles the full she-bang. She said "Your fine" and kept increasing the speed and incline of the running machine. I thought I'm in the right place to keel over so I pushed and pushed. I ran like Forest fuckin' Gump on that machine until she finally relented. I sat drenched in sweat and slumped on a chair holding my chest. I caught my breath and asked the crazy bitch "Did you just try to kill me?"

She said "You're a fit boy. I had to take it full throttle to try and stress your heart. Even in top gear you had more to give. You're perfectly well and fit, if not super fit."
I was shocked and surprised. This was good news and it calmed me enough for me to have a rational, sensible idea. Go to the library and find a book that tells you what to do in the midst of a nervous breakdown.

By the end of the first page I knew I was going to get my marbles back. It said "Just accept that everything your experiencing is temporary. It's just passing through." The advice was "Don't fight it let it wash over you." So I did. I went one better I started praying thanks for the experience and for the life lesson. The book was a real comfort as it described all the symptoms I'd been experiencing I read "Your body tries to con you into thinking you're dying."

Why does the human make up have the capacity to inflict that shit on a person? I'm convinced an attack on a person's nervous system comes from the dark side. That darkness is created by your own actions that generate the guilt that goes on to trigger the murk of a depression. So it's a choice. I could have avoided it all by acting responsibly.

I think this bit of information was a bit of an epiphany in terms of my faith, my understanding of myself and my future conduct. God and Demon are both an inbuilt-part of us. If we press the wrong button we are programmed to shut down and suffer.

I'd had enough of that suffering shit. So I vowed to try to live a totally responsible life from now on. Enabling me to avoid guilt and keep the demons and suffering at bay.

Chapter 55: Bouncebackability

Soundtrack: Rudyard Kipling - If

We landed on my mum's doorstep with all our worldly goods. It was kind of them to cram us into their pint-sized gaff. Mum's fella was in his late fifties and wasn't used to living in a mad house. I told them straight "I feel like a nutter, I've lost my marbles but I do feel it's a life experience that I'm being guided through."

The next day I signed up with three different chef agencies. Then I contacted my inspirational teacher at the college. He told me to come back and do a course with teaching in mind. I loved that guy.

My first chefing assignment was in a five star hotel in Salford. The wife dropped me off and gave me a tearful cuddle. She knew I was shitting myself. My breathing was restricted and I had chest pains. Even though I'd accepted that all the symptoms were fake and were just passing through they felt very fuckin real. My arms were electrified and I could barely feel my hands.

The hotel was short staffed. I was thrown in the deep end I was to join another young cook working a chef's island on view to the public bang in the middle of a busy, modern, all glass eating emporium.

The waitresses had little computers that sent the hungry customers orders up into space and then out of the printer on our chef's island bang in the middle of the restaurant.

We had two hours to prep up the components of the five dishes on the lunchtime menu. The young fella who showed me the ropes had done it before but Gordon Ramsey he wasn't. He did his best to give me a clue.

As the place started to fill up the printer started to growl out its requirements. I was clumsy, my hand eye co-ordination was well out. Every time I spilt, dropped or burnt something I refocused and carried on regardless. The printer was relentless and at one point it had spewed about twenty orders onto the floor. I giggled to myself. I was mad, I couldn't feel my hands, I was under printer attack and I was still getting the job done. I battled through the service, cleaned down and was free to go. I sat out on the waterfront. It was cold and I was sweaty. I prayed thanks. Briefly a different kind of adrenalin surged through me. I recognised it. It felt awesome. It was direct payment for my faith and for my spirit.

The next day started as nervously as the previous sixty but there was good news as my old company wrote me a special letter. It said it wasn't company policy to re-employ people but they would like to make an exception and offer me a temporary part time contract.

My college tutor also offered me a poorly paid teaching opportunity with him and it was tempting but graft and the chance to earn decent dosh was the only way I could afford to go.

I was warmly received back into the fold. I was humbled by the warmth of the staff. I set about repaying their kindness and earning a contract. I was on a thirty hour contract but worked close to seventy over six days and I went to college on my day off.

I was glad to be alive. I was overjoyed to be employed. I was ecstatic my wife and my boy had stuck with me. People were amazed at my joy. "How can you be so happy after everything that's happened to you?" was the recurring question. I never really explained the real reasons that I felt so good. I just told them things could always be worse.

It was a funny situation, nobody at work knew about my mental situation. Nobody noticed I was getting burnt a lot. My nerves improved a little but I was still under attack. The brain is such a complex organ. Parts of it had shut down and felt defunct and crap whilst other parts were starting to buzz.

I started running the six or so miles to work mainly because I was skint and it was free. In the past such times of solitude would inevitably lead to thoughts of self-hate and self-pity. Not now. I may have been a mess but I was at ease with my conduct. I was living by my new rules and slowly my lights started to come back on. I had to take a note pad on my runs to record the idea's that started to fly into my head.

I started praying on the runs. As wind and rain lashed my face I grinned like a Cheshire cat. I loved the feeling of a connection with a greater force. I felt goodness shoot through me every time I thought the right things. Good advice in the form of ideas were my reward. I took note of every single suggestion.

Wifage was unbelievable as usual. She accepted I had to work like a dog. Family time was scarce. I had college and homework. If we wanted to move up, this was the way. She told me it was time to make another baby. No house, no permanent job. I didn't argue she could have everything I was able to give her.

Chapter 56: An unexpected cuddle

Soundtrack: Zorba - Sirtaki

Wifage was strong but she wanted peace of mind. She told me that when she was younger she used to visit a Spiritualist church. She wanted to visit such a place and see if any messages came through from the other side in relation to our girls. I knew nothing about it. I didn't have an opinion. I did what I was told and walked into a small village hall none the wiser. We paid £1.50 each and were told you got tea and biscuits in the deal. This was the first date we'd been on for a while, we were living it up.

The compere for the evening was an immaculately dressed, stick thin, white haired Etonian type fella. He spoke a la de da spiffing type of English. His opening statement had us wetting ourselves. Imagine the poshest male voice you can. A louder David Attenborough: fwar, fwar, fwar..! That was his delivery.

"Welcome brothers and sisters. We are gathered here on this blessed evening to be guided through spirit. Before we ask our medium for this evening to join us I have to regretfully inform you that a local well known spiritualist Thomas Jones sadly left the Earth-plane this week. He stepped out of his automobile and entered a local newsagents where he purchased his favourite chocolate treat: a Snickers bar. Unfortunately Thomas was not concentrating as he crossed the road back to his car and he got splattered. The poor chap was sadly unrecognisable. So let us pray for Thomas and his family." I looked at Wifage and we both thought "Did he just say that?"

The Toff then led the congregation singing 'All things bright and beautiful.' Everyone else in the hall did the usual church mumble-sing-a-long but he sang big, like Brian Blessed. I loved this guy.

He introduced the lady medium who looked like a startled rabbit. She was all nervous as if someone she didn't like was feeling her up. I was very surprised when she sent me the first words out of her mouth "You sir, can I come to you?" I nodded out an alright then type of nod. "I have a very excited Greek gentleman here." Oh my god! Straight away

I knew it was my Greek friend from work. He was a larger than life chef who lost his life in a motor cycle crash the year before. We were close and I was dumbstruck. She said again: "He's very excited!" as she seemed to be barged out of the way by him. Next I felt the warm rush of adrenaline up my arms and a really warm sensation. She said "Can you feel the gentleman around you?" My mouth was open wide a-gasp. I nodded again. She said that he had to embrace me as he had been there with me every day in the tearooms willing me to succeed, frustrated that he couldn't help. She went on to say that he walked around the spirit world cussing and swearing at himself. He was angry at himself for the stupid way he died. Holy shit it all made sense. The poor chap died after offering a 'backy' to a security guard who was admiring his motorbike at a retail park. He got his stepson to give the guard his helmet and took the security man for a quick spin. As they pulled out of the car park a fast car full of youths hit them travelling the wrong way down a one way road. He was instantly killed. The guard was flung to safety and amazingly he was left pretty much unscathed. Tragically the stepson was left waiting and waiting until the police realised he was still there and told him the awful news.

She wasn't finished yet. She told me of my nan and my grandad. She could see them linking arms and she explained that news might surprise me as my nan usually sat in the kitchen while Grandad did his own thing in the living room. They weren't a touchy feely couple. Apparently they were now because in the time my grandad spent on earth on his own after Nan died he had come to appreciate her. So when he passed to spirit he made sure he was always by her side. How nice?

There was more. She reckoned Grandad was flipping me gold coins and even though I'd took a big hit I needn't worry about money. She told me I'd experienced a hard time and I should stay behind at the end for spiritual healing.

She thanked me and I thanked her. I looked at Wifage in disbelief: Did that just happen? Had I just been hugged by my dear dead friend?

Nothing came through for Wifage but the lady seemed to be on the money with everyone else she spoke to. Nobody seemed to disagree with her. I was fascinated.

At the end of the medium's stint we all said the Lord's Prayer and had
a cup of tea and some dodgy cake. The Toff came and greeted me with
a proper stiff handshake. I introduced the wife but he barely
acknowledged her. I watched some people accepting healing. It all
looked a bit Harry Potter to me.

Chapter 57: Education is soul food

Soundtrack: The Who - The kids are alright

The college experience was an odd one. The business dream had gone but for some reason I still felt justified in educating myself in the food field. My tutor was a dude, a really positive guy and I think I just needed to be near him at that time. Wifage took the piss, she said I got all gooey when I spoke about him.

This fella had recently offered me a path to a teaching job when I was in the mire so of course I appreciated the guy. We were prepping veg together one afternoon when out of the blue he told me that when he was a small child he was playing with his baby brother, trying to lift him out of his cot. Somehow the baby got caught on the side of the cot and tragically his beloved brother lost his life. Asphyxiation took him before he could get help and he could be freed.

He told me that his father didn't speak or even look at him for years. His dad finally came round but it was a long and lonely road. He was lucky more siblings came after the death and that they carried the spirit of the lost brother. So although he had always been torn up about it, it taught him that some good could come from even the worst situations. I was touched by his disclosure and he inspired me to make good of my family's situation.

I smashed college and completed my course in half the time of the youngsters. I had to fit my studies around a sixty hour working week so I squeezed five days study into one and would often end up stuck on a P.C. at two in the morning.

I watched the kids giving their weekly excuses as to why they hadn't completed their assignments in wonder. Most of them didn't work and this course was their only responsibility. So it made comments like "My dog ate my dongle" less legitimate and more funny.

Obviously being young and not giving a fuck has its perks. Some of the gang were in the midst of some of the experiences I wrote about earlier in the book: Beer, drugs and nookie and as an old and crusty who'd been down that road I tried to help nudge them the right way. I told them that the very least they should do was graft then party.

My skills were superior to theirs so I found it easy to assist them practically. Some of them were wasting their time in cooking school. They were scared of raw chicken, fish and beef bones. I asked these kids: 'Is cooking really your passion?' If they said no then my advice was "Okay finish the course, get your piece of paper then study something you love. Cooking is a life skill, so you haven't wasted your time here but find your passion and follow your heart." I was repeatedly told I was a sad hippy but I didn't mind. I wore them down over time.

I tried to help one lad more than any other. He had all the passion in the world. He really wanted to be a great chef. He wasn't great but he deserved to be. He had worked long and hard on his knife skills and they were impressive for his age but his confidence was zero. In service he had no belief in himself and he lacked any sense of timing. I took him under my wing but he was a fragile soul. He'd been working in various city centre restaurants for free since he was fourteen to gain experience. In the holidays he did the same living in at fine dining establishments around the country. Each time he came back from such an experience he was more shaky and uncertain he could make it. One day I'm sure he'll suss it out, find his vocation and make it big. I loved this guy and made him my friend outside school too.

He wasn't the only cool kid. What really impressed me about them was their loving demeanour. They were so nice to each other. They all looked after each other. They were much more touchy feely, huggy wuggy than kids were in my day.

The misconception that young people are all feral is just that, a misconception, a myth. Yes at the start of the book I poured scorn on the class of people that don't give love or moral guidance to their kids and I stand by that. There is a small part of our society doing it very wrong and their kids are fighting a losing battle to complete the journey that this book is about. A lot of kids are spoilt too but overall though the young people I was lucky enough to study with were very good company.

The school ran a trip to Paris as part of the course. In Paris they did what young chefs do: Shagging, wine, snails and vomit. It was their time and I stayed out of the way to let them enjoy their youth. Even so I had to drag one or two of my favourites off to experience the view from the top of the Sacre Coeur. It was that windy up there, we had to lean into it. We stood on top of the steps taking in one of Europe's finest views arm in arm, chefs and brothers together.

A tearful but smiling Frog came over to us. We shared his cigar. Struggling to hear his story in the wind I just about understood that his brother had just died from cancer. I told him "That's tough but look at the view: don't waste this, don't waste the rest of your life, celebrate your brother!" He gave me a heartfelt hug and we both leaned into the gale force torrent smiling from ear to ear. It was magical. I felt so alive!

On the trip home a young Sikh lad grabbed the microphone on the coach. He was an overweight cheeky type of Turbanator. He ripped the piss out of all the teachers. One dragon-like hospitality member of staff copped it the worst. He amused us all by telling her that he knew that she thought about him all the time. He felt her X-ray eyes on him in the kitchen. "I feel the same Miss, but we have to try and fight it because my family just won't accept you, it's breaking my heart Miss but control yourself, don't touch me, I am forbidden fruit!' The usually grumpy miss took it well and told him he'd pay back at school. He rolled his eyes and looked like he was receiving a knee trembler "Stop it miss!"

I stayed in the background and enjoyed the show. I got home with a completely clear conscious and it felt very fuckin' nice. I'd finally sussed it: This is the joy of life. Responsible living gets rewarded. A fantastic guilt free experience.

A couple of months later I picked up the 'Student of the Year' award. The college said it was for inspiring the other students. The wife said it was a gift from my boyfriend. I think it was a bit of both. The quals, the award, it was important. Achievement gives you a sense of well being and it unlocks some of the self locked doors we humans close on ourselves.

I didn't get English or Maths at school and that had always hampered my self-esteem. So I decided to smash them next. If you're reading this in book form then I'd like to thank my inspirational English teacher and my two proof readers for helping me believe I could write. If I do get published, Maths had fuck all to do with it. I spent a whole year spending every spare minute trying to get an A grade in Maths. I obsessed my way to a B proving that GCSE's are fairly credible. A Grades go to those who have talent. In Maths you need a Maths mind. Hard graft only takes you so far. So every year when you see the record GCSE results go up, it's because kids are working harder and are getting cleverer. Really!

These quals weren't Oxford or Cambridge bits of paper but I felt the jigsaw of who I wanted to be starting to come together. As a dad I have the tools to help my kids achieve and that feels good in itself.

Soundtrack: Simon& Garfunkle - Feeling Groovy

Even though I was positively charged my nerves still lingered like grandads unwashed socks on the radiator. It would take a long time to wake up not depressed. I just accepted it and luckily for me once I was up, I was calm.

As soon as I'd secured a permanent contract at work, one of the wife's old workmates helped us blag an interest only mortgage deal off a small deposit over forty years. It was important for us to get back on our own feet. Mum had helped me re-find myself and I was thankful that was another piece of the jigsaw complete.

Within weeks I went for promotion at work. In the past I wouldn't have even noticed a position was up for grabs but not now, I was seeing things big. I sailed through the process and secured the job. Somehow I had managed to almost double the wage that I received before I left the company. I raced home to tell the Rock. We both had a little cry of joy and relief.

At this point in life I felt really close to God. My prayers seemed to be getting answered. Not just my requests for stuff. Prayers for advice came back in clear thought. I could hear the prayers of thanks I sent go with a little woosh like an email sent off a smartphone. I really did feel a connection and the spiritualist church buzz seemed like an extra string to my spiritual bow. Up until this point I didn't think too much about the afterlife, it was never something that really troubled me. Even though I'd spent quite a long period of my life not liking myself I had never really considered going to hell. Spiritualism initially confirmed life after death. The experience and evidence of the first service was undeniable. I began sending out messages of love to all my dead relatives and friends.

Every time I went to a service I felt better. Even a poorly attended service felt warm. The attendees were characters. There was no more unique a character than 'The Healer'. He was a lovely looking old fella.

His posture wasn't the best, he was bent over and slightly hunched. He had thick silver hair, interesting eyebrows and long dirty fingernails. Chatting to this fella was an education; he was wide open in terms of sharing his spiritual opinions and experiences: He would tell you who he was in his previous five lives and who he was going to be in the future. Even better than that, he had superhuman powers.

On my second visit to the church after the service he asked me if I'd like him to heal my back. I'd slept funny and my coccyx was playing up. I asked him how he knew I was sore. He told me whenever someone was ill or in pain he could see colours around the affected area. I agreed and was freaked out when his hands felt like a heat lamp as they passed over my back. Sure enough next day I was straight. As he gave me the magic hand treatment he told me he'd been doing this for hundreds of years. I'd not really heard of regression before but this fella reckoned he'd travelled back through time and watched himself as a healer down the ages. It was bonkers but for £1.50 a hit it smashed the shit out of Eastenders. He had another pal there who I found a bit frosty. This fella told me that there are different levels of spiritual awareness. He was really pissed off as he educated himself and meditated himself right up to the top level. He went up all the levels to meet the maker. Unfortunately just as he got there he said he made the fatal mistake of questioning his knowledge. He was cruelly dropped back into an abyss and he tumbled back through all the levels of space and back into his body in his bed. He looked well pissed off about that.

Every week a different medium took the service. They had varying degrees of skill. Some were non-specific and the audience led them where they needed to go but the best ones were very specific, they gave full names and descriptions of your bedroom and which objects in your bedroom that had been moved by somebody in spirit.

Some mediums had specific ways of working. There was an artist who stood there and very quickly sketched the dead relatives of the congregation. When he'd finished a sketch he'd flip the easel around to gasps from the recipient. It was mad.

Another service they did was when you had to bring an object, anything. You exchange it for raffle a ticket, the chap picks up the object and gets a message based upon the energy he feels from the item. Then he picks out the person whose item it is and tells them what number ticket they had. Wifage brought a red rose. The chap picked it up and spoke of holding the rose like the twins. He spoke of the connection between mum and the girls. It wasn't much but Wife got a little comfort from this as it confirmed the girls were in the system. Their spirit lived on.

From that point on she bailed out. She said the congregation was too crackers for her. As usual she kept me grounded. She told me I liked the place because they all blew smoke up my arse and told me I was great. That wasn't it. I was intrigued firstly by the people; the Chairman and the healer were just two of many interesting people. If you think back to biblical times they had no televisions and everyone was doing a bit of healing. I could picture the resident healer doing a bit in Jerusalem. I found it so interesting to hear their far out experiences. The healer was prolific; he spent his days visiting the local hospital zapping people. He'd meet up with other healers when they found kids with severe strains of cancer. They would tag team them. He did animals too. He sat at the local war memorial each morning. I'd often see him there on my way to work. He told me injured animals would often come there for him to heal them. "Brother are you shitting me?" He didn't take offence, he just told me that's what he did, that was his life. He told me that he'd recently healed a fox that looked like it had been hit by a car, it came to him and he ran his hands over the spectrum colours coming from its injuries. He even healed you with his voice as he told you this whacky Dr Doolitle shit. I buzzed off it all.

We have a friend who suffered from post natal depression. She had gone weeks without any sleep. I suggested she should come down and meet 'The Healer. What harm could it do? So she did. Her nan came through in the service with some words of encouragement. She liked that.

After the service I introduced her to the healer. His hygiene wasn't the best bless him; he was looking and smelling a bit funky on this particular night. He had the personality to put her at ease and I looked on as he asked our pretty friend if she minded if his apprentice could help give her a double zap as he was learning the ropes. She agreed and they sat her on a chair with the healer stood behind and the apprentice at the scenic front. I looked on as they gave her a real going over. She sat still and oblivious on the chair while they worked their magic. The real deal packed in after about ten minutes but the apprentice wanted to stare at the young lady's boobs for a few minutes more. It was hilarious when she finally opened her eyes. He quickly refocused his attention back to her face. Perv over.

She rang me the next day. Surprise, surprise. She slept like a baby.

Chapter 59:Hag smashed

Soundtrack: The Troggs - Wild Thing

We were delighted to find out that Wifage was carrying a baby girl. She was conceived a year to the day that we lost our twins. We weren't sure if Wifage was still in working order. So the confirmation that she was still a fully equipped egg layer and it was to be a girl made it feel like an extra special gift. Amazingly Wifage had wanted twins again but I didn't want the double stress of another double pregnancy. I was double happy it was just a single baba.

Six months down the line I talked a heavily pregnant missus into a trip to conduct an experiment. We organised for the Chairman to pick us up to go to a church in Moss Side. My plan was to get him to take us to an alternative service in Denton where nobody could have possibly expected us.

Wife looked seriously alarmed as we traveled down the M60 driving Miss Daisy at approximately 35mph. She was growling at me. I'd never considered my pensioner friend's lack of driving ability. It was too late now so I made light of the situation. Wifage kindly reminded me that I was a prick.

On arrival the hall was full of real people and it felt more pre-show than pre-church. There was a group of girls all made up, heels on, the lot.

A large and bubbly old dear was the medium for the service. She were right proper Lancashire. She had big hair and big earrings. As usual I was the first person she picked out. "Hiya love can I come to you?" "Yes thanks." "I can see your two faces: The man you used to be and the man you're just becoming, please could you stay behind after the service? I would like to have a chat with you." Wife gave me her comedy 'Why's it always you?' face.

The Chairman always got a message. He had a spirit guide for

everyday of the week. That could have explained why he was all so up
and down. He supposedly had five or six spirits pulling him and his
decisions all over the place. He had a picture of one of his guides, a
Chinese fella on display in his home. He said this chap was from the
Shang Dynasty in old China and he had been with him a long time.
Whenever he was addressed by a medium I had to really try hard not to
go into hysterics. The Chairman would try to explain the meaning of
the mediums comments to the congregation. He thought out loud in
fine Etonian tongue and his justifications were usually very
entertaining indeed.

At the end of the show we stayed in our seats and the lady came over.
She told me I was being called to work for spirit. I should decide on
whether I wanted to develop myself spiritually and start willing it to
happen. I thanked her and felt my ego expand like a foie gras. The
experiment proved that some crazy shit goes on in the wacky world of
spiritualism. Whoever sends down the messages has psychic sat nav
that encompasses the whole of Greater Manchester.

The next time I went to church the Chairman was missing. Apparently
he had been banned from church as they had to remove him from the
hall when he stood up in the middle of a service and announced
unequivocally that all the 'Pakis' had to leave. He had lost it and had to
be sectioned.

I was a bit disappointed that his so called friends from church just
made a joke of it. I like a chuckle but there wasn't a hint of compassion
for the man. He'd obviously put a lot of his time and energy into the
place and I felt he deserved better. So I asked them which hospital he'd
been detained at and decided to pay him a visit.

I took my lad with me and we called in at the local N.H.Less mentalist
holding unit. The security was a joke. I asked at the reception if the
gentleman I was looking for was still in the house. They told me
nobody of that name was there. So I explained that "My church says
he's here could you let me in to look for him?" To my utter amazement
the lady said "Okay I'll just buzz you in."

Six foot inside the unit my boy and I were greeted by a little rat like
and dare I say pedophilish looking fella. He said "I'll take you to him"

I asked "How do you know who I'm looking for?" "He's this way."
sure enough the nervous little wretch led us to the Chairman's room.
"He's been expecting you." I thanked him for his help and thought
"shit son we are in a Hitchcock movie!"

The Chairman came to the door. He was immaculate as usual. He
looked me in the eye and had no idea who the fuck I was. I introduced
myself and he lit up. "This is absolutely fantastic news" he said.
"Come in." I introduced my boy and he momentarily acknowledged
him before he asked if he could give me a hug. I obliged and we shared
a clinch that went on a second or so too long. As we came apart he had
a funny look in his eye and it all became clear. Maybe he was gay? If
he was it made no difference to me but it did explain why he rarely
acknowledged the wife.

I had come to the hospital to support the guy on the back of his so
called friends laughing at him. What came next made it difficult for me
not to join in. He asked me if I was familiar with a band called The
Animals. I concurred before being treated to a very posh recital of 'The
house of the rising sun. My boy and I sat on his bed mesmerised by a
sixty five year old performance of a sixties rock classic.

He asked me for another hug. I declined but I didn't want to hurt his
feelings so I offered to bring him any provisions he required. Finest
Toff voice on, he said. "Six bottles of Coca Cola & some finely sliced
fresh lemons." "Quite right brother I'll pop them in for you very soon
pal." Just as we were leaving he hit us with 'Wild Thing' by the
Troggs. It was a great rendition.

I took the wife the next time as a security blanket. We weren't prepared
for scene that unfolded before us. The receptionist explained to us that
the Chairman had fallen over, busted leg and dislocated and fractured
his hip. "Holy shit, can we see him?" "Yes come in." She buzzed the
door.

I was amazed to hear the Chairman's version of events. He was
deliriously happy. He said he had fought off an attack from an evil
spirit. The spirit was a dark one, an old hag. She had thrown him
around like a rag doll. He was proud to have stood strong and seen her
off. My god this guy was seriously injured and he sat there like a cat

with the cream. In his mind at least he had physically battled a poltergeist and won. I handed over the Coke and lemon combo and wished him a speedy recovery.

I gave his mental situation some thought. I noted that even though he was in a right old pickle, he thought he was doing fine. It looked crackers from the outside looking in. Did he have pure faith? Was this Harry Potter style battle his duty? Was he just barking? I believe he saw what he thought he saw in one dimension or another. I found it absolutely fascinating.

Chapter 60: Orbing!

Soundtrack: Starsailor - Good Souls

On his release from the bin the Chairman gave me a book to read about journeys into the spiritual realm. It was absolutely gobbledygook!

Still as my mind became more inquisitive and I started searching for answers the information fed to me in church became more and more accurate. Nearly every week a different medium tried to recruit me. They told me I had the tools. I just needed to open the box.

They told me to just lie in bed and will it to happen. So I did. Each night I laid, prayed and willed a connection towards me. Try this: If you look at a light then close your eyes you can see shapes of light inside your eye lids. Pretty soon I started to see these patches of illumination without a light trigger. They initially appeared in my closed eyes but before long they would stay when I opened them. At first they were unspectacular but the more in tune with the process I became the more the orbs became vivid and beautiful to look at. I would meditate on these until I dropped off to sleep. I felt really nice and seemed to lift the mild depression that usually engulfed me of a morning.

When it came to my faith I searched and studied for answers. I believed in my god but I suppose I still wanted to be in one gang or another. I tried to accept Christian teachings but my love for God just wasn't replicated with the same pure love for Jesus. Now whether it was a dream or vision or a figment of my imagination, one night deep into orb watching and willing territory, a Jesus type dude flanked by a fella on either side of him came to me. It was brief and very powerful. I received a blanket of my old friend adrenaline.

Unfortunately it solved nothing in terms of my beliefs. I just couldn't decide whether it was real or a dream. I just didn't have a true Christian faith or I would have been empowered to stand on a soapbox in the middle of Piccadilly Gardens and share my vision. That wasn't my feeling. Even so I carried on meditating for a week or two more before I encountered another epic phenomenon. This time it was a full wall of light. Again I couldn't say 100% if I was fully conscious but either way it looked and felt delicious. I looked at it for a while and sniffed it. Whether I was dreaming it or not I took the decision not to break on through.

The next day I realised this stuff was getting into life changing territory so I went a googling and read up every opinion on spiritualism that I could find. The mainstream Christian churches all warned against dabbling on the other side. They said Satan cooked the whole gig up to claim your soul. The Jehovah Witnesses really nailed it when they described how such experiences affect your ego. I was really surprised to discover they didn't believe in an afterlife. Their view was that any messages that came through were from the Dark Lord himself. They believed that when you're dead you're dead, there's fuck all else!

After weighing all this up and looking at the impact spiritualism had, had on the Chairman and my ego. I decided I could no longer risk it. Having a Jedi side was fun. It was hard to walk away from but I couldn't risk batting for the devil. I chose to concentrate on enjoying this life and trying to be the best man I could. That was it. I just turned it off.

This didn't stop me going along to church with my friend. I did try and point out to him maybe all this spiritual warfare was just a little bit detrimental to his health but there was no changing his beliefs, he was too far gone and loved it too much. When he was fit enough he asked me to take him to church. I agreed. I suppose it was another experiment to see what the next move was from beyond.

Normally I would urge a message to come through and usually it would happen fairly instantaneously. Now I sat and listened without urge. I had switched off that channel. So I didn't get a sausage. It was also hard to enjoy the service from the nice person accompanying a friend angle because once you buy into the theory that all the people around you are deliriously happy because they are devil worshippers then it becomes a totally different ball game. Although that line of thinking did explain the evil cake offerings. The wholemeal treacle tart was beyond satanic! I went four more times with the Chairman and got zero messages. His health has sadly deteriorated since. He's in the grip of bi-polar. His mum says it all started when he started with spiritualism. Knowing him. Loving him. I feel he's under attack. No question in my mind. The dark side has absolutely robbed him. He's been hoodwinked, conned and spiritually raped.

I pray for his sanity and his deliverance. He's a good man.

Chapter 61: A Stroke of Honesty

Soundtrack: Cat Stevens - Father and Son

I received a phone call from my step mum in Spain. She never rang me so I knew something had happened. I prepared myself for the worst and called her back. She told me Dad was poorly and had suffered a stroke. It looked like a bad one so I needed to prepare myself.

I called my brothers and cracked a few funnies about my old man's powers of recovery. As he'd survived at least five heart attacks down the years so he'd be right.

Only my blood brother could afford to go with me as the flights were ridiculously priced. The next day the two of us landed in Spain. The hospital was much more than the N.H.Less. It was shiny and new, it smelt good and obviously had a great staff recruitment policy: lots of fit, young, sexy nurses. Totally different to the 'suck the life out of ya' institutions of home.

Bless him, my old man looked like a big baby complete with a nappy and a cute saggy bottom lip. He couldn't move but his eyes twinkled when we walked in.

I hadn't really planned what happened next but it just felt right. We are the least touchy family of all time but I had reached a point in life where holding back the love wasn't an option. Step mum and two close family friends looked on as I instructed our kid to get on the other side of my dad and get his hands on his head. I put mine on his face.

"Dad your boys are here. We love you, you're a good man, thanks for everything you've ever done for us etc, etc." We held him tight for much longer than a normal embrace. Brother went to break off a few times but I kept ordering him back on. We went way beyond an uncomfortable too long. He was having it, good style. I told him repeatedly I loved him, that we loved him he was going to be fine. I tried to radiate all the love I had for him into him. It was beautiful and I had a tear in my eye. The other three non-clinchers were a bit taken a back as this wasn't close to typical family etiquette.

We were told he'd not had the worst kind of stroke, the one where you lose your ability to swallow. Even so it was a bad one and it was hard to say if he'd get any left side movement back or whether he would recover his speech.

I didn't like the way they were talking as if he wasn't there. I could tell by his eyes he was alive and computing. Maybe slowly but he was definitely switched on. I encouraged them to communicate with him.

We gave him a few more zaps before hitting the pub to buy the friends who had looked after him a drink or two. In the past such occasions would have started off nice before I would have internally combusted. Not now, my soul was settled. I loved being with my brother. It was a great evening.

The next morning we returned to the grown up baby unit and sure enough he'd significantly improved. He was trying to talk and responded to having a sponge ball squeezed in his hand.

I got back on the love buzz and zapped him for an hour or so. Parents always take pleasure from watching their kids eat so our kid and I ate a lot of hospital food in his company. You could feel his pride, he loved it.

The next and last day was the same. He'd improved again but you could tell he didn't want us to go. He was grumpy because we had to go home. He was like a distressed child wanting his mum. He mumbled some nonsense but all he wanted was more love.

Step-mum and the quacks were amazed in the change in him during our short visit. I don't know if it was love, prayer (God help), positive thought or a cynical coincidence maybe? It mattered little really. Good, loving, right action had made a difference. At least in my head it had.

I took the family back a few months later and dad had been left in a very peculiar state. He had regained 90% speech and 95% movement, interestingly he'd had 100% of his tact removed. He was saying and doing the first thing that came into his head. So if he thought you were a prick he told you. If he thought you had nice tits he told you. It was both disturbing and refreshing at the same time. At least you knew where you stood with him. I just hoped he didn't bump into a City fan with sexy wife any time soon.

More worrying was his too speedy return to driving. He'd always been a natural. His pride had him back behind the wheel much too soon and his gear box paid a heavy price. We all politely sat in silence urging him to change up through the gears before we exploded.

Eventually he got all his tools back. He'd kept his head together and rode the storm. I loved his wife for the way she mothered him and I loved my dad because he was my dad.

My Old Man

My dad's great I said at school
He's massive and he's really cool
Our kid and I were benefactors
Of the dough he earned
From making tractors

7am in his bin man coat
Off to work to keep a float
Thank you dad for all that graft
For building our survival raft

His friends were very special chaps
Smoking, twitching at the match
Mel and Rog and growler Ken
Eavis on the couch again

Crazy days
My days of youth
But now were all
Long in the tooth

You've nearly croaked it
Once or twice
Got lucky when
They rolled the dice

You've shown you're strong
You've shown you're hard
You've had more than
One yellow card

Rugrats dot com
Grandkids galore
If we had any wonga
We'd have some more

It's a awful shame

You're over there
While we get raped
On childcare

But I suppose my friend
You've earned your rest
And with benefits
You have been blessed

So I wish you well
Regain your health
Spread some love
And share your wealth

So enough extracting of the piss
Open your eyes
And take in this
I am not near you
And it makes me sad
Cause I'm your lad
And you're my dad.

Chapter 62: The Spirit of Three

Johnny Mathis-When a child is born

On arrival at the hospital they informed us our precious baby girl was in position. The contractions were a go and it was just a case of waiting.

Wifage and I hadn't spent much time together since our return. I had been too busy trying to re-float the family boat. So the sixteen hours we spent waiting for our little madam were a real treat. I put socks on her ears, sang her songs and generally pestered the shit out her as we waited for some pelvic action. When show time finally came baby was pointing the wrong way again. Thankfully there was a change in midwife, straight away the new nurse spotted our baby was lying cheek first not head first so it was straight down to theatre for a caesarean.

We'd joked all day but when it came to the crunch we held hands very tightly and stared intently, lovingly and desperately into each other's eyes. We both cashed in our prayer chips as we willed a safe delivery towards us.

Things were a lot calmer in the operating theatre this time but we were still shitting ourselves. Thankfully it wasn't long before the soothing goodness of a baby's cry triggered our tears of joy and relief. This time we were presented with the most beautiful healthy little girl.

I will always be proud of Wifage for the way she bounced back to have our baby. It was a real blessing to see her blubbing as she held her prize. The spirit of the twins had returned and for me the predetermined lesson circle was complete. We'd all passed our test, grown from our life experience and had been rewarded in the sweetest way.

The first time I got up in the night to tend to our little princess I took her downstairs and felt the goodness radiating up from her perfect little face. I felt the spirit of her sisters and the thoughts that entered my mind were ones of sanctification. I felt the twins wanted us to love them through her. Right there and then I promised all three of them we always would.

Chapter 63: Five Pints of Guinness and a Protein Bomb

Soundtrack: The Pogues - Fiesta

Alan Wells and 'Chariots of fire' both lit my fire as a nipper. I was fast in the juniors but just like on the tele the black kids accelerated away when I stepped up to secondary school.

When it came to long distance Cram and Coe were safe. I was never going to represent my country, I usually came in about seventh in the school cross country. I wasn't the seventh fastest kid in school but I had the desire to come first and that took me a little bit further up the field than my ability warranted.

Later in life twenty years of footy and five years of raving combined to leave me rather short of functional cartilage, hamstrings and memory cells. My stride pattern became more Albert Steptoe than Roger Bannister.

So when I crawled out of the restaurant post breakdown going back to running was a painful path to tread in more than one way. As I explained earlier shortly after my release from my version of Ramsey's Kitchen Nightmares my first beachside run was a battle not to commit Hari Kari. I had to stop myself jumping out in front of the oncoming traffic on more than one occasion.

I must have looked a sight. I was a milk bottle white bag of bones. I dragged my saggy arse up the seafront sobbing like a wounded animal. Even though I felt no better after the run something within me hinted it was the right thing to be doing. I listened and kept at it.

As my life started to improve so did my running. When I started to tune into God, running started to feel like church. Getting into full flow was a joyful, pure experience. I felt alive again and as I prayed thanks for that I was often rewarded with a beautiful adrenaline connection buzz. I'm a sucker for that feeling and getting it so organically helped me forget about the state of my Steptoe knees.

The more I ran the more I thought about stuff. Ideas flooded my brain and I soon had to start taking a pen and paper on my runs. In the back of my memory were nostalgic family medals. Mum and Dad once ran a marathon together as a team. Something in me needed to emulate that. With this in mind I powered through a storm displaying the facials of an over-happy lunatic. The pen and paper came out and I wrote down the word Mara because my pen was fucked. The time had come to test myself.

In the morning I rang my old pal Mad Head. He was very surprised to be told that we were going to run the Dublin marathon together. He wasn't fit but he didn't argue. The crazy twat rarely questioned my plans. What more can you ask from a friend?

A couple of months later a fortnight before the race Mad Head told me he'd done next to no training but he felt it was important to go out and run eighteen miles so we did. We set off at 8pm on a blowy October night. Ten miles in his knee packed in and we had to walk home through one of Manchester's roughest estates, Partington. We had on a mixture of skimpy shorts, vests, headbands and Paula Radcliffe go faster socks. We looked like a pair of lost kids from Fame. Mad Head was limping badly and I had to support him. Every car that past gave us a homophobic salute. It was the worst marathon prep imaginable. Ten days later we flew over to the Emerald Isle riddled with doubt.

We unwisely met up with Mad Head's paddy relatives and got pissed up before the race. That's how men on weekends away operate and of course this silliness filled us with plenty more pre-race worries.

Mad Head turned to science and spent about £50 on energy supplements. He had gels, powders, bars, plant extracts and protein bombs and an hour before the race he smashed in the lot.

My arse started exploding about an hour before the race. The smell of fear lingered around me like a sour turd blanket. I must have had seven shits and pissed off a lot of people waiting on the other side of that portaloo door.

We stood on the line listening to a wacky Wogan-like Irishman rally the congregation over a PA. He was the most enthusiastic bloke in the world. Mad Head was just coming up after his sports drug binge when the PA called for quiet.

Just as he did a fellow in his mid-twenties broke the silence by sliding up the window pane of his top floor Edwardian flat. He was obviously half cut from the night before. His hair was an electrocuted bird's nest. 17,000 people watched him take about 5 seconds to focus and notice his street had 17,000 people in it and they were all waving at him. He then broke into a huge grin it was a lovely Hugh Grant sort of moment.

Two minutes later we were off. I hadn't planned it but without warning I instantly showed a clear pair of heels to Mad Head. I dragged the poor lad over there only to jib him on the start line. I think I subconsciously thought he may pack it in with his bad leg and I couldn't fail. I knew only injury would stop him though, he was a tough nut.

I bolted and was carried to ten miles on the buzz of the occasion. From that point I started to appreciate people's support. Running through council estates where families had set up their refreshment and party stations for their kids to chuck sweets and bananas at you was heartwarming.

Half way is a mind trick. You get there in okay shape and double the time on the clock. From that point your subconscious sets about scuppering that plan. My initial gallop was reduced to a hobble by eighteen miles as my hamstrings got shorter and shorter. By twenty one miles I was stuck on the railings with a big ball of cramp on the back of my thigh. Lovely people tried to help but I just wanted to speak to Wifage. On the phone the conversation went something like 'I love you, railings, cramp, ready now, bye.'

The last five miles was a 'grit your teeth, and ignore your knees' experience. The crowd full of love and I sucked in as much as I could. I felt love for the ghost of my parents' achievements and as I crossed the line my respect for Jimmy Saville (Before the accusations) became immeasurable.

I finished in 3 hours 48 and I thought I had at least an hour to get a shower before cheering Mad Head in. I was chuffed to fuck when I spotted his gorgeously criminal face bouncing upto the finish line not too far behind. The little twat looked fresh as a daisy.

We embraced and celebrated joining the club. Guts, nuts, will, spirit, friendship, humanity, kindness, spirit, love and a piece of metal on a ribbon. That's what you get!

Then you get two days of cramp and a free pass to the Ministry of silly walks.

Chapter 64: More Bricks

Soundtrack: Talking Heads-Road to nowhere

Blackpool Marathon was a soul destroyer even though the big blue sky and the soothing sun encouraged good life. All around it was grim, grim, grim.

The Prom was being dug up and the sea looked like a shit, pissy gravy. The few people lining the course were grey and uninterested.

At five miles I got pelted with empty beer cans. Some of Glasgow's finest were offended by my go faster knee high socks and the bird that swore the most was not at all sexy. Normally such banter would have tickled me but this bunch was venomous. I detected zero humour in their vitriol. I wondered if hell is like this, a never ending marathon surrounded by a crowd of lost and lifeless souls who had been made to bitterly stand there for the rest of their days. I prayed for the future, for the kids.

The race was annoying too. One chap kept sprinting then walking so he'd pass me then I'd pass him then he'd pass me and so on. It felt like he was doing it all wrong to me. The obsessive compulsive side of me started to overpower the loving hippy side and I had to fight the urge to trip the annoying fucker up or stick the elbow in.

I was excited to see the family at the finish. Wifage wasn't too excited about my marathon career and it showed when they turned up ten minutes after I finished. I smashed my personal best by a whole crappy two minutes. I was never going to trouble Norris McWhirter's printer. The pound shop style medal matched the atmosphere. Shite!

The biggest success of the day was going in to work for eight hours overtime after the race. Wifage thought I was mad. It felt nice. Good life bricks, feel good foundations call it what you want. I liked it. Next race please.

Wifage must have felt a little bit bad about missing my Blackpool dash for the line, as she volunteered to drive me down for the Gloucester

Marathon. I'd printed off some details of local play centres and swimming pools for the kids and it was lovely to have them wave me off at the start. The weather was the usual British fare, hostile and minging!

The few spectators were hard core life enriching people who stood out in the countryside braving the elements to cheer on complete strangers. Humans are the only species on the planet that could be so stupid and so fuckin' invigoratingly fantastic at the same time. I often cried at such love outposts.

At 11 miles I received a phone call from Wifage. She was full of kind encouraging words "You'd better fuckin' hurry up everything's shut and your daughter has the shits. I'm out of nappies and I can't find a fuckin' shop!" I had a chuckle and thought "I love that cranky bitch."

At the start of the race they gave you bands for each of the three figure of eight laps. You chucked one in a bin after every lap so the marshals knew which lap you were on. A mixture of post-rave zero directional awareness and a 'can't be arsed' approach to reading the pre-race instructions combined to somehow enter me in the ultra-marathon. When I got to 28 miles a more cranky wife called again "'Where the fuck are you? I've spent a fuckin' fortune! There was shit everywhere!" She didn't take the bigger race news very well and she ordered me to get to the fuckin' end. At 30 miles a marshal explained I'd taken a wrong turn at 23 miles and to avoid disqualification he'd give me a lift back to where I went wrong. From there I laughed my way to the end and my zombie run didn't feel too bad for some reason.

My prize was two medals. The steward who dropped me off said I deserved them. 33 miles in 4 hours 50. I was tickled. Unfortunately the family was in meltdown, the car smelt a bit turdy. Five hours with unwell kids was easily as tough as my ultra-run experience. We had a wry smile at each other. What a pair of wankers we were.

The Shakespeare Marathon was cool and Loch Ness was the most beautiful and my quickest. Mad Head and our families were on the line and I went through the pain barrier to near on sprint the last mile. Big hugs and a dip in the river Ness was the prize and it was well worth the body damage. 3.35 I was chuffed with that.

Up to this point I'd raised a few quid for charity but my main focus had been on the sport not the causes. One of my heroes is my pal with bi-polar. At his peak in the eighties he set a PB of 3 hours 20. I signed up for a charity place for the London Marathon. I wanted to match his time as a tribute to him. I would have to raise £2500 and it seemed like a lot of dough but my inner ting said just do it.

The paper and pen was soon out on a run to work. My idea was to dress as a 118 man and run on the spot in front of a stereo blurting out Rocky tunes in Manchester City Centre. It turned out to be a winner as I took around £60 an hour off the Great British public. It was embarrassing and yes I attracted every pedophile in town but it was humbling, it was great training and it was my first successful business venture ever. I raised £2700 in two months.

My dad came over from Spain to watch my attempt at 3 hours 20. I was skint so I booked us in a hostel in Lewisham. It was a shocking squat. When I dropped my bag in, there was a romantic couple rattling a bunk bed all over the shop at lunchtime. Okay then! I dropped the bag and went off to meet my old man.

It was good to see him. Unfortunately we watched City do United at Wembley then went out for dinner and arrived back at the rat pit around midnight. It was fuckin' hot. All the multi-national tree hugging wife swappers had congregated under our adjacent top bunk beds. I introduced myself and my dad and told them I was running the Marathon in the morning and I'd appreciate it if they had their meeting in the day room as I needed a pre-race kip. They totally ignored my request. Dad and I listened to a young Yank tell a couple of stoned stories before I took action. I leant out of my bed unscrewed the light bulb and the room fell into darkness they muttered a few insults and fucked off. I smiled into my pillow as I heard dad do a Mutley chuckle.

I tossed and turned and sweated until 1.30am when the loud and now pissed and stoned Yank came back in with young Spanish girl. They had no shame. He started banging her on the pit below. For the next ten minutes my bed became Alton Towers. Years ago I'd have done something crazy but I just decided to pocket the memory and ride out the shag. Luckily they were asleep pretty soon. Not so luckily the

Yank and my dad snored. This accommodation was a grave mistake. All in all I must have got an hour and a half kip and I was dehydrated to fuck. At 5.30a.m I donned my 118 kit and we were gone. I walked to the start of the race and Dad tubed it to Central London.

The London Marathon is awesome. I wanted the 3 hours 20 badly so I fuckin legged it. I high-fived thousands of people and my arm ached for weeks afterwards. I hit half way in 1 hour 25. Then it all went very pear shaped. My eighteen mile tie up came five miles early as cramp kicked in just after halfway. My six minute miles became fifteen minute ones. The sun and the no sleepathon had caught up with me. It mattered little as the people and the occasion were magnificent. A 12 mile slog ensued. The ugly grit face came out and I acknowledged every super human spectator I could. Job done!

Chapter 65: The devil's watermelon

Soundtrack: The Beloved - The Sun Rising

It's funny, when you do a few marathons people start to think you're super fit. I certainly wasn't super fit. I ran to get mentally stronger to feel alive, to feel more in touch with my God, the earth and the elements. To feel the rain and to watch the sun rising. My body was broken down. I'd dislocated my knee at footy eight years previous and the N.H.Less decided not to operate so I was only really functional in straight lines. I obviously had a cartilage deficit too which made each and every stride feel like Russian Roulette.

My bi-polar buddy from the last chapter was convinced I was a superhuman and he passed me a book. I think the cunning old fox knew the book would obliterate any rational self-preservation ideas that I may have had about bodily respect and the possibility of retirement.

The Ultra Marathon Man by Dean Karnazes is an inspirational read. It's the same old thirty year old obsessive dude kind of story as mine but this guy takes running to a ridiculous level. He leaves the house on a Friday and runs non-stop till Sunday eating family sized pizzas and cheesecakes along the way. If his family wants to see him then they have to follow him in a van. The whole book is a tour de force. I knew my body wasn't up to double marathons but as a one off the book convinced me to set myself one monster challenge. When I started to dig for one on the internet one word kept grabbing my attention; Ironman!

I'd heard the word before but didn't know what you had to do to merit such a title. I actually thought it was a bodybuilding thing. It soon became clear. The Ironman was a swim/bike/run event and as soon as I read the potty distances involved in completing these ultra-triathlons I wanted in.

A 2.4 mile lake or sea swim followed by a 112 mile bike ride and a full marathon all to be completed in seventeen hours. It definitely pressed my mad dogs and Englishmen switch.

Swimming was the no no on my CV but I thought 'I bet every Ironman has a no no.' I'd not tried to front crawl since my cowardly scrapping phase. Dislocating your shoulder isn't an experience one likes to risk replicating. Unfortunately when I get my mad dogs and Englishman switch flicked it's a one way valve so I had to have a crack at it.

One of my best pals was Graeme. He was a fierce looking South African. A six foot four brick shit-house of a man with menacing cobalt blue eyes. When he stared people twitched. When he spoke peoples' jaws dropped as he was the campest most deliciously loving creature imaginable. Hugs were his weapon of choice and he often grabbed me in with his monstrous paws and crushed me with his love. He was an unashamed perv and he never wasted an opportunity to have a grope regardless of his victims age, race, appearance or sex. This fella loved all creatures and I loved him dearly. Graeme was a state standard swimmer in his youth in Natal and with that in mind I asked him to guide me through my first attempt at the crawl for twenty years.

I'm an innovator and I came fully prepared. I'd sawn a kiddy's float in half and stuffed it down my shorts. I'd also found ankle floats on Amazon. I decided if I could float then Graeme could instruct my arm movements. It took a while for my coach to get over the half naked man thing but I think the geek float look diminished his perv interest by at least half a percent. Even so I was mightily impressed when he showed me his front crawl technique. He moved through the water like an enormous hungry Great White Shark.

He told me to ditch the float and try a length so he could evaluate my technique. I set off trying to replicate the smooth menacing water splitting technique of the oversized South African. Within 15 flaps I was out of air and shattered. I couldn't believe it I didn't have one 25 metre length in me. Worryingly the Ironman distance is equivalent to 169 lengths of the same pool.

Over the next two hours Graeme tried to give me the basics but I've never been a great multi-tasker. When swimming you have to do loads of stuff at once. If I thought about my arms I forgot about my feet. If I thought about my feet I forgot to breathe. Throw leaky goggles and the threat of a groping into the mix and my feeble mind struggled to compute. I left the pool area in a frustrated state. I hadn't achieved anything and my fears had multiplied ten fold. Even so the devils fruit theory kicked back in. The more I couldn't do it, the more I wanted it. I was fully prepared to narrowly avoid death on this quest if that's what it was going to take. It felt like the final piece of my jigsaw in terms of self-acceptance. The family motto I've brainwashed the kids with is 'You can do anything if you really try!' We were all about to find out if our mantra was an overflowing bucket of steaming bullshit.

Chapter 66: H2o

Soundtrack: Jonsi - Sinking Friendship

They should have made a documentary about my swimming exploits. I was a fuckin' menace to everyone in the Manchester Aquatic Centre.

I looked an absolute Dangerous Brian with my front and back float-stuffed footy shorts. My ankle floats, an over-tight swimming cap, nose clip and ever-changing leaking goggles.

Progress was painfully slow and people were painfully unforgiving. Triathlon is one of the fastest growing sports in the UK and the shipping lanes in the pool were rammed. I was hopeless at staying straight and was constantly heading into oncoming traffic. Not only that, I constantly got cramp which triggered the dying crab routine which involved temporary paralysis followed by a good clattering from the swimmer behind. There was no way around it, I couldn't improve my technique without swimming and my swimming was so bad it pissed everyone off which made me nervous which affected my breathing which upset my stroke which didn't improve my technique. I was caught in a vicious whirlpool swimming cycle of crapness.

By the time Wifage and kids came along three weeks in, I'd lost the ankle and bum floats. I just had one down the front of my undies now. I'd just about developed my take on a stroke. My knee didn't like swimming so I just dragged my legs along behind me. My right hand brawling shoulder was susceptible to dislocation so I had a funny angled turnover so not to stress it too much. The kindest thing you could say about my stroke was that it was unique. I was excited to show Wifage my new skill and I plopped into the family pool and asked her to check out my stroke. I concentrated as hard as I could as I wanted her to take my quest seriously. Five strokes in my fingers smashed into an innocent grandads wind pipe. He started to die in front of his grandkids. It was not a pretty sight. After thirty seconds trying to catch his breath he stopped choking. I compassionately apologised and whipped off my disguise. Not surprisingly Wifage had already done a dog in the fog and I wasn't far behind her. She told me I was a twat. That poor man, his poor grandkids. It was clear I wasn't cut out for swimming and if it was tough on the rest of the world then it was twice as painful on my fuckwit self.

One week later the world struck back. There was a fat bald dude who had a bit of an attitude. He swam breaststroke so he could always see us the water pests coming. He was a tutter and a bumper.

I spotted the nookie bear as I entered the pool. It was 6.50am. Two lengths in he had his first nibble. I carried on regardless. He clipped me twice more. As he overtook me the second time he called me a rudderless cunt. I registered it. "A bit harsh" I thought." but I decided to ignore him and plod on. He waited on the wall for me to surface. I ignored him pushed off and set sail on another wonky fifty. What happened next made me lose my rag for the first time in years. The cheeky fat fucker attempted to swim breast stroke directly over my head. All my swimming frustrations were released as I rained punches down on the bear. It wasn't serious just a 'how dare you take the piss out of me' type of barrage. When I was over him I went back into my stroke. My heart was beating out of my chest. I did three more lengths before I stopped to see what the crack was.

It was 7.20 in the morning and there was every chance the police could walk in and nick me. Nookie bear was long gone. I hoped the daft twat was okay. but he'd gone too far. I took this as a sign to hit the open water. He was right I was a rudderless cunt.

I had two chef friends that started on the swimming buzz at the same time as me. They were both full of muscles and built for speed. They liked having me around as I made them look great. They both agreed it was time to hit the open water and we drove up to Coniston in the Lake District excited to take our first natural plunge.

It was a beautiful English summer's day. In the drink it was less warm and with your head in the lake it was pitch black. It was tough but I felt more at home outdoor in the dark with the fish than indoors with the grumpy human obstacles. This day gave me a little bit more confidence but not enough to not be shitting myself the following week as I lined up for a one mile race in Salford Quays.

It was a minger of a day and the furthest I'd swum up to this point was 800m indoors so I was genuinely scared. The muscles from work were in their natural habitat and they powered away from me with ease as soon as they heard the horn.

The start of the race was mayhem and I swallowed a lot of fishy rat piss water. I got cramped up at about 400m and started to struggle. My technique went to pieces under pressure and my drag technique came into full effect as my new nemesis multi-cramp really spoilt my day down the home straight.

I was twatted. 2.4 miles felt a million miles away but I told myself to chill. I could only do twenty metres a month ago. Take the victory. You can do anything if you really try!

A week later I was glad to get away from the wet stuff. We hit Brean Sands in Somerset and it was predictably wet. There was a brief respite on the first afternoon so when Nan and Grandad turned up we hit the beach which was about Five miles from our Haven caravan.

Brean Down peninsula is a great training spot. It's a thin green piece of land that has about 500 steps up to it and stretches about half a mile out to sea. We attacked it as a family. It is a truly beautiful spot overlooking Weston-Super-Mare and the Bristol Channel. There were cattle, flowers and the inevitable rain.

The next morning it was a quagmire. Skimpies on I set off to attack the Down. By the time I hit the force five gale on the beach I was totally fired up and drenched. I had my thankful buzz face on as I drove hard into the wind and rain. I hit the steps rocky style and ate them up like an incidental nouvelle cuisine starter. I seemed ache-free and painless and totally invigorated. I looked out towards the end of the Down peninsula. A cartoon like storm cloud crackled on the end of the land. I felt its pull and bounded like a fearless, careless teenager out towards its electric epicentre.

I noticed all the cattle from the day before had disappeared. As I approached the top of the Down I'd never been so close to nature. I was in a cloud and it was unloading. I was ecstatic. I looked down through the haze of the deluge at the Napoleonic fort below. It looked biblical. As I started to ski-style skip down the crumbling rock trail to the fort my eyes started to focus and it looked a lot more biblical. I couldn't believe what I was seeing. All the cattle had huddled together out of the rain, sensible cows goats and sheep together.

I got amongst them and started rubbing them. Not in a sexy way just in an it's great to be alive way. I used to think my Yorkshire terrier understood me but this Noah's arc gang were well on my level.

When I got back to the van the mother-in-law gave me a yes you fuckin' loon fake smile as I told them of my pure animal love connection. Beats Jeremy Kyle!

Chapter 67: DIY Ironman

Soundtrack: Denis King-Galloping Home

112 miles in the saddle is a fair old whack. I had no idea if I could do it fast enough to complete an Ironman but I felt I could at least manage the distance. I started off training on Wifage's pink mountain bike. It was a bespoke ten year old Raleigh model and it weighed a ton. It was about a six mile commute to work. I would often finish my shift and try and add an extra ten miles to it. Any further and my knee started to trouble me. My confidence for the cycling part of the challenge came from my experience on a cycling trip the year before.

I cycled the Trans Pennine trail a with a monster of a chef called big D. We both liked boxing and he liked to hit me a lot. He had hands like the Jolly Green Giant and a playful jab from him was like an elephant stepping on your toe.

We went coast to coast starting in Liverpool and we spanked it over three days with beer and curry with our ladies in the middle. On day three I broke the big boy at 80 out of 120 miles of the final leg. He begged me to get the train back with him from Selby but that's not how I operate. The next morning I wouldn't have been able to look at myself in the shaving mirror.

The weather had turned and my knee was in bits but I had to finish. I dug in through wind and hailstones to arrive in the sorry shithole they call Hull around 10pm. I got fish, chips, peas and curry and the train back to Manc. I had to be helped off on arrival, I was in a sorry old state. That memory more than any other gave me Ironhope.

I travelled to the Isle of Man to test myself properly before deciding if I should invest £400 on entering the UK Ironman. I arrived on Friday afternoon and went straight out for a forty mile pink bike ride round the TT racecourse. I was blown away by the beauty of the place. It was old little England at its best. In contrast to that very modern motorbikes kept exploding past me and my lady's cycle. I found the whole place magical.

An early night in a crusty B&B in preparation for 2am rise. Brekky was sucking cold spaghetti out of the can to carb me up ready to try and execute a rather ambitious plan. I wanted to cycle 30 miles, swim for an hour in the sea and get to Ramsey for 9am for the start of the Isle of Man marathon.

I'd underestimated the difficulty of the cycling as it was a lumpy old island and the lactic acid from the day before stubbornly reminded me of the challenge ahead.

I climbed the monstrous hill out of town and looked back over the bay. How things had changed. Once it was just about a grope and a kebab around the town, and here I was testing my body in a very different way.

As soon as the sun came up it was glorious. The cool thing about cycling on the Isle of Man is that you can plummet 600metres from the top of a rocky peak down to the beach in seconds and I must have been clocking between 45 and 50mph on the most extreme descents. Raleigh Shopper; Extreme exhilaration!

I hit the beach about 5a.m as the sun was flooding the Laxey bay. It was as good as any beach experience around the world. I had no wet suit, just my skimpies. I was probably the most enthusiastic person ever to have legged it into the north sea and to be fair it seemed very clean. All that was missing was a dolphin. My swimming was still crap but I was starting to believe. When I got cramp I ignored it and eventually; it went. I was starting to build a pain-taking machine.

The cold sea triggered cramp which took its toll and by the time I'd snaked around the island to the marathon start my bits and bobs were screaming.

Before the run I had 20 minutes to kill so I went looking for someone to talk to. It was a trap. I got chatting to the photographer from 'Runners Weekly' and he told me whoever got to two miles first would be on the front of his magazine the following week. Mr. Balloon took the bait. I was ready to become a one off, world class, two mile sacrificial lamb. I knew it would do me in but that's how I roll. The funny thing was I had no intention of buying the magazine either way. I just like a stupid challenge. I got quite nervous and I spent some time on the toilet de-stressing my bowels.

It was a small field of about 350. Some of them could run so I risked a
lung explosion to try and make it onto the front cover. I was second
when I passed the camera and close enough to have met the criteria.
The balloon within felt fully justified and I must admit I smiled big for
the next mile. I'd loosened up and tried to con myself I should keep a
faster pace going as I must be getting fit. By seven miles I could barely
jog. Both my knees were stressed and my rear right thigh and calf were
tied up from the cramp attacks in the sea.

The last six miles were excruciating. I refused to walk but walkers
were walking past my run. People could sense the depth of my pain.
Everyone that looked me over just went 'oooo!' I comedy ran the last
mile in 21 minutes.

My finish time was 5 hours 20, my worst time ever. I didn't care, the
pain taking machine had been tested. That's what I was there for.

To top it off the taxi company wouldn't take a bike. The direct route
was twelve more miles back to the boat. On the ride I couldn't decide
whether to laugh or cry so I did both.

Chapter 68: A relaxing day in the lakes

Soundtrack: The Beautiful South - Good as gold

A mixture of the pressure of not being naturally equipped for Ironman, shift working, wrong time eating and over-exercising combined with unidentified mild lactose intolerance played havoc with my health and my digestive system in particular.

My system turned acidic. I had constant acid reflux where I burped up the excess acid I produced in my stomach. I had heartburn, gut burn, a swollen tongue and blood shot eyes all of which suggested something had gone tits up.

My GP said it was a common complaint. "Come back in six weeks if you are still suffering." I'd lost all confidence in the N.H.Less so in typical British male style I increased my training and gobbled more milk protein powder. Not surprisingly it got worse, I was dropping unsociable, septic, room-clearing farts all over the place.

That wasn't my only problem. My on loan pink ladies' cycle snapped in half on the way to work, I went to turn a sharp left and the front forks and handlebars separated from the rest of the bike. It was comedy carnage and not for the first time I chewed the floor. Thankfully there were no other vehicles involved so when I hit the deck nothing came over the back of me. My trusty steed was no more. I moved both pieces of wreckage to a safe place. Prayed thanks for my life and legged it to work.

After work I scanned eBay for a cheapo replacement. Nobody was giving a bike away. I was skint. I'd been responsible since my epiphany and part of that deal was no further debt. So I sat at my desk at work and prayed for a bike to come to me. I felt another subconscious woosh of an email prayer delivery inside me and an hour later I nearly fell over when my prayers were directly answered.

I got off the train, walked through the park, down the main road and into the road that linked to our home. Waiting for me lying flat on the pavement were his and hers 'Giant' hybrid road bikes, just what I wanted. I just knew they were mine. I gorped an astonished gorp at the magnificence of this mini miracle.

I knocked on the nearest front door and a fortyish year old bird answered the door and said in a very abrupt manner: "Yes what is it?" "Those bikes." I said pointing at them, "take them!" she replied. She explained she put them outside at nine in the morning for anybody to take as she wanted rid of them. She had waited ten hours for somebody to take them away. Nobody had.

Wifage opened the door to a delirious miracle receptor. She wasn't having it. In her book it was just another spawny coincidence. I was being looked after. I knew that.

With that knowledge in mind heart burn and mega-trumps were never going to stop me entering an official half Ironman around Ullswater in the Lake District.

I had to try out my new upgraded wheels. I called my new steed 'The God bike.' Bicycles were being stolen from work all the time so I garnished my new one by painting it with white gloss house paint then I used a permanent marker to pen meaningful markings all over it.

'God bike', 'Hallelujah', 'please don't steal me', 'I love Wifage' and 'power to the people!' I hoped such vibrant messaging would at least deter any single atheist bike thieves.

So to the race. My great friend Lee was my arch sporting rival growing up. In no particular order we were one and two at everything we tried. We tore it up at primary school and in the Cubs. We carried on kicking lumps out of each other right up to leaving secondary school and it was a lovely surprise to find out we were to face off after all those years. As soon as we discovered we were going to be in the same race we decided to make a weekend of it and take our families camping together. Lee was a weightlifter and he'd got into triathlon through his sixty year old fitness fanatic boss. We were supposed to be past all that locking horns shit but boys will be boys and it felt like the night before the egg n spoon race all over again. Only the egg was a lake and the spoon was a mountain.

My acid problem was getting chronic and thankfully Lee's boss
noticed and issued me with some super strong acid blockers. We had a
barbecue and an early night with our families. What happened next
typifies my life experience. Stuff like this happens to me all the time.

It was summer and the sun came up early doors. The acid had crept up
my chest and was burning my gullet. I lay there at 3am wide-eyed and
twitchy about the day ahead.

The silence was broken by a pissed sounding Geordie dude. He was
singing his own version of Dr Alban's 'It's My Life.' It went something
like "it's my life I'll do what you want to do, you fuckin' bitch." It went
on and on. I looked around my tent and they were all in a coma. The
singer's missus was pleading with him to stop harassing her. Then she
started screaming. "No John, no John." That was me up. I grabbed my
cast iron frying pan and approached the noisy chav tent with the
dishonoured cross of St George above it. As I got closer I could hear
their kids screaming like there was a rape unfolding inside. I made my
intentions clear from the onset. In my best man voice I said "Right
dick head I have an iron bar here. I'm going to do you with it unless
you come out now." "Fuck off!" was his thoughtful reply. His missus
said "Please John just go out." I couldn't risk him hurting the kids. I
unzipped the tent and thankfully the fat wanker was fully clothed lying
over his kids. He spotted me and said "all-reet, all-reet" and he started
hauling his disgusting frame off the whimpering kids. I ordered him in
to his car to sleep it off. He acted like a naughty kid and did what I
said. I thought better of talking to his family. My experience in such
situations is negative, the abused wife would have probably attacked
me. I had a piss and returned to my sleeping bag. My lot was none the
wiser they all looked like they'd been drugged. I would be in the lake
in an hour and a half and here I was, absolutely fuckin' wired! When
the families got up nobody had heard any of Dr Alban's performance.
Why me?

The lake was rough, really rough. Ironman rules stipulated shortening
the half Iron swim course in such conditions from 1.9km to 1.2km so
that's what they did.

My acid situation was bleak. On entering the lake the two foot waves gave me no chance of catching my breath. Every time I came up for air I puked acid instead of taking in oxygen. I was as scared as I'd ever been. The current in the lake was severe and it was a mad scramble to make any progress. Cramp haunted me again too but somehow I made it. I was the first man in and the last man out but I survived.

My guts were in bits and the sports recovery drink I had on leaving the lake doubled me up. As soon as got on the God bike I felt slightly better. I set off in pursuit of Lee, the old juices starting to flow. Out of the two big climbs Kirkstone Pass was the bitch, it went on and on and fuckin' on before we were rewarded with a mega downhill. I caught Lee just before Shap, the second of the two big climbs. He took it well bless him. I felt his heart sink a little as I disappeared into the haze.

The run was a half marathon literally over a mountain. My guts had gone and I was running bent in half. It was a mix of sharp pains, stitches and gut burn. No way was I stopping. One in every thirteen entrants gave up that day. I wasn't one of them, I finished bang on eight hours. Just about on time for a go at the biggy.

Lee made it too. I was dead proud of him. The competitiveness had gone. We'd both earned the victory.

<h1 style="text-align:center">Chapter 69: Bottle Tests & Gas Burps</h1>

Soundtrack: Praga Khan - Injected with a Poison

I can't say I enjoyed the half Ironman but I was proud that I'd toughed it out and that was the real prize I suppose. I was proving to myself that my breakdown was forced upon me. I never give up. My guiding force shut me down for a reason and I was close to accepting that now.

So I took the plunge and sent off a hard earned £430 fee to enter the UK Ironman. I worked the times out from the half distance event and calculated that even in those conditions I was just about on course for the swim. The bike was surprisingly tight and the run was fine. I had two lines of thought going on, the negative one being that the whole Ironman was twice as long and it was unrealistic to hope to achieve the same times on the second lap.

My positive spin was the course I'd just done in extreme intestinal discomfort was one of the hardest races in the world. The chances of the swim being so rough again were slim too. One thing I was sure of was that waiting for a year so that I was in peak physical condition might be a never-ending wait. It was now or never.

When I got my race pack through I was distressed to read that no mountain or hybrid bicycles could be used in the race. My beloved 'God bike' was a no, no. My 'Eddie the Eagle' approach to triathlon wasn't acceptable in the ultra-serious world of the Ironman.

The rule book was very boring. To compete you needed to have a Tour de France style road racing bike. The real players, the dudes with talent had £7000 bikes. God bikes are free and my money was tight but I worked out if I took the interest free finance and sold the bike with all my kit straight after the race. I would be able to pay it off without any real financial strain.

So while the kids were at school I visited a big shiny new bike centre and entered into the most stressful shopping experience of my life. I tested three or four road bikes around the car park and settled on a 'Specialized Allez' model. It was light as a feather compared to my two previous fashion accessories. It was 10.30a.m and after filling in the paperwork they told me they had to build the bike. I was told to come back at 1.30pm.

At 1.30pm they fobbed me off till 2.45pm so I sat around and at 3pm it still wasn't ready so I had to go and pick the kids up from school. So I did what I wanted to avoid and came back with a six year old boy and an 18 month daughter. At 4.15pm they said "Just another 15 minutes and it will be ready." I decided to pick out a gimp helmet and some bike lube for my chain while the kids started to dismantle the store.

At 4.30pm they finally rolled out my Iron Chariot and I must say it looked rather resplendent in Team GB Olympic colours. The assistant stood with the kids while I had a quick blast round the car park. It wasn't God bike good but it seemed fairly rapid.

So I stuck the kids and my carrier bag of accessories in the car then loaded the new wheels onto the bike carrier on the back of the vehicle.

As I walked from the rear of the motor to the driver's side my stomach lurched as through the window I witnessed the fourth suicide attempt in my family in recent years.

My one year old daughter was drinking my bike oil. I flung open the door she'd lugged four out of five inches of it. My instant thought was "she's going to die." My five day binge buddy from the Kavos trip twenty years before was the only human I knew that could drink that amount of poison and keep it down. Speed was key so I drove at warp-edge to the hospital. On the way my boy freely admitted he had decided to crack it open and give it to her. A dark voice in my head wanted me to kill him but that wouldn't have improved things. I'd have no kids left then if this situation turned out as bad as I feared it may.

I was in the palm of the N.H.Less again and not surprisingly they were predictably slow in responding to what I perceived as a life threatening situation. I'd brought the remaining lube with me but it had no ingredients on the bottle. So I sat and watched two nurses mess around on the Internet for fifty minutes without offering any information. I rang the bike store for info. They were unsure of the exact ingredients but said the product was petrol based. I told the Google squad. "Right love." came back the inspirational reply.

Each minute that passed I envisioned the oil seeping in and destroying our baby's major organs. Every bit of petrol knowledge I had haunted me. It cost too much, Man City now had money to spend on players because of it and worst of all I knew it was a cancer causing carcinogenic devil liquid. I tried to stay calm but I was shitting myself.

She seemed happy enough sat playing dollie's totally unaware I was being tortured and she may croak it soon. I couldn't look at my boy as he didn't seem to give a fuck and that was really making me angry.

It was my duty to ring Wifage and she was surprisingly level headed. No swearing or insults. That made it worse as it meant this was a serious situation. She was on her way over.

After fifty minutes the Hogwarts Doomsday Book of Victorian Poison's came out and the nurses informed me that if she'd have spent a bit of time sniffing up the fumes from the liquid then her lungs may have been permanently damaged but the human body can just about handle drinking oil and petrol. The digestive system can handle it as a one off. A doctor confirmed this and told us to hang around for two hours to check her condition didn't deteriorate. I was thankful but I didn't have too much faith in their advice so I just prayed hard till Wifage came.

When she came I explained and she gave me her speciality 'you wanker' look. It was a fair one. I felt like a wanker.

We sat in the kids' play room and watched the Shannon Mathews saga unfold on T.V. It looked like an episode of Shameless to me. The lost girl's so-called family were pissed up spraying cans of Stella over each other in celebration as news came through the little girl had been found. My heart sank for Shannon and the nation. How could they celebrate? She might have been abused for God's sake . This case highlighted to me some of the issues kids face in the UK. Selfish parents! I prayed for the health of my daughter and vowed to somehow try and help young disadvantaged kids in the future. The two hours passed slowly. The little one let out a few gasoline burps but as long as she didn't spark up a woodbine it looked like she was going to be alright.

The next evening I decided to take my son to the local park to play tennis. On the way he dropped his racket. It fell straight between the forks of the 'God bike' and locked the rear wheel sending me into a one hundred and eighty degree summersault. Bang! I couldn't believe it. It felt like I'd broken my wrist just two weeks before the Ironman. I had a chuckle at my lad. We were a right pair of clumsy twats.

So back to A&E. They said it might be broken; it looked like a hairline fracture. They gave me a splint type strap to protect it. My plans for a big training weekend were flummoxed.

I was supposed to swim the 2.4 miles on Saturday and then loop the cycle course on Sunday. My acid situation had continued to intensify making swimming a scary proposition but with busted wrists swimming was now out of the question. It felt like this could be the final nail in the Ironman coffin. I vowed to try the bike on Sunday and hoped my wrist improved.

My fellow half of an Ironman Lee and I set out to loop the Ironman cycling course over the hills of Rivington and beyond. We took turns setting the pace. My wrist was very sore and I placed my wrists on rather than gripped the handlebars.

We were heading up the East Lancs Road which is a notoriously busy dual carriageway between Manchester and Liverpool. It was pancake flat and we were powering along at around 27mph when I hit a loose piece of the road that had come away from what looked like a drain. The handle bars buckled and my wrists didn't have the power to hold it straight. Down I went. Because the bike was new and the shoe clips were set tight I was locked in to the new machine. I took the impact of the fall in my chest, nuts and wrists before my overgrown training partner ploughed in to me. His front wheel smashed into the right side kidney area of my back. Big boy was thrown clear of the wreckage but he landed funny and broke his arm. This ride was not meant to happen!

My life had been spared again because the busy road had been empty enough for the traffic to swerve to our right. Had that right hand lane been full we would have been dead. I prayed thanks for that.

I felt bad on big boy. It was foolish of me to have risked riding in this condition. People who saw the crash encouraged us to go to hospital. I was badly winded, it was a lot of impact to negate.

We decided against an ambulance and both got quite cold waiting for big boys best mate to pick us up. I got dropped off at home while big boy and this pal went off to hospital. I was sick of the place. Three times in one weekend was too much. I set about seeking out divine help and prayed instead. Not just thanks for my life but for my health and a good price for my semi-mangled bike on eBay after the race. If you don't ask, you don't get!

My back was twatted and I struggled to get out of bed each morning for work. I kept telling myself "Keep the Faith."

Wifage kindly drove us south the week before the big one to get some sea training in. My lower back was ruined and it was painful to do anything with my right wrist. I had chronic reflux and gut burn but apart from that I was looking good. I figured a good long swim in the sea should loosen things up.

Wifage dropped me off at the beach in my wet suit, silly hat, snorkel and goggles. It was over cast and the sea looked choppy. She didn't waste her breath telling me I was too injured to even think about tackling that sea. She knew me much better than that. I arranged to swim the bay. It was around 1.5 miles long so it should take no more than one hour thirty minutes. I kissed all the family and took the plunge. I ploughed through the breakwater and did my best not to swallow lots of salty water. Breathing was a nightmare. I had reflux and waves battling to stop me getting a breath. Inevitably I swallowed lots of salty water. I wasn't in any real danger because the water was only about five foot deep. I could have stood up if I pleased.

There was a monster swell going right to left across the bay. Unfortunately I was going from left to right. After about twenty minutes I'd advanced only about one hundred metres. With so much going on the back felt o.k. but the wrist was a bitch. It was nearly real race time so I picked out a church spire on the other side of the bay to use as a spotting guide and got into my stroke. Everything else ceased to matter. I was on it and I repeatedly ground out a stroke nudging slowly round the bay like a slug chasing a snail.

There were few people around on this rainy, windy summers day but one nice old fella had spotted the sole seafaring slug and he came down to the waters edge to check if my unique style was a stroke or a drowning ritual. "I'm alright pal." I screamed when I became aware of him.

I was three quarters of the way there now when I heard the gre-puffle of an outboard engine. I lifted my head up and saw the Lifeguards Rib approaching. The motor started to fade away. "What are you doing? "Training." "Is Your name Pinkie?" "Yep." "You'll have to get in the boat your family think you're dead." My knobby side thought of telling him to bugger off but if they were worried I thought I'd better oblige.

About 600 metres down the beach stood my boy and his Grandad. I smiled, Grandad didn't. I was an hour late. Wifage had scowered the beach and couldn't see me in the swell and assumed the worst. She rang the Lifeguard. This panicked my boy who also got upset. Grandad went on to sulk for the next two days. I understood. He was right, I'm an obsessive selfish knob. My problem was I expected them to recognise that and realise I was too pig headed to die or not finish my swim.

I kept it to myself but I thought it was a fitting end to my Eddie the Eagle training regime.

Chapter 70:Ironcilla

Soundtrack: Cilla Black-Surprise Surprise

Up until now I'd raised money for the big charities and there is nothing wrong with that. One such charity invited me along to the new state of the art local hospital as a sort of thank you for bringing in a decent amount of money for their cause.

I expected to meet some kids and prepared by bringing some magic trick props and a bag full of sweets. On arrival I was told it was not PC to meet the kids as it would be like looking at goldfish in a bowl. I wanted to leave. What a fuckin disgrace. I was quite capable of interacting in a positive way with kids.

A lovely lady then explained the good work the charity does and it was good but the more she explained the funding side of it the more I got the impression the government were milking kind hearted people to pay for basic healthcare while they frittered our dosh away on bombs and all that crap.

The lady showed us around and she told us that the charity's funds were in part used to pay the rent on one building in particular. I asked how much the rent was and she reluctantly muttered the amount in millions. Now here was a brand new purpose built hospital on the cheapest land in the area. The rent was about five times the price of the land. I was drained. In my mind the government had planted a fat cat who was receiving gross amounts of charitable funds every year when the government could have acquired the land and built the facility rent free for a fraction of the cost. That's the way I read it and maybe it's a cynical way of looking at it but without delving too far into politics the public wouldn't pledge money for explosives and I'm sure if they were aware they wouldn't want to be sponsoring fat cat's either.

In the past each time an organisation had accepted my hard earned donation, I didn't really feel like I'd achieved anything. Now I had real doubts and I found that very sad. I hoped my actions and my friends generosity had benefited at least one person's struggle or circumstance. In future I wouldn't take that chance. From now on I wanted my charity wonga to go straight to the person who needed it. I decided I wanted to take a Cilla Black Surprise, Surprise approach to fundraising.

This sort of charity work had long been festering in my mind and when I found out that a work colleague of mine had a nephew with an incurable condition called Menkes' Disease I approached him about the lad's condition and asked what I could do to help the family. We agreed to pledge my Ironman sponsorship to young Mark with the proceeds being split 50/50 between Francis House who are responsible for his care and the family who were planning a Disneyland trip for Mark.

That was the cherry on my cake. Any pain I was about to receive was minuscule compared to the hurt such families with poorly kids face. I was ready to give everything for little Mark. I was inspired.

Chaprter 71: Godspeed

Soundtrack: Andy Williams -The impossible dream

My Ironman experience thus far had been a metaphor of my life experience. The more I wanted something, the bigger the barrier that sprang up to block that success.

I knew I was in bad shape. I was still crawling out of bed in the morning with a bad back. To have a realistic chance of making it my back would need to loosen not stiffen and 112 miles on a bike didn't suggest such an outcome, but I had faith that the force of goodness I call God was going to step in. All these injuries were a test. Walk into the light. That was my focus.

The Ironman experience is a whole weekend buzz. You can attend pasta parties, black tie dinners, expos, briefings, church. I decided I was going to do the expo/registration, the brief, the church and the race. I wanted to involve my mum because she missed out on a lot of this stuff when I was a kid and I needed her warmth and love around me.

So Mum and her trusty sidekick came down to the expo with me at Leigh Rugby club. As we approached the entrance a dude with no legs was coming out. I thought I had a few injuries going into this but clearly I'd got off lightly! I quickly told him he was a legend and an inspiration and he told me he was just a bloke like me. What a guy!

In the hall I picked up a bit of Iron-clobber, got my number and sucked in the pre-race atmosphere. Everyone looked buff. There was a special forces recruitment table which made me chuckle. I couldn't take out a kebab at the moment never mind the Taliban. My acid stomach was now restricting me to a diet of overcooked mushy veg, no dairy, nothing acidic, nothing raw and nothing too cold. So finding 6000 calories to burn became a bit of a struggle. I couldn't even digest bananas which had always been an in race turbo charging supplement for me. My chance meeting with 'No Legs' made such problems insignificant. I just had to crack on.

We met my auntie and uncle from my dad's side for lunch then I went
to the pre-race brief while they all stayed on the sauce. The meeting
was a mixture of boring rules and inspirational stories. I felt a bit of a
fraud as everyone in the room looked granite. They glorified becoming
an Iron dude. It was a sales pitch that worked. Everyone in the room
wanted it that little bit more.

Next up was Ironman prayer service. I rang Mum and they all sounded
a little bit raucous as they had been on the piss now for five hours. I
told them I was hitting the prayer service. If they wanted to come they
were welcome. They agreed to meet me in the mock church over the
road from my uncle's house in a function suite overlooking Bolton
Football Club pitch.

I got there before them and I was surprised to find the room packed to
the rafters. I could tell the room was full of spiritual positive people,
you could feel it. The family arrived shortly after and were dotted
around the room in the last few remaining seats.

The lady who'd organised the service was a carrot crunching English
country girl. Her sidekick was an Italian but the majority of the room
were full on Christians from the US of A.

As she introduced the concept of the organisation it became clear that
this mob were a very well organised God Squad. Carrots explained that
they had arranged synchronised Iron prayers around the world to
coincide with this gathering and the race. Selfless prayer for others. I
love all that. I'd come to the right room.

The Italian picked up his guitar and broke into hallelujah song. It
wasn't really my bag, it was delivered in a very modern Christian style.
It was a slow repeater which went on far too long. Though this lot
were not a tough crowd to please most people including me had a go at
dog shit Karaoke. I saw my uncles eyebrows go up in a 'How did I end
up in here with all these freaks? Kinda way. All this was a bit full on
for him.

After the sing-a-long Bob Dilloni asked if anyone had any thoughts or
feelings they'd like to share. My hand shot up and I shared "Hi
everyone, I'd just like to tell you about the guy with no legs. I'm sure

most of you have now seen or heard about him. He had his legs blown off in Afghanistan. I bumped into him at the registration and congratulated him on his courage. The legend himself told me that his struggle is no different to anyone else's in the race and I guess he's right. I have been plagued by crashes, injuries and ill health. We all have our own personal challenges to face and I would just like to thank God for keeping me on the path. Tomorrow, succeed or fail I will have won because in the face of all sorts of nonsense my faith has enabled me to at least believe. Good luck everybody!" As I confirmed my faith publicly my old friend the 'adrenaline thank you' washed over me confirming my observations and giving me further hope.

The next guy to speak was a cool looking black American. His story was based around his previously overgrown belly. He was half the man he used to be and this was the rubber stamp on his weight loss journey. The yanks whooped him and he took a bow. Run fat boy run, love it!

There were further feel good success out of hardship stories intermixed with more songs and prayers before Carrots and Bob Dilloni joined hands to ask which members of the congregation were competing. Surprisingly less than 20% of the room raised their hands. They then told all the supporters of each competitor to go and place their hands on their victim. If anyone else in the room was not supporting a particular person then they should go and touch a stranger. Then they revealed the plan. En masse we were going to get a zap of the good stuff, The Holy Spirit! The givers were instructed to put as much love into the prayer recipient as they could muster. I don't think my mum had touched me like this for 30 years but after an afternoon on the beer she had no boundaries. She was locked on and loving it and to be honest so was I.

When they gave the command I had members from both sides of my broken family including my life-giving Mum all channelling their love straight into my barnett. Not surprisingly a thunderbolt of feel good engulfed me. I got quite emotional as I connected my own prayer of thanks the other way. The massive 'adrenaline thank you' that followed was a clear sign of divine approval. That was the best meeting I ever attended. Yanks are ace, they all started shouting up thanks to their God. No shame in that. Halle-fuckin-lujah ready to rock and roll.

I got up off my stool like an old man and thanked my team then wished the others a top race. Big hugs and home to bed.

I slept like a baby. At 2a.m I rolled out of bed waiting for the back twinge. It wasn't there. Halle-fuckin-lujah once again. I could not believe it! It was easy to brush my teeth as I was grinning like a Lancashire cat. God is great, faith is great, love is great, Mums are great, cold sloppy roast vegetables for breakfast are not great. I chucked big anti-cramp salt on them for in-lake protection. I washed that down with a bucket of soya milk tea, extra sugar and my eating for the day was done.

I ditched my car and got a last minute hug off my auntie and uncle at 3.50am then jumped the Ironbus at the Reebok stadium to the race start. On the bus was a very cool French dude. He was buzzing. He stripped down to his undies and started gyrating himself whilst rubbing in his sun cream. His wife and daughter had a knowingly proud 'Our mans a nutter' demeanour about them. I decided to try and enjoy the day as much as him.

At the start the conditions were perfect. It was dry, no wind and overcast. Usually I poo a lot before a race; I get very subconsciously nervous. On the day of my biggest race ever I was unexplainably pebbledash free. I looked a bit vain walking down to the lake holding a mirror from the pound shop but I didn't want to be hindered by a wonky mask situation so I took no chances.

The hooter went and I watched with pride as the dude minus his legs rolled off the pontoon in front of me. You had to be inspired.

The lake was pleasantly flat but my reflux problem kicked in straight away and burning puke started to fill my throat. After about 400 metres I stopped to pray. I went still and lifeless and begged for help "Please I am putting my faith in you, please help me." Straight away I felt the presence of Graeme the Great White. I had prayed to God not to my favourite giant homosexual but I had no doubt I could feel big G around me. It was almost as if his big gangly arms started to lift me. I felt light and focused and started to power my way around the course. It was no doubt the fastest I'd ever swum. No cramp, no goggle leakage and no post prayer reflux. I started to tie up a bit on my swim back into the pontoon but I'd made it and I sprang from the lake growling and roaring like a mad man. Seconds later my stomach lurched and my legs went numb. I spotted the race clock and saw I was half an hour early. I ran to a steward and asked him "Have I gone wrong?" "No the lakes full of stewards mate, you can't go wrong." I was freaked. I asked if I could go back in the lake and do another lap and he told me that wasn't possible. If I'd gone wrong I'd find out at the end when I'd be disqualified. For fucks sake! Had I had a miracle swim or had I dropped a bollock? I knew I'd swum around the course twice for sure but I really didn't know if I'd cut any corners. I decided not to worry about it and just enjoy the day. There was fuck all I could do now. If need be I'd just have to do it all again next year.

I enjoyed the bike section. I decided to engage the spectators as much as I could. So I periodically pretended my bike was a horse or a boat and I was a jockey or an oarsman. So I whipped and rowed my way around the course. On laps two and three the crowd started to recognise me as a daft twat and they inspired me with their warming cheers. The dodgy knee started grumbling at sixty miles and by ninety I was pretty lame so I dropped a gear or two for the last twenty miles and smilingly grinned it out. I'd knocked two hours off my half iron split bike time.

About five miles into the run I attempted to run up a canal embankment which linked two parts of the course. My knee buckled and I let out a pathetic yelp. It was messy but no less than I expected it to be. I started with my one legged power hobble. Soon after I passed the ex-fatty Yank. "God bless you fatboy!" He had a sense of humour failure and told me to fuck off!

I thanked almost every spectator I saw. I started to feed off each and every human connection. I had ten friends dotted around the marathon course and they really lifted me. The pain got worse and worse but I started to enjoy the suffering. Nothing was going to stop me now.

I did my usual trick and missed the finish and started on lap four of a three lapped marathon. The stewards noticed I had three lap bands on and turned me round about half a mile the wrong way up the big hill in the race. I had school, work and family friends on the approach to the finish and I decided to disrespect my already broken body by cranking up the power hobble.

I gritted my teeth and tore down the home straight. As I approached the line the compare gave me the good news: "MJ Pinkie you are an Ironman!"

I got mobbed by Wifage and the kids and there were tears all round as we celebrated that you can do anything if you really try.

The swim doubt will forever piss me off but I just have to accept I'll never know if I did do the full distance. That's my punishment for disrespecting my brain cells earlier in my rave career. Ten years on my memory function has improved massively and I'm very organised but I'll always have my "Where's my keys, where's my phone?" side. I'll never doubt that I could and would have done whatever I had to. I finished three and a half hours inside the disqualification time.

I was really proud that I managed to grin and bear the run without stopping as it was a very painful last twenty miles. It was more than worth it for me and for young Mark my charity benefactor. It was an honour to hand over a cheque to his family. I'd found out what I needed to know about myself and I earned my medal. Not as much as Joe Townsend the ex- Marine with the bomb blast legs though. He beat my time by forty minutes. Congratulations to him: Truly amazing!

Chapter 72: Passing it on

Soundtrack: Sham 69 - If the kids are united

The Ironman told me what I needed to know. I could achieve anything I put my mind to. In fact anyone can.

What to do with this knowledge was my next mission. Obviously I brainwash my kids with it I tell them nothing is impossible. They can do anything if they really try. I don't just tell them what they can do. I tell them I love them, I bombard them with it and so does Wifage and it works. They are secure.

Not all kids are this lucky and such kids need an external inspiration. I made such a connection with two teachers at school both of whom took a personal interest in me. The first was the school footy team coach. It was pretty straight forward, he thought I was a decent player and he told me in a way that made my heart sing. He was a photographer and he printed me some really cool footy action photo's. He was an art teacher not sports, he wasn't getting paid overtime for our after school activities, he did it for us and his selfless passion earned him a special place in my heart.

Funnily enough a friend of mine became his business partner later in life and when they discussed our relationship he was totally surprised he'd had such an impact on me. He couldn't remember any sort of bond or special treatment which just goes to show how powerful such actions are. Kids need acknowledgement, purpose and encouragement. Give it to them and it lasts a lifetime.

Inspiration number two was my favourite. He claimed to be a French teacher but he mainly told us stories about his life, his uni days, his wife, his kids, what he had for his tea, his passion for Holt's bitter, his love for the people of France and Germany, the importance of sport and his love for Manchester. We all failed French but he taught us about fairness, passion, joy, friendship and doing the right thing. In our last class I waited behind to thank him. He looked at me like a mum who had just found their nipper face deep in a bowl chocolate. He said

"I don't know what the fuck it is but you've definitely got something."
Then he crushed my hand with a meaningful man-shake. Approval
from this dude meant the world to me and I left his classroom choked
up to fuck.

I waited a long time to find out what my something was but I never
forgot that remark. It's the flip side to
my Milkspermboobswank theory, it stuck in my mind because it wasn't
rude. It was a pure loving comment fired directly into my soul.

It's taken twenty years to suss out that comment but I've finally come
to the conclusion that what I've got is the ability to love. To be like
him, to share that joy and inspire people. So I decided to get into
mentoring.

I can't talk about individual cases but I can give a brief description of
what I do. I get assigned to kids that have somehow been drawn into
the Youth Justice system. It's a voluntary role designed to stop the
youth offending. They train you up on boundaries, safeguarding and all
that jazz. You set achievable goals to work towards and once you've
got them there you end the relationship and start again with another
kid.

Up until now each kid's family hasn't been rich but they have managed
to spoil their kids. Lack of respect for the parents has been evident and
it seems to me the more they give the kids the more ungrateful they
become. So I try and re-educate the kid and the parent that they are
doing it a bit wrongish.

I work shifts so my mentees regularly get knocked up at 5am and
whisked off bleary eyed with a flask of tea to my favourite nature
spots. Kids love boundaries especially from man figures. Their mums
are regularly gobsmacked when their foul mouth little terrors thank me
for a lovely time when I drop them at the door. Little do they know
that I've told them from the start that they need to say thank you for a
nice time, even if it was crap.

Once I've sussed the child's sporting prowess and commitment level I challenge them and get them running up mountains in the rain stuff like that. Testicular development I call it.

Play stations and other such technological play things are the usual downtime tools of distraction for the young 'uns that I've mentored. They hardly go outdoors. It really freaks me out when a young 'un admits to doing something for the first time.

One lad had never laid eyes on a sheep! Up the Lancashire moors he asked if he could chase one. It took all my powers of responsibility not to explain why you should never admit to wanting to do that. Another lad had never seen the sea. So I took him out to see the Iron men of Crosby in Liverpool and played splishy splashy in the north sea. To see him buzzing off it was very emotional. For tougher nuts I take them to Ingleton in North Yorkshire and get their adrenaline going by running around the amazing waterfalls. It's my favourite healing spot and everyone I've ever taken there feels better than before they went.

Going into mentoring my major worry was that the kids would get too attached to me. I did a lot more for them than my two favourite teachers ever did for me. Each child gets up to six months in a relationship and I try to grow them as much as I can. On my first assignment we'd achieved our goals and I was dreading telling him I was releasing him back into the wild. When I did I was magnificently surprised when he said "No probs you're right you should try and help as many people as possible." He wasn't upset he totally got it and that made me ridiculously proud of him.

So whatever lies ahead I'd like to take his advice and help as many lost ones as I can. It's a real privilege.

Chapter 73: Beatlejuice

Soundtrack: The Beatles - All You Need Is Love

This book started off as a state of the nation rant. I was a little bit bitter I suppose that it took me so long to find my peace and happiness.

I worry about the kids in our country. I worry that more and more of them never find themselves. Broken humanity haunts me. Just to back up this train of thought here's a little story. I finished a shift on a Friday night weeks before the 2011 riots kicked off. I was wired after a busy old night at work and as I approached Piccadilly bus station I was troubled to have spotted a pack of teenage hyenas' that we're about to rip apart an isolated gorgeous baby lion.

About fifteen lady chavs had surrounded a pretty girl. The manly looking ringleader was calling her a slag and accusing her of going with some bloke or another. It was a lynch mob and I could tell they were all going to do her in. Two older lads were on the fringes. They kept whispering instructions to the ugly hench bitches. There wasn't a copper in sight and I knew I was going to have to try and save her or she would be seriously damaged. As I moved closer the language was heinous. Everyone else at the bus stop was acting like nothing was happening. Then the bulldog chewing the wasp lit the touch paper. She took off her pound shop high heel and started smashing the once pretty girl's face in.

Pretty tried to stand her ground as each cowardly hyena launched an attack. She managed to rip off three or four fake hair pieces from the barnetts of her over orange assailants. It was a self-defensive wig-rip-fest but within seconds they had overpowered her and her face was a pummelled mess.

I sprinted in and peeled her off the crash barrier she was getting smashed against. I got her in a non-negotiable lifeguard style head lock and started dragging her away at speed. Thankfully a high energy gay lad had joined the raucous on our side and he distracted the mob a little with a sincere high pitched righteousness manifesto speech. "I'm not having this" he kept squawking, bless him.

The blows kept raining in on us both as they chased us into a local shop. The owner ordered us out but I barged past him into the rear of his premises. I sprang the fire exit and set the injured cub free before slamming the door shut behind her. I must have looked impassable as the pack took in my 'don't fuckin' bother you shitbags' face. They backed off and I apologised sincerely to the shop proprietor.

As I walked out of the front of the shop I was sickened to watch the chavs celebrate their victory. They were hugging each other and high fiving. Had I had a machine gun I would have done the honourable thing but I didn't so I just let Dale Winton carry on telling them how sad they were.

I got on the bus wired and troubled. I rang Wifage who understandably said "Why do you have to get involved?" "I can't stand and watch that shit." "Whatever just get home Mr Crimefighter!" Weeks later the real riots started and the worrying state of the nation thing was confirmed.

Even though witnessing such events pains me, I still have hope. Everyone is fixable. Writing this book has made me realise that whatever our start in life, we are programmed to progress. The opportunity for right living is always there. In a lot of ways the tougher the path the greater the reward for sussing it out. I do believe that even people from the toughest backgrounds, the ones who get no real positive life education from their families do still get the opportunity to make good. For me each and everyone of us gets what we need. All the information we need comes from our inner thing, our God, our soul, whatever you want to call it. It comes in the form of our thoughts. Unfortunately the dark side fires bad thoughts at you too! As soon as you suss out which good bits to listen to and which evil bits to ignore, you can't fail. It's available to everyone.

I wish that more than anything else this logic was taught in schools. I think the government should put adverts on the tele. An 'It's A Choice' campaign. To me that's the key to life. Choosing the right positive thoughts to act on and dismissing the negative. As soon as you suss that you get self-respect and become able to love yourself then everyone else. Joy and happiness follow as a matter of course. Love's unstoppable. Believe the Beatles, All You Need Is Love!

Chapter 74: Full Circle

Soundtrack: Kenny Rogers - Lady

Wifage is fit. To me she'll always be 21. She has baldness and dementia on the lady side of her family. So I'm fully prepared for the puzzled Duncan Goodhew phase of our marriage. To me she'd still be fit. End of.

For a woman it's different. Does my arse look good in this? Do I have droopy eye lids? Am I ugly? What the fuck happened to me? All that shit. Wifage has had four kids. She likes food and wine. Even so her body is still in good shape.

After the usual Friday night pizza/Chardonnay work out, Wifage put on the lard arse record again. The time had come to inspire her. "Listen missus The Manchester Marathon is three months away. Sign up today and in 3 months your arse is Kylie's arse!"

Now to say my missus wasn't the most supportive marathon wife in the world is undercooking it a bit. She often told me I was mentally ill for wanting to run in the wind and the rain. She just didn't get it. So when she gave me her 'fuck you, you're on.' face. I have to admit I was rather surprised.

I gave her my best advice, train to be fit over 5 miles, save your knees and tough it out on the day.

Hats off, she was straight into it. She got the clobber and joined the local mums' running club. It was approaching spring and it was lovely to see the first feel good shoots of self-respect sprouting through and manifesting in her after-run smiles.

In the main she took my advice although she did throw in one 11 and one 15 miler both of which were predictably funless and doubt-producing. She got runners knee to test her resolve further but I could never doubt her. She didn't need any testicular development. She's my rock.

Pleasingly she jumped on the Cilla Black fundraising bandwagon and pledged to support a friend who had a similar still born experience to us. She was working towards buying a cold cot for the local hospital so families who lose kids can keep them with them 24 hours a day until they are ready to let go.

The day of the race soon came around by which time I'd just got back on my feet after dislocating my knee for the second time in my life. I used my seven weeks in plaster to whack an Open Uni tin pot degree in youth justice then to write this book on my iPhone.

I'm a great believer in fate and had I not done my knee Wifage couldn't have trained towards a wonder arse and this life story would have probably been on slow burning hold until the end of time. We both grabbed our window of opportunity and I was just about mobile enough to get around the course to cheer on my racing rat.

Race day was fuckin' freezing. It was about five degrees Celsius, windy and wet. You need a sense of humour living with Manc weather but this was unfuckin' necessary. Not to worry, the tougher the test the bigger the reward.

She was up and out at silly o'clock to meet her mum pals and face the music. I was left to marshal the kids and the in-laws. I had them fully drum kitted up at five miles to cheer through the blessed mum pig. It was baltic and I couldn't blame the public for staying indoors. A handful of warm hearted, cold fingered supporters braved the storm to clap the sodden mass of people past the Kellogg's Factory in Stretford. I had been in shit weathered races before and you need a lift so I went balls out to raise the runner's spirits. My drum accompanied chants went, "You can do it..!", "Easy, Easy", "We love Mum, we love mummies bum." and obviously "Your going home in a St Johns ambulance!" Wifage came through looking fit at five. I claimed a kiss and took the freezing kids home to get warm before Nan and Grandad took them swimming.

I dropped them at home and jumped the tram up to Altrincham which was mile 11 of the race. As I got back on my drum it became clear that a sense of humour failure had hit most of the field. Some competitors were crying, some were uncontrollably shaking from the cold. This was sadly turning life threatening for some. I cranked up my sillysongmanship in a veined attempt to give the field a lift, "Singing in the rain, The Hokey Cokey, Manchester la la la!" All the classics. My heart leapt when I spotted Wifage she was looking fit. She looked strong and focused. I limped along with her as much as I could, got a picture and sang her off: "You can do it!,You can do it!"

I nipped home, picked up the rest of the after-swim herbets and rendezvoused with my mum at race mile 20 in Flixton. It was carnage. Some of the competitors were delirious. One old fella ran straight into the drinks station water table. A snatch van was cruelly scooping up 'hypothermic maybes' who were just a few miles from the finish.

I brought back flasks of tea and hit the most needy with lifesaving sugary paper cups of the good stuff. Runners spoke of unavoidable freezing six inch puddles at 15 miles. So with that hardship in mind my boy and I started walking back down the course to find the Wifage. Half a mile in we saw her. She looked fit. Game face on, bin bag on, determinati-on. She was strutting with purpose. Her best pal had done the boxing coach bit, cycling alongside her encouraging her through the worst of the Cheshire frost swamp section. By the time they hit the Flixton turn my Mum and her fella were blue. A decent crowd of good people were gathered through Flixton and Urmston. It was just the job for Wifage. She fed off the love of the people and raised her pace from plod to regal trot.

Back in the car for us to hit the finish line. Longford Park was a fuckin' quagmire. We battled through the swamp to bang the drum once more for my victorious mega-wife. Her lovely friend Helen had braved the mud to share the moment which was lovely.

She powered in recording a very respectable time of 5 hours 34 looking fit! I got in first with a 'You're a fuckin' rock wife-hug before the family group and mate-hug followed shortly after.

We got her home and ran a seductively hot bath. Her arse was like a polar Ice cap. She was still goose bumpy, frozen when she stepped out.

Five large white wines and a Sunday dinner in the pub wasn't the best recovery plan but she wanted to see her friends and family to celebrate the victory. For her efforts she received a bucket of self respect, toned bits (Kylie's big sister) and over £1000 for the great local cause. She wore her medal for two days. A lap of honour that was richly deserved. Due to the shite conditions only half of the eight thousand entrants finished. That marathon was a fuckin' grueller and I love her to the bones.

Running wasn't our only full circle. When I was young I was the party animal in our house. No more. When I drink these days I'm the philosophical giggly bloke. It's Wifage who pulls the moonies now. She's a much nicer party animal than I ever was though and it's lovely to see.

So everything is pretty much hunky dory for us at the moment but that doesn't mean it's easy. Life isn't. I know I'm only ever a couple of bad decisions away from the gutter, from losing everything. Things will go tit's up at some point but hopefully we've built the responsibility foundations to cope with most eventualities.

As for the book and my message, in my perception I feel I'm a normal lad who's experienced a normalish life journey so far. I've been very lucky not to have been legally or emotionally punished for killing someone. So many kids run those risks by fighting and driving in no fit state. I'm not proud of my journey but I am proud of the man that I've become and that's why I've been able to write this book. Some lost and dysfunctional kids in our great country have much crazier shit going on and everyone tries to make the best of their own crazy shit. I'd just love it if one such young 'un read this book and turned their shit into gold. Anyone can!

So if you are living a life where you are drifting from one disaster to another, stop. From this moment on think through every suggested thought that comes into your head and decide if it's a right or a wrong pointer. If there is a negative outcome at the end of your thought then dismiss it and only act on the right ones.

You'll be instantly rewarded by feeling good. Now for anyone that buys my inner God theory, pray thanks to your God for that knowledge. Make that connection and your life will go up, up, up! For believers of alternative faiths or atheists, start talking to yourself, your God or your cat. Whatever you believe in it's all the same shit.

Religious war and all that nonsense is an absolute pile of shit. The Promised Land is within you. Make the choice, walk into it and claim the prize. Do right and keep the faith you can pass any test that comes before you. Whatever your past.

Thanks for everything Wifage

FIT

www.ingramcontent.com/pod-product-compliance
Lightning Source LLC
Chambersburg PA
CBHW072214150726
48002CB00005B/1800